Zero Percentile–2.0

Neeraj Chhibba announced his arrival on the literary front in 2009 with his first book *Zero Percentile* (*ZP1*), which went on to become a national bestseller. Widely read and appreciated, it led to the genesis of his second book *Zero Percentile–2.0* (*ZP2.0*), a sequel as well as one of the first attempts to write about life inside the bubbling Indian software industry.

He currently works with a high-end software services company, Nagarro Software, in Gurgaon.

Zero Percentile–2.0

Neeraj Chhibba

RUPA

Published in 2011 by
Rupa Publications India Pvt. Ltd.
7/16, Ansari Road, Daryaganj,
New Delhi 110 002

Sales Centres:

Allahabad Bengaluru Chennai
Hyderabad Jaipur Kathmandu
Kolkata Mumbai

Printed in India by
Repro Knowledgecast Limited, Thane

Acknowledgements

Acknowledgements are hard to write. So many people contribute to a book's success that missing even one means great injustice to his efforts.

For *ZP2*, I took up the challenge of writing on the software industry by using the characters in *ZP1* in such a way that the readers could appreciate the transition. Believe me, it was not easy. Moving those young characters into the adult world and still retaining their simplicity and earthiness in the complex maze of IT was extremely difficult. Here stepped in Google which added to my limited knowledge (pun intended) and made me write what I believe is a very good story (that's being modest, huh!). Where Google gave me ideas, my friend Vaibhav expanded on them to help me create some very exciting situations in the book. So, thank you, Vaibhav! Then there is this cute surd Leenu who designed a beautiful website and loads of other extremely helpful literature to publicise the book. Recently, he threw away the keys to his car and started driving a Bullet to work. He says this was necessary to fulfil his childhood fantasy and make him feel that he has grown up. What about your two lovely kids, Leenu?

I am also grateful to my publisher Rupa which made *ZP1* the success it is today. I owe a word of gratitude to all the loyal fans and good journalists who found the time to read *ZP1* and said nice things about it that made me take up the gargantuan task of writing *ZP2*.

I would also like to thank my employer, Nagarro Software (*www.nagarro.com*) for its continuous support and engagement. I feel proud to be a part of this company.

In the end, I would also thank Facebook and Twitter. Had they been human I would have fallen in love with them, irrespective of their genders!

A Note for the Reader
You will find occasional asterisks sitting at the end of some sentences. These refer to incidents in Zero Percentile (ZP1) *that were instrumental in shaping the lives of the characters of this book.*

Everything that goes up comes down.
The important thing is to know
when it reached the top of the curve.

Prologue

The stock market crash did not look extraordinary to the common man. Because of the ongoing worldwide recession, people had got used to the frequent and bloody mayhem at the stock exchange. What had happened was a sudden shedding of a thousand points. The trigger was the failure of a certain software company called NumeroSoft to take over the consulting company PureConsultants. Since NumeroSoft was a heavyweight on the exchange, people did not take the news lightly. The share price went into a downward spiral pulling the market down in its wake. It could have fallen more but for the circuit breaker which stopped all ongoing activities in the share market. This happening was so important that it got a mention on the first page of all the leading dailies of the country the next day. After all, it was the surprise failure of one of the biggest software shops in the country to acquire a relatively smaller company. And, the stock market punished NumeroSoft and itself heavily for this.

What also got covered in the following days' editions were four other pieces of news, apparently unrelated to each other, but somehow connected with the happenings at PureConsultants and NumeroSoft. These were stories which covered the turmoil in the lives of Pankaj, Nitin – Pankaj's friend from college, San – a brilliant mind who worked with Motu, and Priya who was a childhood friend of both Pankaj and Motu. What escaped attention were the personal tragedies of Jaanvee and Tanya, since they did not involve blood and gore, and thereby could not bring the shock value necessary to make them newsworthy items.

Motu, as he was fondly called by his friends since childhood, should have read the news of the failed takeover bid over PureConsultants with pride because he was its founder and had successfully thwarted the efforts of a very hostile NumeroSoft. But he was not happy. In fact, he wanted to cry. It was a long, bitter fight for control which went on for a long time, and he was completely exhausted when it ended.

On another front, he had forgotten the bitterness of so many years and was not afraid of picking the threads from where they had left them. He decided to call Pankaj before going to pick him up. The phone rang till it got disconnected. He then tried calling him at his home number, but it continuously gave a busy tone as if it was deliberately kept off the hook. Slightly bewildered, he left home. They had decided to go to the funeral ceremony at 10:00 a.m. together.

The door was opened by the butler. Not surprised, he climbed the stairs to Pankaj's room.

'Is Pankaj awake?' he asked on the way up.

'No, sir. The light in his room was on till three in the morning. He must have been busy with something. So I decided not to wake him up.'

It was 8:00 a.m., unusually late for Pankaj to be sleeping. Pankaj had lived alone for many years after Priya moved out of the house, preferring not to remarry. Motu knocked on the door. It was not bolted from inside. He waited for a few seconds and then entered.

'Hi Pankaj, this is me, Motu. Will you get up now please? I know you don't like me anymore. But you don't have a choice as the stubborn me is never going to go out of your life. So get up.'

Pankaj did not respond. Motu stood on the side of his bed for a few seconds and then reached out to stir him. After that he used his cordless phone to make an emergency call.

Phase I

*Intertwined destinies are a portent of greatness and
a place in history unless certain evil destiny's juggernaut
crosses their path.*

The Period

2006

You can divide Gurgaon into two parts. Old Gurgaon, on the right side of National Highway 8 (if you are going from Delhi to Jaipur) has expanded little with all the development happening horizontally, and new Gurgaon, where development has taken place at a fierce pace with the city growing vertically and beautifully. There is one exception. The local administration forgot to give it a sewage system. Like all Indian cities where big businesses are located, Gurgaon too is a city full of contrasts: a mix of farmers who were under continuous pressure (of their own greed) to sell land to become rich, the Suzuki offshoots including Maruti and its many ancillaries, and the new age IT and ITES companies which were the primary reason for its growth in the first decade of the twenty-first century.

Motu had realised a long time back that if he wanted to attract the best people in the industry he had to build a brand, and he could not do that out of the small office in old Gurgaon from where he started a few years back. So, as soon as he got the opportunity he moved to the new Gurgaon. He was happy that this move had given him the desired results.

Motu was the founder and CEO of PureConsultants. Everyone in the office called him BD, an acronym for Big Daddy. He encouraged people to call him that for two reasons: one, he felt old, which worked for him fine since he felt he could control others better, and the other, it helped create an open culture in his office.

On that day he was in the office at 6:30 a.m., unusually early even by his own high standards. He had woken up with a throbbing at the back of his head – a result of a few mls more than he could handle and a bad dream. He had a premonition that it was going to be a long day at work. To add to his woes, it was a Monday – his least preferred day of the week.

Motu ran his company with the help of five people. He had planned to meet all of them to take stock of things on Monday.

His first meeting was with San (diminutive for Sanjeev), a twenty-four-year-old geek who headed his product team. San was a maverick, liked to live life king-size, and importantly, always on his own terms. He was a dropout from IIT Delhi. He did not complete his degree as ennui forced him to discontinue in the middle of the III year. He was working as a freelancer till Motu heard of him through one of his many contacts and decided to meet him at Radisson hotel. He remembered every small detail of that meeting.

৶

Motu was sitting in the coffee shop waiting for San when he saw a tall, dishevelled young man wearing jeans, a crumpled T-shirt and something that came closest to slippers that men usually wear at night, coming his way. To add to his discomfort, the young man had a three-day old stubble. He suddenly felt out of place in his charcoal grey suit and a black Armani tie.

'I am getting too old to keep pace with these young chaps,' he shrugged and looked at his watch. It was 3:10 in the afternoon, and San was late by ten minutes. Motu was beginning to form hate speeches in his mind when a soft hello broke his reverie.

'My name is San. Since you are the only guy in the coffee shop, I guess you must be Gaurav,' San introduced himself.

'Don't you feel stifled in this fancy suit of yours?' said San unapologetically while adjusting himself in the chair.

'Sometimes, but I thought it was necessary for today's meeting, and it seems I was completely wrong. Why are you looking sleepy?' Motu finished with a question.

'Well! I was working with a customer in the US, and he had me up the whole night. I could get to sleep only at ten in the morning. By the time I woke up it was already half past two. So, I just grabbed the keys and came driving on my bike at a breakneck speed.'

Motu was repulsed by the idea of speaking to an unkempt, unshaven person who had even skipped his bath. He felt claustrophobic and had a very strong temptation to leave.

'So what do you do?' San asked.

Motu willed himself to concentrate (he suspected he had detected a foul smell from San's body whose source he failed to recognise but guessed it emanated either from his armpits or his mouth). He gave San a small presentation on what his company did and then started interviewing him.

What followed was an intense session in which they covered the breadth of technology. By the time it ended Motu was amazed by how much San knew about software. He was very sure he wanted San, minus his bad hygiene habits, in his team at any cost. His only immediate fear was that he would have to shake hands with him again when they parted.

'San, frankly, you are one of the best people I have met and I would like to offer you the role of the product head in my company.' He then went on to explain the product to San. He could see that San was impressed.

'But how do I retain you? I think you know you must be one of the best technology guys in the world.'

'Keep me excited, Big Daddy. Else I will change you like all the women in my life. I am a greedy man. Greed is my biggest motivator. I am greedy not for money, but for all the good things in life. And for a good life you actually need to have some real greens in your bag,' he said simply and smiled. There was no hypocrisy in his voice.

Motu was tempted to ask whether he made love to all his women friends being this unkempt but somehow restrained himself. He stood up and shook hands with San. Two things happened after that – they became good friends and the legend 'Big Daddy' was born.

That was two years ago, and Motu had successfully managed to retain San since. In fact, they had become very close friends. Any time spent with San infused new energy into Motu. There was a faint smile on his face which San could see when he entered the room.

༄

'What's up, BD? Why are you smiling?' Over the years, San had shrunk Big Daddy further to BD.

'It's because of you. You have improved in the last one year. You still wear jeans but with an ironed shirt. You have shoes on your feet and carry the smell of perfume. You have become bearable and look closer to the species you were supposed to be.'

'BD, you will begin to resemble a penguin in a few years if you do not take care of yourself,' San replied, pointing to Motu's ever-increasing belly. San's voice sounded strained and he looked tired, which was pretty unusual for him.

'How's the Babe?' Motu asked. Both of them referred to the product as 'Babe', liking it to a woman.

'The Babe is as sexy as ever, but I seem to have run into a few problems with her.'

'The usual?' asked Motu, slightly perturbed.

'No.' San did not offer an explanation.

'What's the problem?' Motu was all business now.

'The marketing guys didn't know what they wanted when we started with her. Now they want some new features to be added. Otherwise, they feel it will be difficult to sell her. If I try to add these features, then integration becomes a huge problem for me.'

This was a classic case of what the engineers could build versus what the marketing team could sell. But it was not unusual. While the product took shape the demand of the industry changed, and companies needed to innovate to stay competitive.

'How bad is it?'

'It's pretty bad and we may have to scrap her completely and start right from scratch.' San dealt the deathblow. There was silence in the room as both of them weighed the options available.

'By how many days will it set us back?'

'Not days,' San did not venture further.

'Months?' Motu braced himself for the bad news.

'No, at least a year, maybe two.'

Silence followed again. But this time both of them feared breaking it. Two years in software were a huge investment. They might as well kill the Babe and start on something new.

'Is there a workaround?' Motu mustered the courage to ask.

'I don't know.'

'How much more money we need to invest if we have to make her all over again?'

'At a rough estimate, anywhere up to twenty crores.'

Motu had never seen San so gloomy. They had already pumped many crores into the product, and delaying her launch would make it uncompetitive and may even destroy them. Motu's ambition of entering the big league would go for a toss completely. He decided to speak to the marketing head in the evening about this. A smile flitted across his face as he thought of her.

'I should not have told you as yet,' San said.

'Why?'

'You seem to have gone crazy already. I am giving you the shittiest news you may have heard in months and you are smiling,' San cried.

'Forget it. Let me think of a solution and we can speak again tomorrow.' Motu repented the deviation and became serious again.

Motu was a genius with problems. He was nick-named 'Brick Breaker' in IIT, simply because of his great reputation of solving problems. San was very sure that he would find a solution to this one as well. For some strange reason, Motu himself was not so sure.

The next meeting on Motu's agenda was with his COO Arjun Nagpal who doubled up as the head of technology and technical operations. Arjun was a junior from IIT. Their friendship went a long way back. It was but natural for Motu to bring in Arjun when he started PureConsultants.

Arjun, like Motu, had a very humble beginning, though the reasons were different. Motu had a very humble upbringing because his father was incapable to hold on to his fortune, and Arjun, because his father did not have any. Arjun's father was an excellent carpenter. He stayed only a couple of blocks down from Motu's house. The less privileged ones lived on that street.

Their fathers had known each other for years. They first met when Motu's father called Arjun's for renovating his shop in Karol Bagh. What led to a strong bond between the two were their common backgrounds. Both their families had migrated from Pakistan, though under entirely different circumstances. Motu's grandfather and his family came to India on a chartered plane, and Arjun's grandfather covered most part on foot and some by bus and train. The difference in their social standing did not deter them from forming a strong bond over lunch-time breaks at Motu's father's shop, sharing stories of the golden olden days. With hardship being a constant factor in their lives, the bond grew stronger with time.

Motu first met Arjun when the latter's father had come to Motu's house for some work. Motu was into his third year at IIT then. Both father and son worked really hard to get the details of the almirah right. Motu was extremely impressed by their commitment. He continued his father's legacy and invited them to join him for lunch.

'What is your name?' he asked the young boy.

'Arjun,' came back an extremely shy reply. Shyness was an endearing quality he managed to retain many years hence too.

'Why don't you go to school and study?' Motu asked.

'He does study, Gaurav,' Arjun's father said. 'I've had high fever since yesterday. But I had promised you that I'll complete this work today. So he insisted on helping me. And so instead of being in school, he is with me today,' he concluded proudly.

Motu noticed the older Nagpal's bloodshot eyes for the first time. He felt embarrassed.

'But, uncle, this was not urgent.'

'A promise is a promise. I have never failed to keep my promise even once in my life. And I want you to remember this too,' he said looking at his son. That was a quality the older Nagpal bequeathed to his son. That was why in PureConsultants, Arjun never went back on a commitment, nor did he ever delay a delivery.

'In which class are you now?'

'He is in XI. He has always stood first in class,' the older Nagpal replied with his head high. He also topped the Mathematics Olympiad last year and gets a scholarship from the school for securing the highest marks in Class X board examinations.'

'What do you intend to do after school?'

'I will help papa run his business.'

Arjun had no idea what he was capable of. Motu did not want to see him go waste. 'Come with me tomorrow. I will try to help. I hope you don't mind him becoming an engineer?' Motu asked the older Nagpal.

'I don't. Except that I don't have the money to support his education. You know I am too proud to borrow from someone,' he replied simply.

Motu later came to know that all their savings had gone into the treatment of Arjun's mother who was suffering from

Cancer. Cancer, as is its wont, struck both at his mother's body and his father's pocket, stubborn not to leave till it had wrecked both.

Motu always felt thankful to Pankaj who pulled him out of the rut at the right time and helped him join Inside Education. With no support from his own family, he might have ended doing something similar to what Arjun was inclined to. He knew if not guided properly Arjun would drift apart and another one of those beautiful minds would go wasted. While speaking with Arjun he thought of a plan. Though at that point he did not know whether it would be easy or difficult to implement it, he wanted to give it his all, if not for anything else then to absolve himself of a feeling of indebtedness to Pankaj. Motu's mind, as is the case with all young people, had no acceptance for stereotypes. He began to identify Arjun as one of his own, breaking the societal barriers which wrongly divided them on the basis of what they did, giving no importance to the dignity with which they did it.

Arjun arrived at Motu's house immediately after school. They ate aloo parathas made by Motu's mother. While Motu ate seven, Arjun managed to eat only one, which Motu's mother took as an insult to her cooking. Motu later explained to her that it was only because Arjun was an introvert and his eating less had nothing to do with her culinary skills. After the feast was over, both walked down to the office of Inside Education.

It was three years since he had left the institution, but Senior sir still looked as formidable to him as when he first walked through its doors so many years ago.* The mentor-protégé relation did that to people, he thought.

'Hello, sir!' Motu said.

'Hello!' he replied from his chair while poring over some books. He sounded irritated, not liking the disruption.

'It's me, Gaurav, sir,' said Motu, still gasping for words like earlier.

Senior sir looked up from his books. 'It's been some time since you last visited,' he said with a smile, though Motu heard the complaint in his voice. Motu counted while looking aimlessly at sir's balding head. It was exactly nine days. 'They will all be gone if you take as much time to visit me again next,' Senior sir said, catching his glance.

'How's it going at the IIT?'

'Hectic, sir,'

'Who is hiding behind you?' Senior sir asked, looking at the shrinking figure of Arjun.

'He is Arjun, my friend.' Motu then narrated Arjun's story to him.

'Hmm! What can I do for you, Arjun?' Senior sir asked.

Arjun felt dry in his throat. He tried to say something but words refused to come out. Motu realised he needed to take charge.

'Sir, can he study at our institute?'

'And who will pay his fees? It is very expensive studying here.' Both of them knew that he will not charge a penny from Arjun, but still continued with the charade.

'Sir, we shall figure out a way.'

'I will waive off your fees if you promise to study really hard.'

'I promise, sir,' Arjun mumbled. 'I also promise that I will repay every single paisa I owe you with interest,' he said, his eyes brimming with confidence.

'I don't need the money,' Senior sir barked.

'I don't need it either,' pat came the reply.

For once, Senior sir was left speechless by the unassuming Arjun. He decided not to argue with him.

Arjun appeared in an entrance test (made especially for him) ten days later and cleared it easily. He later cleared the IIT entrance test with a rank in the top fifty, and selected Computer Science as his branch. He paid the fees for IIT as well as the loan he had taken from Senior sir, by taking mathematics classes throughout the four-year period at IIT. Thus the son of a carpenter finally became a proud, debt-free computer science engineer in 1997. By the time he had finished his degree at IIT, he had also saved a neat seventy thousand rupees with which he bought himself his first computer – a brand new Pentium II. And since he was in a mood to indulge, he also got himself a cute pair of speakers to listen to his favourite music.

ᔑ

Many of Motu's friends had asked him why he had not given the charge of the Babe to Arjun. Motu had realised a long time back that there were no real rules in business except that it needed to succeed. With so many things on his plate Arjun wouldn't have been able to give her the attention she needed. So Motu had taken her out of his purview and given it to an outsider. He had later called Arjun to his office to explain his decision, and Arjun had accepted it graciously, not betraying the slightest sign that he did not like the idea.

Since their paths did not cross very often, the relation between Arjun and San was cordial. There were sometimes a few arguments on the architecture and platform in 'Knowledge Sessions', held very frequently in software companies to share information which would otherwise become extinct under silos of everyday work. These sessions were the meeting grounds where best practices were shared, useful experiences were discussed and hot debates on the future of technology took place. San won most of these arguments as he had more hands-on experience in technology than Arjun, who, faced with the constant pressure of timely delivery of various projects could not keep himself abreast of the latest and the greatest. The arguments were quite infrequent and held in the right spirit.

'How's it going, Arjun?' Motu came straight to the point.

'Things are fine. How are you?' Arjun was the type who took it slow, always spending time over pleasantries. Motu realised he had to bear with it.

'I am fine too,' replied Motu, suppressing the impatience in his voice.

'I sometimes wonder how difficult it is for our friends to survive in the US. We have a whole ecosystem here which helps our children grow – grandparents, parents, maids, relatives, friends at home and school. And they are almost alone there,' Arjun carried on with the small talk.

'In the US our friends and their wives stick to each other for good. They are well aware that they only have each other to fall back on in times of need. Then there are parents who frequently fly to support the newborns in their families.

'But don't forget, parents visit, their visas expire, and they return. There is no replacement for friends; they win over families hands down and are always around when needed.'

The warm memories of his childhood friendship with Pankaj flashed through Motu's mind,* but he shut the thoughts out before they gave way to bitterness that had seeped into their relationship over the last few years.

'Why criticise the US? Even here, especially in metros, it is becoming pretty much the same. There are nuclear families, live-ins and crumbling relationships. We are fast catching up,'

Motu blurted out. He regretted his words immediately realising that Arjun's marital life was not going smooth.

✑

As it happens in most love stories with a good ending, Arjun married early. He was picked up in 'Rendezvous' by the highly energetic and bubbly Muskaan. Rendezvous was meant for introducing the students of IIT to those of other colleges, and especially, the ones from the opposite gender. Strangely, both he and Muskaan studied in IIT, but never crossed each other. As luck would have it, Muskaan liked his serene smile, and decided to break the protocol and introduced herself to Arjun.

'You are extremely lucky that I like you,' she said.

'Why?'

'Boys are dying to date me,' she said.

What she had said was actually the truth. With one of the poorest girls-to-boys ratio in the world, a girl with even the slightest pretensions of being beautiful was feted as 'Miss World' in IIT. Though that was not true in case of Muskaan. She was a rare combination of mind and matter, which enhanced her appeal.

'And what if I say no?'

'I will find a way. I am very ambitious. I hate failure.'

Arjun thought hard. He could not find a reason to say no. But he missed the most important and obvious ones – her ambition, her obsession with perfection, and her refusal to accept failure.

After he passed out of IIT in the late nineties, it was but natural for Arjun to join Motu. Motu's consulting business had begun to flourish and he was looking for good people, and

Arjun was an obvious choice. He assimilated extremely well into Motu's scheme of things and became the backbone of his business. He worked really hard as he always felt indebted to Motu for changing the course of his life and considered it a means for repaying that debt. Motu, Pankaj and Arjun formed the crux of the company. It was ironical that he became one of the main reasons for the rift between Motu and Pankaj later.

Arjun's marriage to Muskaan proved to be a blessing in the first few years. They loved each other like crazy and continued to discover new aspects of each other's personality, thus making their bond stronger with each passing day. While Arjun's simplicity and intelligence, which helped him understand the most difficult of problems, easily impressed Muskaan, her innate understanding of the politics of life, her fierce desire to conquer it and live on her own terms made her dearer to him. Life could not have been better. What added to their happiness were the first signs of morning sickness in Muskaan.

When it was finally confirmed that Muskaan was pregnant, they actually began to believe that they were the happiest couple in the world. But god, always watchful of the right balance of joy and sorrow for everyone, decided it was time for them to experience their share of sorrow through their child.

Except for happiness, the only thing they remembered of the day when their daughter was born was the unusual thunderstorm, rain and the blinding streaks of lightning that swamped the sky throughout the night. She was born exactly at 00:00 hours.

'Let's call her Diyaa – the carrier of light,' a tired Muskaan whispered when she was wheeled out of the OT.

'That's a great name. She has come at the time of absolute darkness. Doesn't she look angelic?' an emotional Arjun said in one breath.

Diyaa did touch the lives of many people, but in ways neither of her parents had expected.

⌇

They were a happy family till after four months from the day Diyaa was born. That was the first time Arjun commented on her development.

'Isn't it time she started reaching out for the toys?'

'I agree that Diyaa's generation does things faster. But it's still too early, you know!' Muskaan smiled. The fleeting moments of worry passed but only for some time.

'Musky, haven't you noticed that she has not started turning over or crawling. Isn't it late?' Arjun brought up the topic again when Diyaa was eight months old.

'Yes, I do.' This time Muskaan could not disagree with him.

'Let's go see the doctor tomorrow,' Arjun decided.

The doctor examined Diyaa very carefully. He checked the growth of her muscles, commenting on the shape of her legs once. Then he began asking them pointed questions about her daily activities. They tried to reply accurately, but with growing unease and sense of concern. When the doctor started asking questions about her birth – some very detailed ones – it struck Muskaan that the circumstances surrounding Diyaa's birth could be far from normal.

'I cannot say anything conclusively right now. We will need to wait till she is at least eighteen months old. But yes, I can see that she has problems. Her movements are not normal. We would need to keep her under observation. But whatever she may be suffering from, she is a lovely child,' the doctor concluded with words of encouragement.

'Thank you, Doctor,' both of them said feebly. Arjun noticed with anguish that Muskaan did not try to pick Diyaa up from the doctor's table.

'Where do we go from here?' Arjun asked her.

'Let's visit the lady who gave birth to her,' Muskaan said.

They went straight to Muskaan's gynaecologist from the paediatrician's clinic. The doctor did not have any patient at that time. Muskaan barged into her cabin in a combative mood.

'Hello, Muskaan, is everything alright?' The doctor was surprised by Muskaan's unannounced visit.

'What happened on the day Diyaa was born?' Muskaan was not game for pleasantries.

'I do not understand your question,' The doctor asked, nonplussed.

'She is slightly upset,' Arjun, deeply embarrassed by Muskaan's outburst, tried to calm frayed nerves.

'Yes, I am upset. Now you tell me what happened on that day. You had said that it was a special day for you, and that you had already delivered three babies before it was Diyaa's turn.'

'Oh yes, I did! But what does that have to do with you?'

'You were overworked, Doctor. By the time you came to deliver Diyaa, it was already late in the night. You had an unusually hectic day after the delivery of three babies. You were extremely tired and drowsy. Diyaa's case required you to think; you needed a break, instead you got me. Your tired mind was not up to it.

'What also must have played a role, though a small one, was that you are an ethical doctor. You had mentioned to me that you did not want to go for a C-section unless it was absolutely necessary. So you delayed the decision till it was too late for Diyaa.'

'Push harder and the baby will be out in a few seconds,' the doctor faintly remembered telling Muskaan in her tired state.

'And those few crucial seconds killed the brain of my daughter. Did I summarise it correctly, Doctor?'

'Yes, I made a mistake that day. When the baby came out I thought everything was fine, but it seems I was completely wrong,' the doctor surrendered meekly.

'But what have you come here for today?' she asked, fearing the worst.

'We only came here to learn the truth,' Arjun interjected, not wanting the situation to worsen.

Even if they wanted to, they would not have been able to sue the doctor. First and foremost, the Indian mindset of equating the doctor to god, and then the intricate web of relations and recommendations (the doctor was recommended to Muskaan by her sister who had come to know her through her sister-in-law) would not have given them the freedom to take her to court.

'What is the extent of the damage?' a strangely relaxed doctor asked.

'We still need to find that out,' were their last words as they walked out of her cabin.

⟨⟩

Muskaan's and Arjun's attitude towards Diyaa changed after that day. Muskaan began to keep away from her. At a time when Diyaa needed support, Muskaan began to withdraw from her. Nothing changed in the conscious world, but Arjun could sense it from the sudden increase in the number of hours she put at work and her always keeping busy when Diyaa cried for attention. Though she tried to hide the fact, Arjun still realised from an inadvertent remark from her to the maid that she had stopped breast-feeding the baby as well. It was as if she were waiting for some conclusive evidence to cut the umbilical cord forever.

'What's the matter, Musky? Why do you look so detached from our daughter?' Arjun had asked once.

'Your child gives you the chance to cherish the innocence of a golden period which you could never appreciate as a child yourself. I can't see this happening with Diyaa.'

That was the end of the conversation on the topic.

While Muskaan distanced herself from Diyaa, Arjun started getting closer to her. He took it onto himself to take care of her smallest needs and found that he loved doing it. Diyaa's eyes attracted him immensely. They were very big, the darkest shade of brown, almost bordering on black. What made her eyes unique was that they talked. She expressed easily through those two communication channels which constantly conveyed something. Most of the times, it was pain and sadness, but sometimes it was happiness. She would be happy when Arjun would hug her, kiss her and play with her. Arjun realised that there was a very fertile brain that guided the eyes to do the things she did. She followed every word that Arjun spoke and understood the meaning behind it. She understood who lizards were and blinked a yes when Arjun added the number of lizards right and mocked him when he did it incorrectly. She was only twelve months old then.

Eighteen painful months passed away, and they again made the dreaded trip to the doctor. Meanwhile, Arjun monitored her condition constantly. Close supervision showed that Diyaa was not doing many things that children her age normally do. It was difficult for her to drink milk. Arjun suspected that her legs were taking a rather unusual shape too.

'Her condition has not improved. And she has all the symptoms of a special child. We may not be able to conclusively establish anything unless we do an MRI. I will talk to you after that,' the doctor said.

The idea of a small helpless child going into the big machine made Arjun squirm in his seat and a strange wailing sound originated from deep inside his stomach. That was the first time he cried openly.

Muskaan sat through the whole episode impassively as if she had turned to stone. It was Diyaa herself, through the expression in her eyes, who finally comforted Arjun as if saying, 'I will be alright, Papa.'

A few days later they went back to the doctor, this time with the incomprehensible MRI report.

'It is difficult to say conclusively but I very strongly suspect that your daughter suffers from cerebral palsy. The part of the brain which controls the movement of different parts of the body has been damaged. She may face difficulty in communicating and recognising the people around her. The complete effect on her body needs to be seen as she grows up.' The doctor sounded extremely repentant as if he was the cause of their problem.

Arjun rued the delay of few seconds in Diyaa's birth for the rest of his life. Those few seconds would have made her a healthy child who went to school and lived a normal life like all the other kids. The delay in Diyaa's birth also killed their marriage. That she had given birth to a 'special child' sent Muskaan into a state of shock, and she was never able to reconcile herself to the fact. She considered this as the only failure in her otherwise spotless life.

'I cannot take care of the baby any longer. I don't think I will ever be able to love her,' Muskaan said one day after the visit to the doctor.

'But, Muskaan, Diyaa needs help. You cannot leave her like this. Will you be happy without us?' Arjun asked, sounding defeated.

'Yes, I will be happier without her. Why don't you take the responsibility of bringing her up? I am through with her.'

Both of them thus decided to part ways. There was no shouting, no blaming each other. What remained was sadness that things did not turn out the way they should have. They began to live separately after that. Both of them did not seek a divorce. It was as if they did not need the freedom that a divorce provided.

Muskaan's departure had a positive impact too. It made Arjun resolve that he would not allow Diyaa to become a vegetable.

✍

'So how are things shaping up?' Motu subtly signalled an end to the preliminaries bringing Arjun out of the painful past of his broken relationship.

'They have generally been good, except that I am losing many of my good guys to stiff competition and at salaries way above what the market is giving. I don't know whether it is planned or just a coincidence.'

'Must be because of the boom in the job market. Is it bothering you too much? Who are we losing them to?' Motu asked quickly, wanting to get down to the core of the matter.

'They have all been joining a very small company which seems to be doing work similar to ours. And I fail to understand why does a small, less than a hundred people shop need five of my best architects and ten of my best managers?' He was exasperated.

'Try to look up its website and figure out who are the people behind it.'

'I did, but the website does not tell much. Strangely, it does not tell anything about the promoters too. All my googling led me nowhere.'

Arjun was right. A hundred-people company would at most need a single senior architect and five managers.

'You should be happy that you are helping others grow,' Motu chuckled, trying to play it down.

'I would be, except that I have a hunch that someone is out to destroy us.'

〽

The next on Motu's list was a meeting with his CFO. Jaanvee was a dynamic thirty-six-year-old woman. A graduate in economics from St Stephen's, she finished her MBA in finance from IIM Ahmedabad. She was a genius with numbers. A beauty with brains, she could easily qualify to be among the top five in the 'thinking man's most wanted women's list.' To everyone's surprise, she had chosen to stay single and concentrate solely on her career. Inquisitive, idle, past-their-prime aunties, and men of all ages tried to enquire about the reason behind her staying single. They were usually cut short before they reached halfway through the first sentence. The combination of intelligence, beauty and her single status added to the mystery of her persona. Women both admired and envied her, and men lusted for her. The fact that she was not conscious of her physical charm only added to the magnetism. In office, she was a no-nonsense woman and commanded immediate attention and respect from her superiors (not many), peers and juniors.

As she walked into his room, Motu immediately snapped to attention to welcome her.

Unlike Arjun, Jaanvee did not need the preliminaries to start a serious conversation. Knowing this, Motu was all business immediately.

'Where's all our money going, Jaanvee? Have you left us with anything in the bank?' Motu started in a lighter vein.

With back-to-back meetings throughout the day Motu realised it was always better to start off humorously, with issues which weren't that important, giving people the necessary time required to switch their minds to the meeting at hand. Also, that was the only time they usually got to recoup their energies.

'The usual, BD. Most of it you distribute as salary and what is left is spent on ferrying your employees to office, providing 24x7 air-conditioning and paying the increasingly greedy landlords of Gurgaon,' she replied in the same vein.

Motu suddenly remembered his father's small dingy shop in Karol Bagh.

In a single sentence Jaanvee had summed up the four biggest expenses of any software company: salary, rent, power and transportation. Welfare of the people being the biggest concern of all software companies, they innovated to provide their employees with the best possible facilities. Motu was worried about the ever-increasing property rents. Land sharks of Gurgaon had realised that companies would have no other choice but succumb to their demands after investing so much money on their property. Not everybody knew that rents in Gurgaon competed with those in the Silicon Valley minus the infrastructure that it provided. Salary was another area of concern. They were ridiculously high as compared to other industries. There were brilliant people in automobile and construction too and they worked an equal number or more hours to produce world-class products but at half the salary of what people in software demanded and got.

'So what do we do about them?'

'Maybe we should buy our own piece of land and move away from here.'

Both of them were not sure if it was indeed the solution.

'Hmm … okay. Right now I want you to work on two things.' Motu changed the topic.

'San has run into a few problems with the Babe. Can you sit with him and figure out the cost of changes he is suggesting to make?' Motu paused.

'What's the second one, BD?'

'There's a small company which is doing work similar to us. Many of our ex-employees have joined there. You'll get the details from Arjun. I need all the information about this company. Can you do it for me?'

'How much do you want to know?'

'Everything you can lay your hands on.'

'And how soon do you want it?'

'Very,' Motu said with a sense of urgency.

'And which one is more important?'

'Both.'

❧

Nitin was in a sour mood. He headed the administration at PureConsultants. He firmly believed in the theory that there was no job more thankless than that of an administration head. He had multiple problems at hand. He was always short of money. He had bought himself a big house whose EMI he could not afford. He periodically sent money back home to Kolhapur to support his retired father. Apart from that, he had to partly bear the burden of his treatment. He realised that he might not get fat salary hikes any more. He was frightened to think of the day, which he knew was not too far, when he would need more money and support than he could get. He reminded himself to speak to Motu in the meeting about a possible salary hike. One more reason for his unhappiness was that his manager had gone away from work unannounced, and he was doing things which otherwise he would not have been involved in.

'I have not stolen anything. What I have done is my right. I service the generators (diesel-run captive power generation units) on hot summer afternoons. If I sell the oil which nobody in the company needs, am I a thief? Did I ever say anything when they sold old newspapers and pocketed the money?' cried Ramlal, the electrician, not realising that blood was oozing from the gash in his forehead, thanks to the twenty-year-old engagement ring of the burly security guard.

Generally, an admin manager's job in a software company is cushy as the problems are less complex because of it being populated by educated people, many of whom have travelled across the world, thus leading to a more mature outlook towards things. Nitin called the admin supervisor and enquired about all the old newspapers and cardboard boxes in the office. He feigned ignorance. At the same time, he looked harshly at Ramlal which gave Nitin some clue as to what was transpiring in his head. Nitin realised that the newspapers must have been sold by him but had no proof to back it up. He always suspected that there were small mafias running parallel to each other in the company and were controlling the fate of a few lakh rupees – one belonged to the drivers who operated the company vehicles and left him suspicious about the unaccountable few hundred litres of petrol every year; the second one was run by the admin supervisor Suresh, in connivance with the security officers, who smuggled anything out of the office that they thought was not useful for PureConsultants. The third one, which had surfaced recently, was the gang of electricians who he wondered must be pocketing the biggest amount as they had control over more than a hundred thousand litres of diesel. The genesis of today's trouble lay in Ramlal's refusal to share the spoils with the rest of them which became the main reason of consternation among the other two mafias. This was why Ramlal was caught and the matter was brought to Nitin's notice.

Usually, the amount involved was not very high; so Nitin turned a deaf ear with more pressing issues always eating into his time. Today was different. It was the first time a theft had been reported and he had to act in his official capacity. Normally, he would not have taken such a harsh decision but he was badgered with problems from all sides and was not thinking rationally.

'Ramlal, you are fired. I expect you to return all the company things in the next one hour and leave. And you take care that he is out of the building in the given time,' Nitin gave orders to Ramlal and the burly security officer in pristine blue dress in one breath.

'Yes, sir,' the security officer was left confused by the brazenness of Nitin's action.

On his way to BD's office, Nitin thought he saw a smug smile on the face of the admin supervisor, but there was no doubt as to what he saw in Ramlal's eyes – loathe. He had never seen so much hatred in anyone's eyes and it left him worried.

Nitin's association with Motu went back many years when Motu, Pankaj, Nitin and Arjun worked together in a small office. His eyes moistened when he remembered the old days, and lately he had been thinking of them quite often. He liked and respected Motu immensely. In fact, he had always been a little in awe of Motu. He felt a deep sense of gratitude for Motu for helping him find a place for himself in the big bad world. He was unconditionally loyal to Motu but always felt dwarfed by his personality. This was the main reason he could never discuss his own problems with Motu which he thought were much smaller than what Motu faced (running the company) every day.

'Hi, BD!' He smiled at Motu on his way in.

'Your smile looks laboured. Is anything the matter with you?'

Nitin told him about Ramlal and he also wanted to tell Motu how he had fired him when he realised that Motu had lost interest because of the bigger problem of the Babe not shaping up well.

These days Motu felt pangs of guilt whenever he met Nitin. He always thought that he could have done more for Nitin. Apart from the woman he loved, Nitin and Arjun were his only link to the painful past. Memories of his friendship with Pankaj were still vivid in his mind.* There were others too, but he considered them only his associates and he liked to keep a clear distinction between the two. All his associations failed to cross that boundary. Pankaj and Priya and, to a lesser extent, Nitin and Arjun emerged as the only true friends he ever had.

Motu had realised that Nitin had peaked out. It was becoming increasingly difficult for him to find a place for Nitin in his rapidly growing organisation. He also realised that Nitin needed money for his treatment. He was very often caught between friendship and his role as the CEO and so far the friend had won each time.

'BD, I wanted to ask you something?'

'Yes, go ahead.'

'I need a raise as I am finding it difficult to meet my expenses,' Nitin stuttered; he always did when he had to talk about money with someone. It was only five months since Nitin had got his last raise.

'You are asking for too much, Nitin. You know I cannot do this. I need to justify my actions as the head of this organisation. I think you realise that you are already drawing a salary higher than what your peers are getting in the industry.

Nitin did not reply, but Motu sensed that his tall frame had shrunk immediately.

'I am sorry, Nitin! I had a bad day,' Motu was contrite, not daring to look Nitin in the eye. When he actually did, Nitin had already walked out. He was again filled with remorse for Nitin. 'It's a hell of a day,' he muttered to himself.

⟡

This Monday had been unusually bad for Motu. It was almost five in the evening. He decided to call New York and finish the last call on his agenda. He relaxed suddenly and dialled the number.

'How are you?' His voice was very soft.

'Good, but I am still half asleep.'

'When are you coming to India? It's been some time since I last saw you,' Motu said trying to hide the longing in his voice.

'It's been so many years but you still don't forget to wake me up,' she said in her sleepy yet seductive voice.

'That's because I know you will get late, and that is something I cannot afford – a productivity loss,' Motu said humorously.

'But I feel like sleeping some more! Is it Monday already?'

'Yes, it is and that too not a good one,' Motu pulled both of them out of the reverie.

'Give me ten minutes.'

Motu put the phone back reluctantly, letting his fertile brain run wild, imagining all sorts of things she would be doing in those ten minutes. He loved her. Perhaps his love for her was enhanced by the distance between them. She, incidentally, was also his 'chief of marketing' in the USA. She did not happen to be there because of nepotism. She was one of the most deep thinking strategists he had ever known, an expert in the pharma domain where most of their business in the US came from and a big part of the Babe's success depended on how much conviction she had.

New-age Indians had for long stopped inducting undeserving family members and relatives into the mainstream of their businesses. They realised how professional the business environment had become. They also started respecting the guys on the other side who rose from the ranks, had an entrepreneurial spirit, a professional degree to back it up and were ready to soil their shirt. The bane of the Indian business was the 'License Raj', which when abolished, led to the release of huge amount of positive energy and talent into the Indian business sector.

It was high time that the country of over a billion which had 330-million deities began to hero-worship deserving business gods. This begun in the 1990s with every organisation boasting of many heroes, if not gods, and businesses striving hard to win the confidence of the common man. The average age of business honchos dropped to between mid-thirties and mid-forties with the unleashing of the power of the youth.

↬

The incessant ringing of the bell brought Motu back to the more immediate problem. 'If only phones could transfer smells?' Motu said.

'They do images at least. Why don't you switch on the video conferencing?'

He saw her, mint fresh and looking lovely as ever in a white top and jeans, her favourite dress for years.

'So what's up?' It was strictly business after that.

'What is your opinion on the Babe?'

'How do you want it?' she asked.

'Raw and naked.'

'It will be difficult for me to sell it the way we have made it. The competition has made a more comprehensive product. I went to my friends in the top five pharma companies for their feedback on the Babe and I did not return very happy.

'All of them said that a lot more still needs to be done before it can turn into something worthwhile for them. Mind you these five companies together are worth one thousand billion dollars. You cannot afford not to listen to them. They are the gods,' she summarised. The voice was still soft, calm, undramatic and without a quiver. It was difficult to grasp the damage if one was not listening seriously.

'I have been hearing the word "competition" for a few weeks now. Do you remember when we started with the Babe there was no competition. Now suddenly there is, and everyone is so acutely aware of it. I feel something is not right here,' Motu blurted, remembering the days when they conceptualised the product.

'You are actually right. We had researched the market exhaustively and there actually was no competition,' she spoke haltingly, trying to recall the exact sequence of events, memories that had faded, ravaged by the constant stream of other important pieces of information filling her mental space every day. And this was just a few years ago.

'Again till about six months ago too, there was no competition. Products this size don't get made overnight. How did we not get to know about this earlier?'

'You are right.'

'Have they sold anything till now?'

'Nothing that I know of,' she said trying to think hard.

'Now on to the most important question, who else is making a similar product? Is it one, two or has the whole industry started making one?'

'I don't have an answer right now,' she replied, completely on the back foot now.

'Then find out,' Motu said brusquely, realising that much of what happened in their future was linked to how the Babe fared in the market.

It often happened with them. While discussing work, they would completely forget their relationship. Sometimes, they would argue and fight furiously on what they perceived as right but at the end of it they got back to normalcy. They never took these arguments to heart. Their respect for each other had survived their tough professional relationship.

'How's it going otherwise?' she asked after the business was over.

'We have lost a few key people. San is unusually stressed, and I am feeling guilty about not being able to help Nitin anymore,' Motu summarised the meetings that happened during the day.

'I have a premonition that we are running into bad weather. We need all the toughness we can gather to survive. Remember, when times are tough, one thing or the other snaps. I hope nothing does in our case. Just be careful,' she said.

'Of what?'

'I don't know. We just need to be wary, though.'

Motu's heart sank. Her hunch usually came true. And he really wished this one did not. He wasn't naturally courageous or aggressive. His courage came from the knowledge that he had the means to handle the system. Pankaj was both, and had an instinct for handling the toughest of situations. Motu wished Pankaj could be by his side to see this through.

Motu had been bruised badly after his separation from Pankaj. Then he was young and ready for the fight. This time it was different. He had gotten older by a few years and battered by the tough daily battles in the office. An outright war at this stage was something he wanted to avoid. He knew, he had great people who were ready to fight till the end with him, but as the chief of marketing he had to be vigilant. And the feeling that there may be a mole in his organisation made him all the more uneasy. He did some arithmetic and realised that the only outsiders he had in his close circle were Jaanvee and San, and it was difficult for him not to trust both of them.

༄

Nitin was a totally depressed man by the time the day ended. Monday had been terribly harsh on him. He dreaded the look in Ramlal's eyes when he left the office. He felt guilty of firing him, whatever may have been the provocation. Someone told him that Ramlal belonged to the warrior Rajput community and was also related to the local MLA. He was not going to take things lying down. All these thoughts playing in his mind left him uneasy. But the final skirmish at the gate of the office made Nitin's resolve of not taking Ramlal back at any condition stronger.

'Sir, you made a wrong decision by firing me. You still have time to reconsider if you want.' There was neither respect nor regret in his voice.

'No, you're out. And that is final,' Nitin was determined not to change his decision.

He pushed the negative thoughts away for some time. He was scheduled to have a routine check-up with his doctor that evening. And that remained on the top of his mind for the moment. As he drove off to the doctor's chamber, he was feeling nostalgic about all the good things that had once been a part of his life, and he wanted to cry.

'How am I doing today, Doc?'

'Not very well, Nitin. The HIV infection is seemingly becoming resistant to the antiretroviral drugs I had prescribed. We may have to change the treatment once again.'

'Does this mean the medicines will become more expensive now?' Nitin shivered.

'I am afraid, yes,' the doctor said.

After returning from Russia, Nitin had remained off medicine for a few years as HIV did not bring the count of the immune cells down by much. But when he went from stage IV to stage III of the disease in the early years of 2000, the doctor advised him to start the treatment. The dosage was complex and he had to be very careful in sticking to the regimen. He remembered asking the doctor how much time he had, to which the doctor had replied, 'An able-bodied young man like you can live for twenty more years before you actually become infected with AIDS. You have a lot of healthy living left in you, young man.'

That was five years ago.

'The immune cells are falling rapidly. At this rate, you may move to Stage II very soon. That is the reason why we need to change both the regimen and the combination of drugs. But I am surprised by the rapid decline in your condition. The immune cell count does not fall so fast. Are you taking your medicines properly?' the doctor asked, frowning.

Afraid of a rebuke he did not tell the doctor that he had missed a few because he had to save money to send it back home. Little did he realise that the HIV developed a resistance to drugs because of an irregular regimen.

'Nitin, you may not admit it, but I think you are not serious about your life. If that is the case, you are going to die faster than it takes to wink.' He looked straight into Nitin's eyes.

'My father needs money to sustain his dying cloth mill,' Nitin blurted.

'And you need it to live. All my efforts and time mean nothing if you don't take yourself seriously. Remember it's not cold or cough that you can ignore; it's AIDS we are talking about,' the doctor shouted.

'Yes, sir, I promise to be more careful in future.'

'You'd rather be if you want to live. I hope I have been able to drive home the enormity of the situation.

Nitin nodded his head quietly and then asked, 'Your fees, sir?'

'Use it for your medicine. You still have a long way to go,' the doctor's voice softened finally.

The doctor, a forty-year-old man with a golden heart, knew about Nitin's family condition, and so never took money from him unlike the usual practice in the medical fraternity, which has industrialised medicine and has made saving lives a hugely profitable business. He decided to speak to the AIDS Foundation for providing financial support to him. It was founded by a rich industrialist who took considerable interest in Nitin's case.

A dejected Nitin got up to leave. Two pairs of eyes followed him to his car. One, the doctor's – moist with concern, the other, a stranger's – glistening with revenge.

As soon as Nitin left, the doctor called the industrialist. He was funding the treatment of many such patients. This made the doctor optimistic that getting Nitin a benefactor would not be a problem.

'I want to recommend someone for treatment.'

How bad is the case, Doctor?'

'Not good. The guy seems to be losing the will to live, and that may prove to be counter-productive.

'Apart from the medicine, can we do something else?'

'Give him hope and a reason to live.'

∽

Jaanvee had her plate full. But she, unlike many people, loved challenges. By the time she walked out of BD's office she had already begun to size the magnitude of both the problems at hand. The first was a meeting with San which brought a smile to her face and the second, investigation of the mysterious company, made her frown. She decided to attack the more pleasant one first.

'How's the mood today, San?'

'Belligerent.'

'It doesn't seem to be the right time to discuss the Babe today then?'

'And what else can we discuss? We don't seem to have anything in common.' San picked one of her lines she had used once to kid him.

'San, we are in serious trouble with the Babe and you know that as well as I do. I have a very busy schedule today, so let's cut the crap. We need to make a plan to feed the Babe till it grows up to be self-sustaining.'

'You think the Babe is an artificially injected chicken leg? We cannot make it fatter faster and ready for sale by making a financial plan. It needs time and nurturing. Anyway, let's meet in the evening when you are finished with your busy schedule,' San backed off a bit.

Jaanvee regretted her outburst, but she was in a no-nonsense mood. She was always like that in the first half of the morning, tightly knot brows slowly relaxing as the day progressed. She liked San for his youthful energy, intellect and his ability to converse on any subject, from weather to women to wine to politics. What she detested in him was the aggression with which he tried to enter her inner space, which she had guarded fiercely, and till then had strictly been a no-man's land, constantly challenging her resolve to stay single.

She had successfully warded off all the previous attempts. Those attempts were from seasoned, highly successful and filthy rich older men and she had devised a successful mechanism to deal with such men. She knew her way around them, did not feel threatened by them and knew how to handle them. But San was none of that. He was young and had enough money to splurge which he complained was never enough. He was still learning how to climb the ladder of power. Somehow Jaanvee, intelligent as she was, failed to decipher him and was thus always tentative with him. Maybe it had something to do with her inner turmoil, but she still had not found the answer to the mystery called San before her meeting with him that day.

Jaanvee's day was typical for a finance head. She looked at the financial risks involved in different projects. She found that they were within manageable limits. The profits looked decent. The only worrying factor was the position of cash. Her customers were negotiating with her for longer payment terms which would lead to tight cash-flows. She decided to speak to her banker for help.

'Hey, Siddharth! How about redrawing our cash limits? The proposal is pending with you for a long time now,' Jaanvee asked the CEO of the bank after the preliminaries were over.

They often met at seminars and had developed a cordial relation bordering on professional respect for each other.

'Yes, I know. I will ask my team to hurry this one up,' he sounded evasive.

'Sid, I have a very healthy balance sheet. You must be a fool to turn a customer like me away,' Jaanvee was angry.

'The bank will not shut down if it stops doing business with a certain Jaanvee,' Sid retorted.

Jaanvee knew she needed him at the moment, and should do nothing to piss him off. 'I am sorry for my outburst. Just a little stressed out on the "Manic Monday" as they call it,' she apologised.

'Okay, Jaanvee. But you should learn to differentiate between your subordinates and a banker. You know being impolite to a banker can do you more harm than good,' Sid answered playfully, but Jaanvee could identify the threat in his voice.

'Yes, I know,' she sighed into the already dead line.

She told herself to be patient. The decision may be taking time as the amount she was asking for was a few hundred crores. She had no other option either. All the other banks had already refused her and Siddharth looked like her last and only hope.

❧

Nitin had remained awake deep into the night thinking of how he wanted to lead his life. His biggest problem was that he did not have the support from family and the society that he so badly needed. Whenever sad, he remembered the days in Russia prior to his getting infected with HIV. His mother, Pankaj and Motu were the only people he could look up to for support and all three supports had withered away. Mama, as she needed financial support herself; Pankaj, as Nitin almost did not see him anymore because of the different paths their lives had taken; and Motu, as lately he had become more of a boss than a friend, which Nitin always tried to understand but couldn't. But, in spite of everything, he still loved all of them. For him, the perfect harmony in life was being in a state of happiness whatever the circumstances. He promised himself to get Motu and Pankaj together before he died, if only once. He went to sleep still swaying between despondency and hope searching for that reason to live, his tall frame shrinking as if wanting to go back to the comfort of the womb from where he had come so many years ago, a carefree child.

Nitin woke up the next morning ready to go to the office, willing himself to think that the worst was over. The spring in his feet was back. On his way inside, he saw some unusual activity in the office. The security guard at the gate was not his usual cheerful self and avoided looking him in the eye. The same happened with many of his other colleagues; their greetings restrained as if avoiding him. During the day wherever he went he saw small groups of people, engrossed in heated discussions, suddenly going quiet on seeing him as if they did not want him to know what they were talking about. He was bewildered by their reaction, dismissing it as their angst against him for firing Ramlal. The same behaviour continued till about 4:00 p.m., when not being able to take it anymore, he approached Julie – a colleague and a very good friend.

'Hi, Julie, what's going on?'

'Nothing much.' She too avoided looking him in the eye.

'I can feel something is wrong. Please let me know what it is?' His eyes begged her. Julie chose not to respond and stepped back a little. 'Please, Julie. Is it because of Ramlal?'

'I don't know any Ramlal. It is because of you,' she blurted angrily.

Nitin heaved a sigh of relief, clearly missing the bigger problem. 'What about me? Are my trousers torn?'

'Nitin, you have AIDS,' Julie almost shouted.

By that time a group of about fifty people had already surrounded them. Each one of them had loathe in their eyes. 'I don't have AIDS. I am only infected with HIV,' Nitin replied, meekly taking support of the handle of the chair on his right.

'Don't lie to us. Do you realise how much damage you would have done by now? You sit with us, eat with us and we shake hands with you every day.' Julie was crying now.

Nitin sat down on the floor, not knowing what to say. Except for Motu, Pankaj and his family nobody knew he was infected. 'It is nobody's business. Let's keep this to ourselves,' Pankaj had advised him many years ago. And that's how they had kept it for so long.

The group swelled to a hundred-and-fifty. By then all the other activities on the floor had stopped. Nitin helplessly looked at the crowd. He had realised no logic would work so he decided to shut his mouth. To make matters worse for him, Motu was not in the office. What saved him from a physical assault was that people were afraid to touch him.

'You need to get out of here right away,' someone from the crowd shouted.

Nitin was crying openly now. He stood up and began to walk slowly, his legs refusing to support his weight. Now he understood the look in the security officer's eyes in the morning. While backing his car, he thought he saw Ramlal in the rear-view mirror, standing close to a van with a satellite disc on the top, saying something in the mike in front of him with a smug smile on his face.

$\backsim$

By the time Jaanvee finished with all the regular items on her agenda, it was already late in the evening. The office had only a handful of people left. They were people who had to meet customer deadlines, take status calls, and also people from administration who needed to ferry employees to their homes. It is rightly said that a big software company is like a metropolitan that never sleeps.

'Are you free, San? Can we meet now?'

'I have been waiting for this moment. Shall we go out for a candlelight dinner?'

'For now, the boardroom will do. Don't forget to bring your notes with you. The unorganised person that you are, you will need to refer to your notes regularly since your brain rarely works, more so in the night!'

'Try me. I am a nocturnal creature. I only just began to feel alive,' San started flirting, realising she was more relaxed now than in the morning.

'What is the problem?' She tried getting official. 'I want every bit of it. Don't try to hide anything from me. I will get to it eventually.'

'Did I ever hide anything from you? he said, refusing to forego the chance of flirting. 'It is the other way round. You are the one who is holding back. When will you open up to me, Jaanvee?'

'I am not sure about what you like in me. If it is my beauty, it will wither away with time. What will survive the onslaught of time is my soul and you haven't even started to know it yet.'

'Please open it to me, Jaanvee. I have been dying to ask you this question.'

'I just realised that begging got sophisticated and corporatised too.' Jaanvee burst out laughing.

'Don't you think it's time you fell in love?' San ignored her comment.

'I do, but I don't want to end up dating juveniles. I have a career to take care of. Even if I do get interested in you, rumours such as your obsession with saving water haunt me and really kill my curiosity,' Jaanvee said, suppressing a chuckle.

'I take bath at least once.' San was on the defensive now.

'But isn't that your weekly average?' Jaanvee was enjoying the banter.

'Can't you smell the perfume on me?'

'Mixed with the odour of your sweat, it is something else now.'

'That's not sweat, that's musk.'

'Try launching a musk range of toiletries then,' Jaanvee laughed again while San looked at her.

He was tempted to ask her to make love to him. Her frank demeanour served as an invite, making him feel that he could ask anything of her and she would not refuse. But he knew that behind the veneer Jaanvee was tough and unyielding. 'So what's the problem?' Jaanvee broke his reverie.

'The Babe needs to be revamped. Otherwise it does not stand a chance,' San said.

After that he ran Jaanvee through every detail of the problem. He spoke continuously for two hours telling her that most of her features were written in older, replaceable code making her outdated, slow and unacceptable to the industry. Both of them wondered how the change of certain rules by the USFDA – the regulatory body responsible for controlling, among other things, the safety of drugs and the behaviour of the pharma behemoths, made the Babe unusable in its present form.

'In short, whatever we have done to build her into a world-class product will come to naught if we do not make the necessary changes immediately,' San seemed frustrated.

'You love her, don't you?' Jaanvee said.

'I do. Apart from that, it does not make business sense to dump her now after putting so much money into her.'

'But it also does not make any business sense to put money into something which has gone into a coma with no signs of a revival,' Jaanvee replied.

'The Babe is not dying!' San shouted.

'I know. What I just said was only hypothetical. You know I like this never-say-die attitude of yours. I hate to lose and be associated with losers.'

They kept on talking deep into the night. They talked some more about the Babe and a lot about each other with San again managing to break into her inner space. By the time they finished it was two in the morning.

They said a soft 'goodnight' to each other and departed. Both of them remembered the night very well but for different reasons. The fact that Jaanvee hated defeat struck San, while she realised that it was only a matter of time before she would fall into an abyss. She could see that happening sooner than later.

'Let me try and see if I can love him from a distance,' Jaanvee muttered to herself.

She checked the time. It was 4:00 a.m. in the morning. She had still not started the second important assignment given to her by BD.

∽

Nitin's exasperated look got splashed on the front page of the national dailies, which unfortunately for him was the first day of the weekend, a Saturday. Pain, torment, fear and helplessness were written large on his face in the photograph. Instead of sympathy, he invited public ire. Opinion polls were conducted on him with an overwhelming (and uninformed) majority declaring that he was on the wrong side. Mass opinion portrayed him as a shrewd 'corporate villain' who indulged in deceit and lied to people about his condition for many years. He became prime time news for Saturday and Sunday in the absence of any other significant news. For the news-starved media, he became the most discussed and debated personality. The debate also took a political hue with self-proclaimed moral groups holding protests in major metropolises. The first one in Delhi was led by Ramlal and his MLA relative enjoying their moment of glory. They set his effigy on fire and stomped it in broad daylight under the full glare of the weekend cameras. In short, Nitin was killed before he had even begun to die.

Nitin confined himself to his apartment, not daring to venture out. He even switched off his cellphone dreading unsolicited hate calls. He stopped eating, drinking and taking medicine, not caring anymore about his fragile condition.

A week later, someone knocked at his door. It was hope. He had heard a few people knock earlier as well, but he didn't open the door fearing the worst. This knock was uncanny, soft and intriguing.

'Are you there, Nitin?' He did not reply thinking it was someone from the press.

'Nitin, I am Tanya, and I assure you I don't represent anyone,' her voice carried through the cracks under the door. Nitin still did not reply.

'Oh! I forgot to tell you one more thing about me which makes me so special, I don't bite.' Nitin could imagine her smiling.

'Do you want me to disclose everything about me while standing out here in the heat? If you delay opening the door you will not be able to see my new dress before ...' Tanya did not get to complete the sentence.

'What do you want?' Nitin's voice was brusque, business-like. It had been days since even sunlight had got a look in, and he was in no mood to let that change.

He looked dishevelled, his seven-day old stubble had begun to look like a beard; his eyes were swollen and full of despair.

'Wow! You still have a lot of machismo left in you,' Tanya barged into his large four-bedroom apartment, pushing him aside.

'Tell me one thing. You are infected with HIV. To top it up you are unhygienic and unattractive. I don't think anybody will ever marry you. Then why do you need such a big shack?' she said while taking a tour of his apartment.

'How do you know of my condition?' Nitin said, desperately wanting to hide the facts from her.

'The whole country knows it,' she said nonchalantly.

Nitin was amazed by her confidence. What attracted him towards her was that inspite of being dressed in a simple light blue-coloured T-shirt and dark blue jeans, she looked extremely beautiful. He was also impressed by her child-like exuberance and innocence.

'Well, when I bought it I had money to invest,'

'Hmm! Bourgeois is trying to play Mr Cool. You don't look like you ever take a bath, so what's the need of a towel?' she said as she folded one and put it back in its place.

'Don't touch my towel, you may catch the virus,' Nitin replied playfully, opening up to her. He tried to recall the last time he had smiled.

'I will not. And this is exactly the reason I am here. I want to tell the whole nation that you have done nothing wrong if you don't go out spreading the virus. That you are well within your rights to keep it private and that you need compassion to survive. You need to be accepted, not shunned.'

'Why do you want to do it?' Nitin asked, looking at her disbelievingly.

'Because they raped you on prime time television and there was no one to defend you. I want you to tell your side of the story to the whole country. But before that I need to know it.'

'Who are you? A doctor?'

'No, a lawyer,' Tanya said.

'Were you thrown out of your job? Don't you have anything better to do in life than try and save me?' Nitin was still sceptical.

'For your information, I was a top-notch lawyer till I left my cushy job with this famous law firm. When I was leaving they told me I could come back and join them any time I wanted to.'

'Then why did you leave in the first place?'

'Because I was defending all the wrong people. They were men with money and power, who abused both to create more money and power for themselves. I just walked out one day vowing never to go back. And here I am,' she said moving her hands frantically in the air.

'And when was that?'

'That was four years ago. In the meanwhile, I have rehabilitated four orphans and brought water to three villages. Luckily for you, I was free and looking for my next project when I saw you on tv.'

'Am I only a project for you?' Nitin asked gloomily.

'Yes, but a very special one. I will tell you why at the right time. Let me tell you about my one weakness. I tend to get romantically involved with all my projects.' She winked at him trying to lighten up the atmosphere.

'Now tell me how you landed in this mess. You look like a decent person to me.'

Nitin told her about his freewheeling days in Russia,* about his getting deported and then spending a few traumatic years back home in Kolhapur where he was ostracised by everyone including his family. He also told her how he was called by Pankaj to work with him and Motu, and how he was facing a financial crisis of late.

He told her everything, every little secret he had. There were a few interludes of tea and tears in between, both his and Tanya's. In the meanwhile, the sun had set somewhere behind the trees and darkness had taken over the street, but they did not bother about the time. He shared with her all the pain of the past so many years, of keeping his darkest secret to himself, the pain of solitude, of being left alone when he needed support, and the pain of answering uncomfortable questions about his bachelorhood which seemed to be in stark contrast to his affable and charming image. He kept on speaking till there was nothing left to be said.

'It's midnight already. You are such a gentleman that you did not even ask me for food,' Tanya said standing up.

'My cook also left me in the midst of this crisis. I can make something for you if you want,' Nitin offered.

'No, let's go out to eat. I will treat you to the best food of your life. Go, shave and take a bath. We do not want to tell the cruel bastards of the world that we have lost to them. Do we?'

Nitin complied without protesting. He felt light inside after so many years. He bathed himself with the best perfume in his collection and wore his best striped shirt with dark grey trousers.

'Wow! You look like you are dressed for your wedding,' Tanya said, embarrassing Nitin with her comment.

'You are dangerous. You know exactly what is going on in the other person's mind,' Nitin replied coyly.

Both of them went out of his apartment laughing.

∽

Jaanvee woke up at 7:00 a.m. on Tuesday morning feeling heavy with both guilt and sleep. She decided to skip office in the first half and concentrate on the second assignment given to her by Motu. Jaanvee, very often, worked from home when she needed to research on the Net or strategise. The only weapon she had was her laptop.

The new-age Internet-savvy entrepreneur relies very heavily on search engines for information and Motu was the first one to realise its immense potential in decision-making.

Jaanvee liked to work with Motu and considered him to be one of the best leaders in the industry. She was also a little worried after her meeting with Motu. Over a period of time she had fallen in love with PureConsultants, maybe because of her motherly instincts. PureConsultants was her surrogate child, replacing the physical, in-flesh one. She could not tolerate anything bad happening to it.

She started with the website of the company. It had the usual information about the areas it worked in. There were no details of the promoters which was pretty unusual for a software company. Small software companies attracted business based on the strength of the resumes of their promoters. Its website was also done shoddily, in stark contrast to the world-class work they were pitching for. She looked into the minutest of details for a clue, but could not find anything. It was two hours since she had sat down for the analysis. She got up to make coffee because she wanted the break to think.

Something did not seem right. She could not figure out what it was. Then suddenly it hit her. PureConsultants prided itself on being on the first page of the search engine on all the relevant keywords, but when Jaanvee put in the same keywords and looked at the results she found that PureConsultants was beaten in ranking by that small unknown company by the name 'Software Builder.' Then she realised that the website of Software Builder was almost identical to NumeroSoft's. It was like they were stalking them and copying every single move of theirs. She was flabbergasted. So Arjun's hunch was right. She had found an affirmative answer to the 'if' but not the 'why' when she reluctantly broke off for lunch at 4:00.

⌢

Tanya took Nitin to the best hotel in Gurgaon.

'What will you eat?' she asked.

'Anything and everything this place has to offer,' Nitin said.

They ordered the finest Italian delicacies and waited for food to come. Meanwhile, they began to think of different ways of hitting back.

'We need to tell the press our side of the story as well. I have a few friends in the media who can help us do this. Let me try and talk to them and see what can be done,' Tanya said.

'It's half an hour since we placed the order and the food has not yet come,' Nitin wondered.

'It's not even peak time. Food should have come by now. Something is not right here … and I think we know the reason,' said Tanya, looking around and fixing her eyes on something.

Nitin followed her eyes and he stopped at a small group watching tv in the far right corner, which was running an old and much battered story on Nitin. One of them pointed at Nitin, and the other at the picture on tv. From a distance they could make out that the duty manager had been called. In a few minutes, they saw him approaching them.

'Tighten up your belt. We are in for some fun,' Tanya said.

'Sir, you will have to leave our hotel,' the manager said, his voice polite but firm.

'May I know why?' Tanya hissed.

'Your being here is not good for the image of the hotel,' the manager said again.

'I understand you are in a difficult situation and sympathise with you. However, I promise you will find yourself in an even more dire situation if you do not allow us to eat here which, I believe, is our fundamental right,' Tanya was taking control.

'And how will you do that, madam,' the manager asked.

'I am a lawyer, the best in the trade. If you insist on throwing us out on some flimsy ground, I will sue your hotel. And the amount I will sue you for will run into crores. And when your hotel will lose this suit, it will fire you in no time.' Tanya was now completely in charge.

'Sorry, madam,' the manager took a few seconds to answer. Then he turned to his subordinates and said in a hushed tone, 'It's late in the night. Let's pretend we never saw them.'

'Thank god they did not call your bluff; otherwise we would have been out of here in no time,' Nitin told Tanya.

'I was not bluffing and if you want to die with your head held high, know your true worth,' Tanya replied in all seriousness.

The food tasted exotic after the small but significant victory.

The victory at the luxury hotel changed the way Nitin looked at himself and the world after that. He was backed to the hilt by Tanya. He began to believe and rely on her completely. Egged by her he was more confident and ready to take on the world. Full of hope he sat down with her to plan their next move.

'This is war. And if you don't take it as one you will be annihilated,' she advised him. 'Let's start with your office.'

Motu was back in office after spending ten days in Singapore for a conference and business meetings. He had caught Nitin's trauma live on tv. He tried calling him at least a thousand times, but always found his mobile switched off. He even sent someone to search for him, but without success. Nobody opened the door. After three days of trying he stopped, praying to god that everything be alright with him till he returned.

It was his first day in office after coming back, and he wanted to finish everything fast so that he could go down and see Nitin. It was only ten in the morning and he had been asked many uncomfortable questions already, 'Did you know about Nitin's medical condition, BD? If yes, why did you hide it from us?' The question was either in everyone's eyes or on their lips. He told the ones who asked that he had thought of telling them at the opportune moment.

'I need to go and find Nitin. This whole thing is making me mad,' he was muttering to himself when the intercom rang.

'Sir, Nitin has come to see you.' There was contempt in the operator's voice.

Nitin was ushered in by the no-nonsense security officer. He again wore a pristine blue uniform and a very confused look. To Motu's utter surprise Nitin was smiling. He was followed inside by a vivacious young lady with an angelic face.

'You stupid man! Where the hell have you been? I have already gone mad trying to find you,' Motu said. Nitin saw the concern and his soft side after many years. This made him cry again.

'Don't cry. This too will pass,' Motu tried to placate him.

'You will not understand the reason behind these tears,' Nitin smiled, leaving Motu puzzled. 'Anyway let me introduce Tanya.' Nitin and Tanya then spoke frantically to Motu for the next five minutes.

'Do you think we can pull it off?' Motu asked.

'Can you think of anything else?' Nitin retorted.

༄

After her small, lonely and simple lunch Jaanvee sat down to work at her laptop again. While nibbling at her food, she yearned for company which she never had the need for earlier, always preferring solitude and her own companionship to anyone else's. She began her research afresh. She had tried almost everything but had come up a cropper till now.

'You are getting old for this kind of stuff,' she rebuked herself.

She went back to the website of Software Builder and looked up their telephone number. She called the first number not knowing what to expect. She tried all the given numbers one by one but no one picked up.

'Strange! The office doesn't work at 4:30 in the afternoon!' She threw her hands up in frustration. She called one of her team members Sree, whom she always looked up to in tough times. 'Drop everything else. Find yourself a seat on the next plane to Bangalore. Go to Software Builder's office. See what you find. Report to me as soon as you have something,' she barked into the phone not heeding at all to his muted protests. She knew his wife was into the ninth month of her pregnancy but this was not the time to take decisions based on the personal circumstances of people.

Then she called Motu.

'Don't ask me for an update right now. Give me time till Friday though I am trying hard to find the answers earlier,' she told him. She could have given him some details, but did not want to share inconclusive findings with him.

Motu knew better than to set a deadline for Jaanvee.

'By the way the main reason I called you was to ask a question. Who are the people we have lost to Software Builder? Give me the last dossier you have on them.'

Motu promised to email her all the information she needed. His email landed within minutes of their conversation. One more example of how fast he was.

All the names in Motu's email seemed unfamiliar except one. She had met Shankaran a couple of times and had found him to be pretty intelligent. She sent him an email requesting him to contact her, not having any contact number of his.

She had taken all the actions she could. She had one more idea which she wanted to try out but deferred it till she got more information from Sree. She was sure he would be able to find something substantial. He was a smart cookie.

She had worked late into the night catching up on other important work. Being a very important cog in the PureConsultants' wheel she did not have the luxury of working only on one thing and delegating the rest to others.

She was woken up by the incessant ring of her cellphone and the strong sunlight which had managed to break into the room from behind the very dark curtains. It was 12:00 p.m.

'Jaanvee, if you are looking for some exciting news you are going to be disappointed.' It was Sree. 'I went to the address you gave me. The place is located in a residential complex in upmarket Bangalore. To add to my misery, it was locked. There were cobwebs around the door. Looks like nobody had been there in years,' Sree spoke in one breath.

'Looks like it is a dummy. Can you do me another favour please?'

'Only if you give me something more exciting to do. You know my daughter will not forgive you ever if she doesn't find her father by her side after she is born. And if she gets to know that you sent her father to visit closed doors and look at cobwebs, she will murder you for sure,' Sree said, always referring to his offspring as 'she'.

Jaanvee laughed heartily inspite of her tensed state.

'Go to the regional office of Company Affairs. Get the tax returns of Software Builder. Bribe someone if you have to. And I will kill you if you come back empty-handed. In this case, your daughter will have no father instead of a father who missed her birthday,' Jaanvee hissed into the phone.

'Yes, madam,' Sree resigned to his fate.

'And if you find some time go visit your mother-in-law. That will make your wife happy.'

'You are so nice even in difficult times,' Sree said sharply.

She commanded immense respect for Sree to have refused her and she knew it. He knew that her threat to kill him was made only to stress upon the importance of a point but with no malicious intent. She was known to love her entire team and stand by them in tough times.

Sree returned the next day with a well-compiled dossier which was surprisingly thin.

'How much did you have to shell out for this?'

'It cost me only two-hundred rupees and that too for the photocopies. The local chap was very cooperative unlike the people here.' Jaanvee had temporarily lost interest in him. It was a sign for Sree to leave.

Her heart was beating very fast against her ribs when she started leafing through the papers. The dossier was thin because Software Builder was formed only two years ago and had filed only one tax-return. It did not have any income and almost no assets. She was right. It was a dummy company. She went down to the director's report. It contained a lot of shit about the progress made in the previous year and its false future plans. That was not what she was interested in. She flipped another page and found what she was looking for – the name of the directors. One of them was Shankaran.

~

Being the technology head in PureConsultants was demanding to say the least. What differentiates the IT industry from others is the fast pace of its growth with new technologies emerging every other day. A technologist needs to read extensively and update himself constantly, otherwise he would soon be outpaced and sidelined by a more hardworking but not necessarily an equally intelligent colleague. Similarly, Arjun faced the additional burden of keeping himself updated along with the routine responsibility of taking care of a growing company like PureConsultants.

With Diyaa taking almost all of his spare time he always found himself too busy. He felt guilty when he spent more time in office than with Diyaa. He felt a tender love for her – maybe because she was completely dependent on him. Her big eyes seldom complained, only requesting, never demanding favours. The only exception to her behaviour was when Arjun came home late. That was when she began to throw tantrums, refusing to eat and complaining with a groan as she struggled to speak fully comprehensible words. But Arjun knew she was quick to forgive him.

Diyaa's condition led Arjun to subconsciously take the decision of not competing on technology with others who had more free time. He instead decided to control the multiple deliveries that happened every day, ensuring that releases went out to customers error-free and on time. That was one reason that though he was slightly hurt he did not feel very bad about Motu giving the Babe to San. He understood Motu's reasons and did not complain. In fact, deep inside he almost felt thankful to Motu that he did not give him the choice to decide. His pride would not have let him refuse Motu and he knew with the constraint on his time he was in no position to do justice to her.

This did not mean that he liked San. Arjun was envious of his carefree lifestyle and his devil-may-care attitude. Both of them had managed to keep their paths separate most of the time, so the altercations they had were too few and far between to really trouble anyone.

After his meeting with Motu, Arjun went back to handling regular issues. First, he checked the more than a hundred releases that were planned to go out that day. There were no red flags and things looked under control. All of them would go out to the customers as promised at different times in the day. Some customers would appreciate their work through emails sent to project discussion boards, others would come back with criticism of their code for not meeting the desired standards of quality which would later be corrected and delivered to their satisfaction. There were very few escalations that reached him and he could go to sleep in peace unlike the earlier days when he had just begun work with Motu and Pankaj.

He had very explicitly told his managers not to leave any project without satisfying the customer. Because of that there were even fewer customers who ever turned to litigation to get the desired results from them. The whole machinery had been fine-tuned by him and everybody knew his job. This had been achieved with years of building knowledge banks, trainings, and defined coding guidelines. So, Arjun did not bother about one bad delivery or a customer email because he knew that things would be sorted.

'Arjun, I have a slight problem with my project, and I wanted to discuss it with you,' his messenger window popped open. It was one of his toughest managers who could handle any customer.

'Okay! Why don't we meet in Renaissance?' Arjun referred to one of the meeting rooms.

'So much for the less stressful days,' he sighed deeply, raising a few eyebrows in an almost silent hall. He preferred sitting in the open with his engineering team. That helped him connect with his people and keep a tab on the regular buzz.

'What is the problem?' he asked the delivery manager.

'The client says we have screwed up and have not delivered what we had initially promised. It is an important project and this is a big release. We are delivering almost fifty-thousand hours of work. There were multiple components that had to be plugged together to make it function. One of the most important components is not functioning well.

'Whose fault is this? Fire him immediately?' Arjun was furious. A howling customer was what he could never forgive.

'We don't need to. He has left already and that too abruptly. He did not give even a day's notice.'

Never before in the history of PureConsultants had a senior manager left them in such haste. He had always worked with responsible people, and he took pride in putting the right people at the right place.

'Do you know where he went?'

'No.'

Arjun suspected that it must be Software Builder. He was left stranded again.

'What is the impact on us?'

'This project has the personal backing and interest of the customer VP. He is putting his reputation at stake for this. In case you have forgotten he is expected to be one of the first clients for the Babe as well. The impact on this project is going to be immense in terms of actual as well as collateral damage.' The delivery manager need not have spoken the last lines.

This further consolidated his conspiracy theory which Motu had dismissed with a laugh. Arjun was still confident that they would be able to salvage lost ground as the customer had been a friend since many years. He knew both Motu and

Arjun and had helped them when they had only started out as a small company. At the time, Motu, Pankaj, Nitin and Arjun were all working together; their single-minded focus in life was NumeroSoft and their friendship. But even the customer would not be able to help them if the project was not put back on track immediately.

'Yes, you are right. Who is the best guy we have for solving this?'

'We have San but he is completely occupied with the Babe. He is out, I guess. Then the next best guy we have is involved in one of my other projects. I can pull him out of there and put him onto this one.'

Arjun agreed. San was out of question. Had he been the only choice, Arjun would have put aside his personal feelings and propagated his transfer to the project, but in the current scenario it was not the best choice considering the importance of the Babe for PureConsultants.

Of late he had come to resent the idea of shuffling people from one project to the other. Since this was an emergency and the project was one of their biggest revenue grossers, he agreed. Demand on the time of their best resources was one of the dilemmas that the technology heads of software companies faced and they were under constant pressure to utilise them in the most efficient manner. So, these people were used sparingly in difficult projects when the situation got out of control of the delivery managers.

'Do you think we shall be able to control the problem with this movement?'

'Yes.'

Arjun dismissed the manager and reached for his cellphone to provide more proof to Motu about his conspiracy theory. 'Can you change the managers' figure to eleven?'

'What?' Motu said exasperated, not understanding what Arjun implied. 'I just lost one more and my gut says it must be Software Builder. You don't dismiss this as routine now,' Arjun said.

'I won't dare to,' Motu said squirming in his chair.

Motu was not afraid of a fight because they were common within a framework with a defined set of rules. But this was war. He desperately wanted Pankaj to be beside him.

After Motu met Nitin and Tanya, an email was sent to all the employees of PureConsultants for the 'town hall' on the next day. Town halls were a regular feature in PureConsultants (as in many software companies) and were conducted whenever the whole company wanted to meet formally or informally.

The atmosphere was abuzz with excitement – some of it positive, mostly negative.

'We are meeting under extraordinary circumstances today,' Motu cleared his throat while trying to count hundreds of heads in the hall.

'I take immense pride in the fact that we are a democratically-run company. We give a fair chance and platform to every individual before arriving at any decision here. But this democratically-run company hanged someone last week without giving him a fair chance to explain his side of the story.

'We failed collectively last week, and I feel ashamed that it happened in our company, which we have all so painstakingly built together. Do you want to cleanse your conscience and give that someone a chance again? You are free to announce your verdict after that,' Motu concluded sincerely.

Nobody spoke but nodded in support.

'Then I will call Nitin, a colleague and one of my dearest friends, to this platform.'

Only the sound of air-conditioning and the flash of the cameras of the media persons who had come to cover the event could be heard in the silent hall.

'Everyone commits mistakes in his life. Some mistakes affect our life; others affect the lives of people around us. We apologise when we have in some way harmed them due to our mistakes and caused them pain. We are either forgiven or banished. Forgiveness is given if their capability to forgive is greater than the pain caused.

'Long ago, I committed the mistake of having unprotected sex. I got afflicted with HIV. I apologise to my family every day because my mistake has made them suffer. They have forgiven me and they love me like they did before I caught the virus. This is the reason I am still alive.

'But I do not say sorry to you because I have not caused you any pain. At the same time, I look up to you for support and love. For me, survival is already difficult. Please do not make it more difficult by discriminating against me,' Nitin ended with a plea.

Nitin's small speech was powerful, emotional, and awe-inspiring. For a few seconds, no one could gauge the mood of the audience. But a small clap from the back of the hall egged on the educated software community of PureConsultants to finally accept Nitin as one of their own. They understood him and liked him for the courage he displayed in coming out in the open. Amidst the applause, no one except Nitin noticed that Tanya who was earlier standing in the right hand corner of the hall was missing.

Tanya had decided to take a backseat and let Nitin be the hero of the day. It was she who had suggested not to make the speech apologetic. Somewhere during the middle of the speech, she realised that the gamble was paying off and it would go down really well with the audience. She also realised that if she stayed any longer in the hall she would break down. So she went to the restroom to wash her tears.

'When will you learn not to get emotionally involved with everything you do?' she chided herself as she wiped her tears. Nitin was special for Tanya. She had lost her father to AIDS when she was eleven. Her father had caught the virus on his only visit to a brothel on the East Coast in the US. Instead of help he had got the boot.

'I am dying. Don't throw me out,' he had pleaded with Tanya's grandfather.

'For me, you are already dead,' Grandpa shouted at her father.

'Grandpa, please let him stay,' Tanya had pleaded with him, not wanting to let him go after losing her mother to an accident only a few years ago.

'Tanya, you keep out of this. You don't know what he has done.'

That was the last she had seen her father. She heard later from someone that he had died on the street with no one to look after him. She always regretted that she could not do anything for him. When she heard about Nitin she was reminded of her father's condition. And the orphans, villages and water stories were just cooked up to impress Nitin. What she did not tell him was that she had left the cushy job only to be with him and help him live a respectable life.

Her chain of thoughts was broken by a loud knock on the door. 'Tanya, are you inside? The security officer told me you came here.'

'Just give me a minute,' she said.

'People came and shook hands with me. I feel alive for the first time after so many days. This is all because of you. Thank you,' Nitin said when she came out.

'You were not there towards the end. You should have seen the applause.'

'Now what do you want me to do, clap for you? Will this make you happier?'

Nitin was shocked by the angst in her voice. 'Let me drop you home. You seem upset,' he said softly.

'It's okay. You are back where you wanted to be. The project is over,' she said.

'Does that mean our relationship is over too?'

Tanya did not reply.

∿

Jaanvee was not shocked. She had seen enough in life not to be stunned by anything anymore. What she did not understand was that why would Shankaran join 'Software Builder.' So far as she remembered he left the company on good terms.

'I am looking for bigger opportunities which I don't believe PureConsultants can offer at this stage.' He had told Jaanvee when he was leaving. The determined look on his face stopped Jaanvee from asking him any more questions.

'I want to control lives which can only come with absolute power,' he had said as if answering Jaanvee's unasked question, his eyes burning with ambition.

Shankaran had told people that he was starting his own company. So his name as a director of 'Software Builder' did not surprise Jaanvee. But starting a dummy company did not give him the power he sought so desperately.

'There is something bigger behind this,' she muttered to herself.

Sukumar, the other director of 'Software Builder' was not known to Jaanvee. His name did not ring any bells. She googled his name. All she could get was the name of his college and the year of his graduation. He almost did not exist both on the Internet and in reality, which was quite eerie. For all the hype around the millions working in the software industry there were only a few hundred who you saw in conferences, seminars and on other public platforms. These people networked well, never hesitating to share information, because they know they may need the other person some day. So Jaanvee knew almost everyone at the top either directly or through someone. But she had not heard of Sukumar anywhere.

After coming to a dead end, she went back to researching on Shankaran. There was no updated information on him after he left PureConsultants, which was again uncanny. For any person in the position of power, a dossier builds up on the Internet over time. It was unavoidable. Not finding any information on the two of them made her uneasy. Maybe both of them had consciously tried to keep themselves off the Internet and had succeeded in doing that.

'This is not logical.' She threw her hands up, as if admitting defeat. 'You are a clumsy woman. You cannot get anything straight,' were the last words she spoke to herself before going to sleep.

꙰

Over time, in consultation with Diyaa's doctor, Arjun created a full support team for her.

'Diyaa is disabled. Don't label her a handicap,' he clearly remembered the doctor say this to him.

'What can I do?' Arjun had asked.

'Give her full support. You will not be around forever. You must make her independent,' the doctor had advised him.

The doctor's words clung to him. By the time Diyaa was three, she was taken care of by a team comprising a speech therapist, a physiotherapist and an educational therapist. Arjun took the last role onto himself and left the rest to professionals.

'Let's set ourselves a target, Diyaa. We should be completely independent in two years.' Diyaa groaned in reply, her head slumping to one side.

Two years of effort on the three fronts yielded miraculous results. The drooling reduced tremendously as the sessions with speech therapist began to show results. He had said it was only a matter of time before she started to speak.

'The muscles are stronger now, and I think she should be able to support her weight in a few months,' the physiotherapist too had predicted.

Arjun had never doubted that Diyaa was an extremely intelligent child and she had never done anything to prove him wrong. She had tremendous interest in her surroundings and recognised almost everything. She was good in Maths and that made Arjun extremely happy.

'The daughter takes on her father,' Arjun smiled at her while she drooled (only slightly) in reply.

Arjun remembered the day when Diyaa uttered her first word. That night after Diya was fed, Arjun kissed her, covered her with a sheet and was about to switch off the lights when he heard her rumble.

'What, Diyaa? Do you need anything?' She rumbled again as if trying to speak something. 'What, honey? Can you repeat what you just said?' Arjun encouraged her.

'Papa,' the first clear word that came out of her mouth was loud, slightly unclear, but unmistakable in the enunciation.

Papa hugged his daughter, a symbol of victory which came after a long, painful struggle. He realised that both of them had tears in their eyes.

⟋

Jaanvee's gloom continued into the morning. She got up and looked around. There were two open boxes of mushroom pizza on the table in the corner with leftovers; one from the afternoon and other from the evening. Two-day old unopened newspapers were lying next to the pizzas. After the advent of Internet she used newspapers mostly for cleaning mirrors.

'You are going crazy,' she continued with her soliloquy while reaching for the phone. The two SMSes in her inbox added to the gloom.

'What do you do when you don't sleep the whole night? You think of the reason, so I thought about you all through the night' followed by 'Do you know why I hate nights? Because they make me come home and sleep which stops me from thinking about you.'

'You lousy bastard, when will you stop bugging me,' she said as if San was standing in front of her.

She knew she was punishing both San and herself. She had been resisting him and that was one more reason for the frustration – both hers and San's. She knew it was very difficult for her to unshackle herself from her past and embrace San. As always, she chose not to reply to both of San's SMSes. The bitter memories of that day so many years ago stopped her from doing so.

⟡

One more year passed. Diyaa had turned five. Her words sounded clearer with every passing day. She had also begun to walk with the help of braces as the physiotherapist had predicted. Social acceptance was still some time away with apprehensive parents not willing to send their children to play with her.

'What would you like for your birthday gift, Diyaa?'

'Papa, what is a school?' she replied with a question.

'Baby, school is the place where children are taught. How did you come to know about it?' Arjun asked, slightly perplexed.

'All the kids in the park go to school, Papa. They mocked me when I told them I don't.'

'Oh!'

'And what is a class, Papa?'

'It's where all the children sit together to study,' Arjun replied.

'Do you think I can go to school?'

'Of course, you can,' Arjun said encouragingly.

'Then it is decided. I want to go to a school and a class,' Diyaa gave the war cry. Her innocent big black eyes shone with determination.

Arjun took her to the best school in the region. They directly went to see the in-charge of the Junior School. The in-charge was confused when she saw Diyaa. She looked at her and Arjun as if the two of them had lost their way.

'Yes, how can I help you?' The in-charge was visibly upset with their arrival. It usually happened to her when she was taken out of the confusion of daily life and forced to take a difficult decision – something she had stopped doing a long time back.

'I have come here to request admission for my daughter,' Arjun said.

'What is your name, little one?' The in-charge looked at Diyaa.

'Diyaa,' she said in her slightly slurred voice.

'She needs special attention and I'd recommend that you take her to a special school.'

'She doesn't need a special school. She needs a normal school just like all the other children.'

Diyaa looked bewildered throughout the whole conversation, not actually grasping the exchange but intuitively sensing something was not right from the pain in Arjun's voice and the grimace on the in-charge's face.

'Look, sir, she will not get the attention she needs and deserves in this school. She will be better off in a special school,' the in-charge insisted.

'Why don't you put her through the drill just like the other children, and then take a final decision?' Arjun requested.

'That will not be possible,' came the curt reply from the in-charge.

'And may I know why?'

'She is handicapped and not normal. Can't you see?'

'I think it is you who can't see. She is not handicapped. She only has a disability and she has tried really hard over the years to not let the disability turn into a handicap. The only problem I can see with her from your perspective is that her speech is not clear. She will take that too as a challenge. She will be back here one day, I promise you. You will not be able to say no to her the next time.' The flabbergasted in-charge could not utter a word.

'How much time before we come back again, Diyaa?'

'Six months,' Diyaa rumbled.

The proud father and daughter walked out hand-in-hand with a very strong determination to come back and meet the in-charge in six months' time. Both of them knew the next time it would not be easy for the in-charge to refuse admission.

With all the other parameters clearly under control, father and daughter worked very hard on her speech. They tried innovative ways to strengthen the muscles of her face and tongue. The results were again extraordinary. Diyaa's speech got clearer with each passing day. People who did not know of her condition would never have known that she ever had the disability. Except for the occasional drooling from the mouth and a sudden slumping of the head, she looked absolutely normal. The unpredictability in the timing of their appearance was Arjun's biggest concern. The frequency had decreased so much that he was prepared to take the risk again.

'It's time to go back to the school,' Arjun told Diyaa after the six-month period was over.

They reached the school the next day. This time the in-charge was ready and in an awful mood. 'I had discussed your problem with the principal and the management committee. We unanimously arrived at the decision that such cases should indeed go to special schools. I acknowledge Diyaa is a wonderful child and has immense potential, but this is not the right place for her.'

She lied but Arjun did not know it. He got up and began to walk back despondently. 'Papa, why don't we go and meet the principal?' Diyaa took his hand in hers reassuringly.

The principal was tall and fat. His weight was directly proportional to the power he had acquired over the years. He sat impassively in the chair. His face did not betray whether he had a heart. Arjun decided to give it his all, realising that this was his last chance.

'Diyaa wants to study just like everyone else. She is a child with above average intelligence. I feel she is brilliant, but these are preposterous assumptions of a biased father. But just because she walks awkwardly and started her life with a disadvantage, she should not be deprived of a chance to study in your school,' Arjun almost begged the principal.

The principal summoned the in-charge of the junior wing.

'You guys don't give up easily, do you?' the in-charge commented on her way in, trying to be jovial.

Arjun and Diyaa looked at each other and smiled. They were asked to wait outside while the in-charge explained the whole episode to the principal inside.

'If we do this for them, the parents of every special child will insist on enrolling their child here. We may not be in a position to say no to them once we give admission to this girl,' the heartless in-charge warned the principal of the consequences.

Arjun and Diyaa were called in again. The decision had been taken.

'I respect your spirit and your desire for parity for your child. But if you look at her walking in braces and with a slightly twitched face, anyone would be able to see that she is a special child and needs care and attention. You will not be doing justice to her by admitting her to this school,' the principal said in his very convincing baritone.

Arjun got up to leave realising there was nothing more he could do. 'Sir, I agree I am a special child,' Diyaa began hesitatingly, her tiny palm slipping into Arjun's for support and strength.

'Earlier papa used to help in every little thing. But I have worked hard so that I can do everything on my own. Now I can comb my hair, put my shoes on, hold my books in my hand and do all the little things children my age do.

Arjun prayed for the head to not slump.

'My papa is helping me a lot. He says if I try I'll become perfectly alright. Then no one can call me a special child. I promise I will work very hard. I want to study here. Will you not give me a chance?'

Her thoughts expressed through the movement of her hands, the wideness of her eyes, and her clear speech shut both of them up. Even Arjun was taken by surprise.

That she did get admission to the school and began studying like everyone else, leaving behind her disability became one of the legends of that school. The missing part of the legend was that Diyaa was happiest about the fact that she was able to hold the saliva in place, willing it to not do anything without her command. Her new-found confidence also helped her make friends with the one thing she feared the most and which she later lovingly began to call 'Chimpoo'. That it was a cockroach and roamed freely in the bathroom when she was around did not deter her from doing so.

∽

Six months into her first year at school Diyaa came home deeply disturbed.

'What's the matter, honey? Why do you look so sad?'

'Papa, all the children in my class tease me about my age. They say I am old and instead of nursery I should have been in class I. Is that true, Papa?'

Arjun realised that the best approach with Diyaa was to be honest with her. 'Yes, Diyaa, you began school at a late age. But that does not make you less intelligent than the rest of them.

'But, Papa, will they tease me forever? I feel very unhappy when they do this. Is there no way of stopping them?'

'Of course, there is. I am surprised I did not think of it earlier. In fact, that is the only solution we have.'

'What?' Diyaa asked impatiently.

'Diyaa, do you love challenges?'

'Yes, Papa. You know I do'

'Then you will try and complete two classes in one year till the time you catch up with children your age,' Arjun said.

'Do you think I will be able to do this, Papa?' Diyaa asked doubtfully.

'I am confident you can do it,' Arjun said with conviction.

'Then I am sure I will be able to. Even if I fail to do this, at least we'll know that we tried,' Diyaa said innocently, excited at the prospect but apprehensive of her own ability at the same time.

It was time to meet the in-charge again.

᳁

After that day in office Nitin felt torn. On the positive side, he was everywhere, and for all the right reasons. He appeared in debates on right to privacy and peaceful existence for people infected with HIV. He also appeared in many awareness campaigns on AIDS. His simple 'I am still the same – tall and dark, then why am I not handsome anymore?' slogan caught on like fire. He became the flag-bearer of hope for those afflicted with the virus in the country. Even international channels and dailies regularly carried stories on him. He seemed to have found his place under the sun. But paradoxically, he was not at peace. Tanya had refused to speak with him after that day in the town hall. Her phone would always be switched off. As he had no other contact address for her he was not able to reach her. It was as if she had deliberately strangled their relationship.

Two years had passed since he had last spoken to Tanya. He had almost lost hope of seeing her again.

One day he was invited to appear again on one of the most prestigious shows on national television called *Hope*. It carried special features on ordinary people who did extraordinary things. *Hope* always ran to highest TRPs and almost everyone who liked tv switched channels to watch it.

'Welcome to the show, Nitin,' the showmaster said.

'Thank you.'

'How has living with the dangerous HIV affected your life?'

'The only effect I have had has been external. With the constant support from my doctor I feel just fine inside. It was as if the virus was not inside but outside my body.' Nitin laughed remembering his ostracism from society.

That set the tone for the half-an-hour interview.

'Nitin, one last question before we end the show. You have been a source of hope for the millions carrying HIV. All of us are very interested to know who has been your inspiration for the fight-back.'

'It was like that special role in the movies – a cameo – where the hero comes for a few minutes, plays his part and then disappears. She was destined to happen to me. I was going through the darkest phase in my life when she came, showed me the way and then abruptly went away. She made me the hero I am today.'

The atmosphere in the studio suddenly became tense. It was not orchestrated, like the manufactured emotions shown on tv every day.

'Would you like to send her a message through our channel?'

'I would, though I don't know whether she is watching this show or not. Even if I was only a project for you, why did you have to leave like this?' Nitin paused. ' I still thank you every night after I switch off the light and before I go to sleep. Suddenly he was kneeling, face towards the camera and said, 'Tanya, I love you from the core of my heart. You have revived that feeling, stirred those emotions which I thought had died so many years ago. Please come back to me. I am incomplete without you.'

The host, a lady who had a few hundred interviews behind her, who was used to plastic smiles and glycerine, was all tears herself. Nitin was still on his knees when a copyright notice signalling the end of the programme rolled in the background.

❧

Jaanvee was eight years old then. The memories of that day were still vivid in her mind. The experience was surreal. Her bruised soul constantly reminded her of the pain. She still remembered her paternal house. Her father and her unmarried uncle lived with her grandparents in that big house until that day when everyone had to attend an important marriage leaving her, suffering from fever, with her uncle who chose not to go. She remembered being fondled, touched, caressed and kissed. It was all very strange. Even at that age, she remembered, she got confused at first and then felt afraid. After fifteen minutes of torment, she somehow managed to push her uncle away and ran to her room. She locked herself in, afraid and palpitating. Thankfully, her uncle did not come for her after that. He must have been jolted back to his senses.

She clammed up after that, refusing to discuss the incident with anyone, not even her mother. Nothing changed in the world around her. Her uncle got married and lived happily as if nothing had happened. The only person who suffered was she. After the incident, Jaanvee began to detest both herself and all the men she came across, neither forgiving nor forgetting, with her father too becoming an unsuspecting victim. She felt used like the fancy porcelain cup with the last cold sip of tea in it. It looked great from the outside but nobody wanted to drink from it until it was clean again. The problem with her was that she thought she would never be clean again.

With age came wisdom and she began to realise that not everything in the world was bad and in order to live she first had to forgive herself. She did that but vowed to never let a man rule her life.

One of the lasting consequences of that incident was that she never felt a tingling in her loins on seeing a man, any man for that matter. She thought she had turned frigid. That was until she met San. He had shaken her and left her in a state of indecision. She did not know how to handle her feelings for San. With nothing going right, she decided to leave for office. She heaved a deep sigh and got ready to meet Motu.

Motu waited anxiously for the meeting. With the premonition that things were not going right and a very strong sixth sense about the outcome not being under his control, he saw Jaanvee enter the room.

'Which topic do you want to start with – the Babe or the …?' Jaanvee deliberately left the sentence incomplete.

'Let's start with the less stressful of the two,' Motu suggested.

'We need to decide how far we want to go with the Babe, BD,' Jaanvee said.

'In its current form and shape, if we went out to repair it, she will take a huge amount of money and time. And with our hundred-crore line of credit still not coming through from the bank, I am very, very cynical about putting in more money into this. The future months are going to be bad for us, so I will suggest not to be extravagant with the Babe.'

'You are right. My hunch says the same. But we cannot wash our hands off her completely. That would be suicidal and does not make business sense. She is very important for the industry, some of our biggest customers want her and her launch is awaited as the culmination of the dreams of hundreds of people at PureConsultants.

'Killing her will kill all those dreams and demoralise the whole company. I will speak to a few people who drive this industry and keep only her most important features, the ones the industry cannot do without, the ones the USFDA will not let them live without,' Motu said.

'I agree. What about San? I think this decision will impact him the most,' Jaanvee said.

'Yes, it will ... drastically. You don't worry too much about him. I don't know how he will take this, and I don't even want to think about it now. He has to grow up and face the realities of the world. He cannot afford to live in a utopian world and pretend that everything is alright. I will tell him to go slow with her for now.'

Jaanvee's heart bled for San. But the software industry was brutal. She herself was a hardcore professional. She knew since it was unethical she would not tell San anything until the right time. She also knew that the power equation in the company would change as the Babe was the most visible product in PureConsultants. So it inevitably made San very powerful in the company. That was till then. As soon as the news about the pruning of the Babe reached people, tongues would start wagging and San would stop being the uncrowned king of PureConsultants.

Thus she was partly relieved to hear that the Babe was not being shelved completely but would come out slightly modified, maybe not as defining for the company as it was earlier but still important enough. She also realised that one day they would have to tell the shareholders about the change in the plan and vision of PureConsultants. She feared that it would bring down the price of the shares further. She willed herself to be strong and tried to concentrate on the more immediate and difficult task at hand.

Jaanvee then ran Motu through the whole sequence of events, without creating any brouhaha about the long nights she had spent trying to get the information. It was plain, matter-of-fact reporting.

'I am sorry. I do not have much except the fact that we are heading for a storm whose scale and magnitude we are not aware of. I will keep looking though.'

'Don't kill yourself. Take a break. We shall survive this,' Motu commented on her unusually sullen mood.

'Sure, it's just a passing phase,' Jaanvee replied.

None of them believed it.

ᔐ

The in-charge was not happy at all on seeing them again. Being lethargic and a slow-learner herself – someone who gains expertise through experience and practice – she did not like situations which were demanding and fast-paced. Arjun and Diyaa always came with a difficult problem and when she saw them enter her room once again, she flustered within.

'The two of you do not believe in the 'live and let live' policy.' Diyaa and Arjun looked at each other and shared a secret smile. 'I am sure you have come with a new problem today. How can I be of assistance?'

'Madam, we respect you immensely and believe that you will find a solution to our problem, just like you did last time and …' Arjun stopped midway when Diyaa pinched him on his arm which was dangling under the table. Father and daughter exchanged a mischievous glance again.

'Diyaa wants to take exams of two classes at a time so that in a few years she could study with children her age. Can you please allow her to do so?'

'I need some time to think it over,' the in-charge replied. 'I promise to get back to you in a week's time.' She was not happy.

'Do not take too long to decide as Diyaa can now find her way to the principal's office. And, as you have seen yourself, she is very convincing when she begins to speak.'

The in-charge, as Arjun had suspected all along, came back with a 'no'. The premise on which her refusal was based was that it would burden Diyaa too much, and that the school did not want Diyaa to disintegrate in the very first year.

'This decision has the consent of the principal. So don't bank too much on the knowledge that you know the way to his office,' she smiled impishly.

'What can we do this time, Papa?'

'We shall be making enemies in the school. But if it's necessary, we'll have to do it. We shall go to the management committee. Before that let's learn what the children in your class are still to learn,' Arjun told a despondent Diyaa.

'And how's that going to happen, Papa?'

'Let's prepare as if we are going for an entry directly to class I.'

The five members of the management committee, each at least in his fifties, were almost copies of the in-charge. They too loathed change but relented when they were told by Diyaa's class teacher that she indeed was a special child not because of her disability, but due to the superiority of her grey matter. The committee finally relented and gave Diyaa a date after three months to prove herself.

Diyaa laboured through the content of the books for KG as well as class I. She was able to grasp most of the topics in her books easily. Her biggest problem was the English language where words always sounded differently from the way they were written. She easily understood what was logical, but it took her a Herculean effort to understand the abstract. Perhaps the left side of her brain was more developed than the right, Arjun summarised to himself.

One day short of the big day, both father and daughter were very tentative as to whether they had done the right thing.

'We made a decision. Maybe we were wrong, or maybe we were right. On the battle ground we may win or lose. But our biggest achievement will be that we had the courage to take the challenge and the ridicule that comes with losing, head on. Let's not worry too much about this and get back to work,' Arjun spoke with the confidence that he did not really feel.

Diyaa looked at him with awe, trying to comprehend the full meaning of the words he had said and then went back to rehearsing the poem which had been troubling her the most.

The members of the management committee looked more imposing behind the long mahogany table and Diyaa tinier than she really was in the big auditorium. This is what people call the big stage, Arjun thought.

'The Diyaa Test' as it was called was conducted openly so that nobody could question the outcome. It received some unwanted attention in the school because of Diyaa's unusual circumstances and an even more unusual request. The gathering of more than a hundred people in the auditorium did not help Diyaa's cause. His profusely perspiring palms told Arjun that he had hurried through this one. He spoke to her five minutes before 'the Diyaa Test' to ask her to call the whole thing off.

'Diyaa, you think you want to do this?' he asked holding her tiny hands in his in a secluded corner of the auditorium.

'Yes, Papa. You told me yesterday that to have the courage to do something is bigger than the actual achievement. I will definitely try. Don't be nervous ... we shall win.' Diyaa smiled at him.

'How do you know I am nervous?'

'Your palms are sweating?' Diyaa smiled mischievously.

Arjun was surprised by her keen observation and her words gave him the confidence that he did not take a wrong decision.

He went back to his seat in the crowd barely able to hide his tears and fear. He prayed for his daughter to do well in the test and hoped that she did not get scarred forever in case the outcome was negative.

The questions came in thick and fast. She answered most of them, looked confused about a few and did not have the answers to some. The committee was stolid, not at all revealing what it was feeling.

In the end came the request for the poem which someone later told Arjun was taught to the children towards the end of class I and which Diyaa had been struggling with throughout. Arjun realised it was the end of the road for her because English recitation was extremely tough for her.

Diyaa kept silent for a few seconds in which Arjun's heart sank. Then she began hesitantly, creases forming on her forehead. Arjun knew in this cruel world you are remembered only for your last actions. He did not want his daughter to be crucified for the weak recitation. But Diyaa was born tough. She did not want to give in easily. She prayed to all her gods and then began. She reached the last four lines of the poem without forgetting anything. Arjun prayed while Diyaa recited the final lines:

Family keeps the love alive,
Father makes you want to fly,
Mother brings the family nigh,
Together the family takes to sky.

Arjun was shocked. He sensed the sadness she brought to the intonations while reciting the poem. It must have come naturally from the loneliness that she felt inside. Whatever he may have done for her, he was still a single father who would never be able to love her with the tenderness of a mother. The melancholy in Diyaa's voice carried straight to everyone's heart. There were a few wet eyes behind perfumed handkerchiefs which did not want to be seen crying publicly.

Strangely, both Arjun and Diyaa did not give a damn about the results anymore. For them proving their point to the world was enough. The managing committee took one hour to announce the verdict.

'We are delighted to say that for the first time in the history of this school we are allowing this very, very special child to take the exams for two years at the same time. In case she wants to cover more classes later we will allow her to do so. This decision has been taken unanimously with the consent of all the members of the committee. Let us all get up and cheer this wunderkind.'

On that day one more inspiring chapter was added to Diyaa's life. Both father and daughter were happy. They went to sleep, jokingly fighting over the fact that Diyaa must have a piece of paper with the poem written on it hidden somewhere which helped her recite it so well.

❦

The episode of *Hope* featuring Nitin ran to the highest TRPs ever in the history of the channel. It became a beacon of hope for the many closet sufferers and lovelorn people.

One month had passed since *Hope* was aired for the first time. Nitin had finished watching the 12:00 a.m. repeat telecast about an hour ago. Since it was a Friday he could afford to sleep late.

He had been accepted wholeheartedly at the office. If anyone had any inhibition, they never betrayed it. He was no more an outcast. Still there was a void which was difficult to fill. He wanted to be loved, he wanted his face to be held between the palms of a woman with her breath caressing his lips. And he wanted that woman to be Tanya.

'Thank you, Tanya, for helping me sail through the toughest phase of my life. Will I ever get to see you?' he muttered his daily request and had almost dozed off thinking of her, when he heard the doorbell ring.

It was Tanya. 'I saw your programme today for the first time. I never realised you miss me so much,' said she as she entered his house. She looked dishevelled.

Nitin was too stunned to say anything. 'Does it matter at all?' he mumbled and broke down.

'It does matter. I stopped seeing you because you were no more just a project for me ... I got so emotionally attached with you ... It has been so long since I last saw you but still I can't think about you dispassionately,' Tanya said.

Nitin was too overwhelmed to say anything. He couldn't believe what he was hearing. 'Tanya ... have you come back for me ... do you love me? ' he finally managed to speak.

'This is what it looks like, moron,' she said half-laughing, half-crying.

Then for the first time in more than a decade someone hugged Nitin. That her breath almost caressed his lips was god's second gift to Nitin that night.

❧

Nothing significant happened in PureConsultants since the day Jaanvee was asked to track down Software Builder, except that PureConsultants kept on losing more good people. Jaanvee could not break through the mystery called Software Builder. But there was no more bad news until one day she called her company secretary (CS in short) for a formal meeting which she had been postponing for some time because of other bigger problems and because she got informal information everyday on what was happening to PureConsultants' shares in the stock market. This time she decided to meet the CS for three reasons; one, the CS had been pestering her for long; two, she realised a formal session was needed to analyse the movements of the last three months, and finally her instinct told her that the meeting would throw some surprises.

'So how have our shares been doing?' asked Jaanvee.

The CS went ahead and churned out numbers which she soaked in very fast.

'We seem to be in good health and the price of our shares has increased in line with our results, not bad at all,' the CS said. But that was his judgment. Jaanvee knew she had to scratch the surface to see if there was some hidden devil in the data.

'Now show me the report of all the people who are holding more than one per cent of the company.'

There were the usual names, a few banks, mutual funds and top employees of PureConsultants whom the company had rewarded for their loyalty.

'So Sid's bank has decided to lower its stake. He is losing faith in us,' Jaanvee commented jokingly.

Then there were a few new entrants which was also not unusual in case of publicly traded companies. She was not really worried till she got down to the bottom of the list. There was a new buyer for the shares of PureConsultants – Software Builder.

'Software Builder has begun to woo you. In fact, stalking will be the right word,' Jaanvee explained the development to Motu.

'What can we do?' asked Motu. Deep furrows appeared on his forehead.

'The percentage that it holds in our company is too small to worry us at the moment. But looking at its penchant for all things related to PureConsultants, it will not stop at this,' Jaanvee summed it up.

'Can't you somehow break through this jinx?' Motu asked, helplessness showing clearly in his voice.

'I don't know. Let me try. Maybe the problem will go away on its own and it will lose interest in us,' Jaanvee said with no conviction in her voice.

Jaanvee tracked the company's share position almost every day from there on. She did not like what she saw. Software Builder's holding in PureConsultants increased steadily, rising to two per cent in the first month, then to 3 per cent in the second month and reaching just less than 5 per cent by the end of the third month. It was buying everything that was available in the open market, but keeping just short of the percentage required by SEBI to disclose its identity to PureConsultants. It was preparing to launch a full-fledged attack and waiting for the most opportune moment.

'They are spreading like a virus. This is an attempt to take us over,' Jaanvee declared.

'I will never be a slave and work for someone else,' Motu said.

'Then we have to find a way to stop them.'

'How can we do that?'

'We need to figure out the percentage of shares held by us and our loyalists. Then we need to start buying from the market to reach an impregnable number between now and when they come out in the open with a takeover bid ...' Jaanvee paused to see Motu's reaction.

'Go on,' said Motu.

'We need to hold fifty-one per cent of PureConsultants' shares to defeat them,' Jaanvee said. 'Are you ready for it?'

'I don't know. I am not sure.' Motu sounded despondent.

They departed on that note knowing that it was almost impossible for them to achieve that percentage.

∽

As Diyaa became increasingly independent, Arjun began to feel a strange vacuum in his life – something he had never experienced because of his preoccupation with her. As she took charge of her life, he realised he had more time to do new things. It also occurred to him that Diyaa had started to miss her mother and that she would need her all the more as the days passed. She needed her to share small things that girls generally talk about – the dress to be worn for an occasion and various other girly things.

Diyaa had realised that Arjun found discussions on silly nothings boring and never had anything to contribute. One weekend over a cup of milk (in Diyaa's hand) and tea (in Arjun's) she cornered him with a question she had on her mind for some time.

'Papa, do you think mama will come to live with us if we request her?'

Arjun was taken aback by the seriousness in her question. 'Your mother does not love us anymore. I don't think she will ever come back. Why do you ask?'

'I thought if we asked her ... maybe she would,' Diyaa replied sadly.

That was the end of the conversation but not the loneliness that both of them felt inside. However, Arjun did try to contact Muskaan and tell her about the latest happenings in his and Diyaa's life.

'Oh! Really! This is all very nice to hear. She still wears braces on her feet, doesn't she?' Muskaan had killed the conversation immediately with those cruel words.

Arjun hesitantly told Diyaa about his discussion with her mother and immediately repented it. Since that day, she seemed very distraught. Diyaa's forlorn look and his own loneliness forced him to do something he would never have thought of doing otherwise. The intent was not what it ultimately led to, but what happened through the course of time was completely unexpected and changed the course of their life.

He decided to mingle with women through chat rooms on the Internet. Being the technology head of a company Arjun knew all about online chats, but till date he had only thought about them from a technological perspective. The latest circumstances at home forced him to enter one of the chat rooms with the chat ID 'Superhero007'. The chat room he entered was 'Single ready to mingle'.

It was well past ten at night. Diyaa was sleeping. Arjun's heart beat wildly against his ribs when he entered the chat room.

'What the hell am I doing here? What is wrong with me?' He almost signed out at one point but somehow gathered the courage to ping one of the IDs which looked like that of a woman.

'Hi,' he said to her.

'ASL,' pat came the reply.

He was utterly confused. He replied with a question mark.

'How old are you?'

'Eighteen,' he lied.

'If you were eighteen you would have known what ASL means. So stop lying,' replied the girl on the other side with an angry emoticon.

'You are right. But please tell me what does ASL mean,' he begged her. But she had signed out by then. It took Arjun five more attempts in which he was greeted with different emoticons expressing anger, surprise and confusion when one kind girl did find the time to help him.

'It is a standard exchange between two chatters to know the other's age, sex and location before they start chatting,' she said and went offline, not wanting to be bothered by

Superhero007 again. He turned around sheepishly to see if someone had seen him being rebuked, inspite of knowing that there was nobody except him and a sleeping Diyaa in the house.

Arjun left the chat room because he feared that someone might throw him out of it physically. The next chat room he entered was 'Lonely Hearts'. With his new-found knowledge he went about introducing himself to different girls till he chanced upon one from Delhi, around thirty and not married who had only just entered the chat room. She called herself 'Sorriso75'. There was something in her name which he could not place but was familiar enough to make him stop and ponder.

'What do you do for a living?' he asked her.

'I am a freelance photographer,' came back the answer after a pause.

He tried to find a profession which would excite a freelance photographer. The technology head of a software company looked extremely boring in comparison.

'I design websites and am learning animation,' Arjun replied.

'Designing is chic,' she wrote back.

They chatted for one hour after that. That is how Superhero007 and Sorriso75 became online friends.

He found this dual life very exciting and an outlet for all his frustration. He enjoyed talking to her. Still, there was something about her name which bugged him constantly.

Chatting with Sorriso75 before he went to sleep became a daily habit of Superhero007. They talked about many things, but strangely both of them did not broach the topic of love or sex in their conversations. Arjun attributed his behaviour to his upbringing, but he did not understand why Sorriso75 was being conservative. He had been calling her 'Sorry' of late. The first time he called her by that name he had been greeted with a mock threat that she was leaving the chat and a reciprocatory 'Supper' as a nickname.

Both of them were content talking about things that were not at all related to the professions that they had said they practised. Sometimes their conversations turned philosophical, sometimes theological. Whenever their discussions accidentally touched the work place, one of them deliberately steered the conversation away to something stupid or nonsensical as if both of them did not want the other to realise that they were lying. Arjun observed over time that Sorry was far more intelligent than her online identity portrayed her. She was becoming a bigger mystery with each passing day and he really wanted to solve her.

'Hey! Sorry! Why don't you tell me something more about your life away from the Internet?' He decided it was time to break the unwritten rule of chatting between two strangers.

'I don't prefer talking about my personal life,' she replied.

'But you must tell me something. There must be a really strong reason for someone like you to be chatting at 1:00 a.m. in the night.'

'You are doughty, aren't you?'

'I am.'

'Well, I live alone and my only passion now is work,' she replied.

'That means earlier you had more passions in your life,' he picked up on her words.

'Yes, I had many. One of them was loving my husband. I was married once. But something happened that spoiled everything. Now don't ask me what that was.'

'What spoiled it?' he asked.

'You are a stubborn bastard.'

'Yes, but what spoiled it?'

Sorry then wrote something completely out of context. 'Have you been to the mall that opened last week in Gurgaon? I'll go there this weekend.'

Arjun had heard of the new mall. With an irrational belief that he would meet Sorry he decided to take Diyaa there for their weekend outing.

They bid 'goodnight' to each other and signed off. Strangely, Arjun was happy that he was talking to a woman who still seemed to love her husband. The fact that it mitigated his chances somehow did not bother him so much.

⌇

Nitin was not sure of what to do next; so he only followed what Tanya was doing and put his arms around her. He was tentative at first, then held her tightly as if locking her in his arms would ensure that she would never go away.

'It's been so long since someone embraced me,' Nitin whispered softly in her ears.

'You will break my bones. Maybe that's the reason women keep away from you,' Tanya replied playfully.

'You know what the real reason is.' Nitin was slightly hurt.

'Sorry, baby. Of course, we know what the actual reason is. It's ignorance and insensitivity.'

Then she did the unthinkable. She put her lips on his and slid her tongue into his mouth.

'Have you gone crazy?' Nitin pushed her away.

'What is wrong in this?'

'You might get infected.'

'Of course not, Nitin. You should know by now that your saliva is not a carrier of HIV unless it is mixed with blood. Now please let me do what I have been thinking about for the past few months,' she said, her voice heavy with passion.

'So it was not love but this that forced you to come here.' It was Nitin's turn to be playful.

'OK! We are even now. Let's call it quits,' Tanya replied. Both of them laughed heartily.

Nitin noticed for the first time that she was in her pyjamas. The light coming in from behind silhouetted her figure. He felt a stirring in his loins, familiar but forgotten, something which he had not felt in a long time. He held her close and their mouths locked for what was a long wet kiss.

'It was heady. But this will be the only time,' Nitin pushed her away, not knowing whether what they were doing was right.

'I want to go all the way,' Tanya was adamant.

'Have you gone crazy! This is impossible.'

'Why?'

'Let's just put an end to this.' Nitin was stern this time. He could not afford to risk Tanya's health.

They kept on talking through the night. Tanya told him how it was impossible for her to live without him. When the conversation finally ended, dawn was ushering in a new day. Nitin chaperoned her to her home.

'Where do we go from here?' Tanya asked the parting question.

'I don't know. Just let things be for some time,' replied Nitin.

ॐ

Post her meeting with Motu, a period of hectic activity started at Jaanvee's office.

'Can you bring a mattress, lots of coffee and a few clean shirts to last you a week? When I say a week, I mean seven days,' Jaanvee said to the CS as soon as he entered the meeting room.

'What is the matter?' The almost retiring CS looked flabbergasted.

'We need to buy all the shares that are available in the market till we reach the magical figure of fifty-one per cent. And if this information goes out of this room you are gone too,' she threatened the CS.

'What are you planning to do?

'How many shares do we hold right now?' Jaanvee answered with a question.

'The promoter group and our loyalists hold almost thirty-five per cent of shares. Software Builder has twenty-two per cent; the public holds eleven per cent and the institutional investors have the rest.'

'So it is a race for sixteen per cent,' she said to herself.

'Yes, unless our loyalists shift alliance,' the experienced CS corrected her.

Jaanvee knew what the CS said was correct. When the fight got down to the wire, with huge amounts of money at stake even the best of friends would get tempted to switch sides. After all, this was business.

'Call all our broker friends and tell them that we are interested in buying as many shares as they can lay their hands on without giving any hint of our plans.'

'There are a few hundreds of them, maybe thousand. Do you think we can do this?'

'You are getting old, sir. Take Sree's help. We have to do this come what may. Remember, you should speak to all of them by tomorrow evening. Also give me a list of all the institutional investors along with the contact details of their decision-makers,' Jaanvee told him.

'By when do you need this?' The CS expected a reprieve till the next day after having been loaded with the enormous task of talking to all the brokers.

'One hour, maybe two?'

Jaanvee had to act fast before things got out of hand completely. She let the difficult thoughts take a back seat for a while. She was looking forward to unwind by spending an evening with San.

Of late, she had allowed San to take her out, letting both of them observe the situation and see how the relation grew. Inspite of all her fears, no antagonistic feeling had risen inside her till then. This was indeed surprising. She was happy that she had lain to rest the demons of the past. She also cautioned herself that it was premature for her to arrive at any conclusion about San.

'Why do you bring me to such dark places?' Jaanvee commented on the lighting in the restaurant when they went out in the evening.

'This is not dark, and the lighting is called candlelight. For your information, candlelights are supposed to be soothing if not romantic.' San looked hurt.

'Oh! Really! I did not know.' Jaanvee laughed aloud.

'Why do you always have to begin on a sarcastic note?'

'Because I am testing the strength of your character, and you have been coming up a cropper till now.' She laughed again disporting herself.

'And when will you stop treating me like a child?'

'When you will grow old enough to be called a man!' she said jokingly.

San wore a sullen look. Jaanvee sensed that he was seriously hurt. The difference in their age was becoming a big psychological block for Jaanvee. They had entered a complex maze whose exit key they did not have. Jaanvee was apprehensive about San due to his younger age. She also knew that sarcasm was her defence against the romantic onslaught of San.

'I am sorry, San,' Jaanvee softened and reached for his hands.

Then they spoke for hours, their reverie broken by the unwelcome interlude from the waiters for taking the order, then laying of the order, and then cleaning the table. The candlelight indeed had a soothing effect on both of them and the discussion was less hostile, bordering on the romantic.

Arjun and Diyaa went to the new mall on Saturday evening. It was huge. Whenever a new one opened Arjun wondered if it was there to stay. He had concluded that each new structure ate into the footfalls of the previous one as if telling it that its time was over. They had reached the food court when Diyaa stopped.

'What happened, Diyaa? Why have you stopped?' Arjun asked.

Diyaa seemed to have not heard him. She looked at something ahead. Arjun followed her eyes, and his heart stopped beating for a few seconds. It was Muskaan. She too was looking at them with a stunned face. Then slowly, she got up from her chair and moved a little towards them. Arjun too walked towards her with Diyaa in tow. As he reached her table, he gave her a weak smile. Muskaan too smiled slightly before turning her attention to Diyaa who was silent all this while.

When Muskaan smiled at her not knowing what to do and say, Diyaa broke the awkward silence by asking, 'May we share this table with you, Mama?'

'Of course,' Muskaan replied, slightly taken aback at being called 'mama'.

'Do you usually come here, Musky?' Arjun asked.

'No, I am here for the first time. I needed to buy a couple of things for my trip to Italy,' Muskaan replied.

'You still go to Italy?' Arjun asked.

'That's where we get all the business from. Don't have a choice.'

Arjun remembered that as the head of the IT security firm, and the best one at that, she had some of the biggest Italian banks as her clients and had to undertake regular trips to Italy as a consequence. He remembered she loved the country even in her college days and had been fluent with the Italian language.

'Let me bring Diyaa something to eat. Do you need anything?'

'No, I am fine.'

Arjun stood in line for his turn.

'I am going to school and I do all my things on my own, Mama,' Arjun heard Diyaa telling Muskaan. Her face was glowing as she spoke. Arjun had not seen her so excited in a long time.

As for Arjun, he still felt dazed at this chance meeting with Muskaan. He asked himself whether he hated her for leaving them. The answer was 'no'. Not that there was no bitterness, but it was directed more at life than her. It was strange. Arjun and Muskaan lived separately but none had requested for a divorce. They were not insecure being alone and somehow still trusted each other. Though strange, Arjun had never held any grudge against her. He knew in his heart of hearts that the decision Muskaan took had affected her the same way it did them. He still considered her his closest friend and she would be the first person he would call for help if the need arose.

'And then, Mama, they asked me to recite a poem. By the time I finished everyone in the hall was crying. The principal called me a very special student. And how's your work, Mama? Diyaa spoke animatedly.

'Give her a break, Diyaa; let her eat,' said Arjun as he returned. 'Musky, we can move to a different table if you want?' Arjun offered her a reprieve.

'No, I am fine. Keeping very busy, Diyaa. In fact, my life has become very boring and predictable with work being my only companion,' Muskaan replied, regretting it immediately.

They sat together for some more time eating their food. Diyaa told her of all her achievements till Muskaan looked at her watch and stood up to go. She didn't know what to say to both of them.

'You are very sweet, Diyaa,' Muskaan managed to say.

'Mama, the three of us miss you a lot.' Diyaa held onto her hand. There was a stream of tears rolling down her cheeks.

'Diyaa, let her go.' Arjun tore her hand away.

'Three?' Muskaan was surprised.

'Yes, papa, Chimpoo and I,' Diyaa replied.

Muskaan laughed heartily as she came to know about Chimpoo. Do you want me to bring you something from Italy?'

'Yes, Mama,' Diyaa replied.

'Tell me what do you want?'

'Mama,' Diyaa stressed on 'mama' this time to make it clear what she wanted.

Muskaan walked away dazed, leaving them waving sadly at her fast-disappearing shadow. Diyaa was inconsolable. She cried all the way on the drive back home. 'She did not even once call me baby. She doesn't love me,' Diyaa complained.

'If you set Chimpoo free she will love you more for your compassion. Maybe she will call you baby then,' Arjun told her just to distract her. On the other hand, a certain excitement began to build inside him. He thought he had found the missing piece to the puzzle. He wanted to reach home as soon as possible so that he could solve it. After putting Diyaa to bed he opened up the dictionary on his laptop and looked for the meaning of 'Sorriso.' His gut said it was an Italian word. He was right. The translation was 'smile.' He had heard this word a few times when he and Muskaan were together. It had not struck him before. Muskaan's year of birth was 1975. So Sorriso75 could actually be Muskaan. The revelation made him feel light. For the first time in life he wanted to believe in the hands of fate.

'This cannot happen by chance. I don't have an answer to why this happened, but it must have a bigger meaning behind it,' thought Arjun.

Despite Muskaan's obvious awkwardness while meeting her daughter, he felt the evening had been a success. He adjusted the air-conditioning to a more comfortable twenty-eight degrees, wrapped the crouched Diyaa properly, put the strand of hair that was repeatedly disturbing her back in its place behind her ear. That night he went to bed a happy man, though a certain uneasiness kept gnawing at his heart. His only worry was Diyaa. It scared Arjun to see how much she missed her mother. But he pushed aside every thought for that moment. He was waiting to chat with Sorisso75 again.

When he woke up the next morning he saw that the bottle which had been Chimpoo's home for more than a week was empty.

Nitin and Tanya met every day after that as if they were trying to make up for all the lost time. They hugged and caressed each other but could not do what was a natural culmination of all normal relationships – make love, move in unison, climax together and dissolve into each other. Nitin never allowed their relationship to move to the next level and this was the biggest cause of friction between them. They dodged the inevitable question that was on their minds till one day Tanya told him, 'Next week it's your birthday. We need to celebrate it in a unique manner. We know we love each other. And no relationship of love is complete without lovemaking.'

'No, Tanya, it's very risky. It might ruin your life. And it will be difficult for me to live if anything happens to you.'

'What do you propose then? We keep on getting frustrated like this every time we meet. I want to feel whole, complete. And this cannot happen without you making love to me,' Tanya blushed as she said this.

'Tanya, I know if we take protection it is safe for us. But somehow I feel it's not right. I don't want to take that risk even if there is one-in-a-million chance of it happening.

'I propose a solution.'

'What?'

'We shall use two condoms when we make love.'

Nitin was taken aback. He started laughing hysterically but stopped midway when he saw a determined expression on her face.

'I am damn serious, Nitin. In fact, I have been thinking about it for a long time now,' Tanya said.

Nitin was extremely confused. He postponed the discussion till the time he visited the doctor. He trusted the doc and wanted to take a decision based on his advice.

'Take whatever advice you want, but you will have to decide by your birthday because this is the priceless present I am planning to give to you,' Tanya's parting words echoed in Nitin's mind.

～

Arjun was getting desperate. It was more than a week since he last saw Muskaan online. He was angry with himself for not asking her about her return date from Italy. He left her an offline message on the eighth day telling her that Supper had been waiting for her every night at 10 p.m., and that he was surprised she had not logged in for so long. Their chat session at ten had almost become a ritual for them, and they had a tacit understanding about the time of the chat.

On the ninth day she was exactly on time.

'Where had you been?' Arjun expressed surprise. Now that he knew Sorriso75 and Muskaan could be the same person he had to be very careful not to express those facts which he knew about Muskaan as Arjun.

'I was visiting my relatives.'

'Where?'

'Italy.'

'Wow! You have relatives all over the world,' Arjun replied, smiling to himself. The 'Italy' connection confirmed his belief Strangely, what added to his happiness was that she found it difficult to tell the truth to a stranger.

'Can you promise me one thing, please?' he continued.

'What?'

'That you will never ever miss our 10 o'clock chat.'

'Okay,' Muskaan replied with a smiley.

'Now that you have made this promise, I feel you consider me your friend. Don't you think that a friend can ask another friend about what went wrong with her married life?'

'I shall tell you when it's the right time.'

'Let me guess. Your husband must have turned impotent. All middle-aged men do.'

'No, I have a daughter just to prove people like you wrong,' she wrote back angrily.

'Then why did this happen?'

Maybe meeting Diyaa had made her emotionally vulnerable or she had really begun to trust Supper that Sorry opened up after that as if she had been waiting for the slightest provocation. She told Supper everything about her life, the reasons associated with her separation from Arjun. In the whole process, Supper became her adviser, her confidante, and her only friend.

After that day Sorry shared everything with Supper. He always managed to know her weekend destination during their chats, and more often than not, both he and Diyaa magically appeared at those places, each time managing to express genuine surprise at the frequency of the coincidences. Diyaa always got that twinkle in her eyes when Arjun offered to take her for an outing knowing she would definitely meet mama somehow.

'Mama, I topped twice this year,' she told Muskaan once.

'How?' Muskaan was surprised.

'I cleared two classes in one year. Now I need to take one more exam to be equal to kids my age,' Diyaa was animated as usual on seeing Muskaan.

'Wow! That's great.' Muskaan looked really pleased. 'And, Arjun, how's your work going on?'

'Well, it's getting tough. The responsibility is increasing with each passing day. Moreover, right now things are really patchy at office. It looks as if someone is ready with a knockout punch. He wants to throw us out of the ring for good.' He then went on to tell her about the happenings at PureConsultants while Diyaa made desperate attempts to be a part of the conversation.

Later on, they said warm goodbyes to each other, unlike the frosty departure of their first accidental meeting in the mall. Diyaa was still slightly upset that mama had not called her 'my baby'.

Arjun was eager to get back home to know the feedback of their meeting. Sorry was already waiting for Supper.

'How was your weekend?'

'You know I met my husband and my daughter again. Every time I see her, I feel more drawn towards her. She looks so much like me.'

'Then what is stopping you from going back to them?'

'What will happen to you then?' Sorry teased Supper.

'Don't worry about me. The more I get to know you the less I want to ...' Supper replied, deliberately leaving the sentence incomplete. He then asked, 'But tell me why you can't go back to them.'

'I don't know. I find it very difficult. She still wears braces. And that reminds me that I failed to deliver a normal baby. '

'But, Sorry, that was not under your control. Both of them love you, don't they? Looking at the number of choices you have, with not even me standing in queue, you are running out of options.'

Sorry did not reply as if she had been offended. Arjun had deliberately been harsh in his choice of words as he wanted to make her realise that life was not perfect. She had to try to adjust to the situation even if it was not to her liking. He just needed a final extraordinary situation to break through her softening outer shell. He knew the solution lied with Diyaa. Arjun realised that he would have to brace her up for another challenge.

ℐ

Somewhere during the evening, as always happened with San and Jaanvee, the conversation moved to business and, unavoidably, the Babe.

'Jaanvee, do you remember when we met some time ago and discussed the Babe's future, I asked you something,' San reminded her.

'What?' Jaanvee tried to evade the topic.

'You forget easily. Let me try and clear the cobwebs in your memory. It was a romantic night like today and instead of talking about love we were discussing the Babe. Infact, I had something else on my mind throughout. That was the first time I opened my heart to you. Now do you remember?'

'Oh! Yes, I do now.'

'By the way, you still have not accepted my proposal. '

'This means the time has not yet come,' Jaanvee cut him short. She usually did so when he tried to get too romantic with her.

'As you wish, madam. Now can you tell me what do you think of the Babe? Have you made any plans around her?'

Jaanvee did not know what to say. She began to sway between what was right professionally and emotionally. She decided not to tell him the whole truth, but enough to get him ready for the bad news when it arrived.'

'San, we are passing through a bad phase. The banks are not extending us the line of credit that we expected would come through easily. I suspect you may not get an entirely free hand as earlier when you started working on her,' Jaanvee spoke hesitantly.

'Can you be explicit?' San asked pointedly. The Babe was his life and he was always confused between who was dearer to him, Jaanvee or the Babe. He was surprised that he could never decide between them.

'You should be prepared for all the eventualities. That's all I can say,' Jaanvee repented saying more than she intended to.

'How can I work if a sword is always hanging on my head? I am a creator, and a creator can never be bogged down by the rules of business. I can understand if time is a problem. I shall ask all my people to work double the number of hours. But you cannot stop the dough. That would be disastrous. It will kill the Babe when she's ready to blossom into a beautiful young lady, ready to charm the world.'

'San, please don't overreact. This isn't the end of the road for her. Nothing is final till now. The whole scenario may change if the money comes in,' Jaanvee tried to placate him.

'You only have one shot at greatness. If I miss this one chance I am gone forever. The whole company will know that the Babe isn't the same anymore. She will come out emaciated, an underfed child. I'll be crucified for its failure. I know BD wants that ... the cool, calculative, heartless BD. They told me not to trust him in my darkest hour. The idiot I was, I always did. Now I know how wrong I was. '

Jaanvee reached for his hands and took them in hers. 'Things will be fine. What I was hinting at would be an extreme case. Please stop worrying,' she said softly.

He had broken down completely and sobbed into her scarlet red top which she had specially bought for the occasion only the previous day.

'You have ruined my best dress ... the stains will never go away.' There was a quiver in her voice as well. After that, she spoke incessantly for half-an-hour on different topics to divert his attention. He had returned to some normalcy when she showed him off to his car.

Jaanvee was feeling heavy in her heart. She was very sad for San. She realised that she was hopelessly in love with him. She could no more hold herself back, and more importantly, she didn't wish to. San was the only man she would be able to spend her life with. Jaanvee decided to express her feelings when she met him next. At the same time, there was something in her conversation with San which didn't seem right. Jaanvee couldn't put her finger on it. It kept playing on her mind even when she went to sleep. The whole thing annoyed her immensely. She wanted to think of love and San, imagine her life with him, but that small irritant did not let her do that. She was still looking for the elusive answer when sleep engulfed her.

The Past

It's when you get close to the furnace that you
begin to feel the heat,
And when you know people too closely that
relations turn insipid.

The Period

From the year 1998 till just before PureConsultants was formed.

It had almost been six months since Pankaj had returned from Russia. Meanwhile, he had tried his hand at different things but nothing had taken off successfully for him except his love for Priya which had rekindled and helped him forget Sveta.* He had decided not to use his only expertise – doing business in Russia – to survive as he had lost all inclination to keep any ties with his friends there. In the absence of any real choice, it was but natural for him and Motu to join hands and give the much needed impetus to Motu's consulting business.

'Pankaj, the basis of our relationship is trust. We shall individually make many tough decisions in business, but we must always take them in the right spirit. Our business partnership should not affect our friendship in any way. If it ever begins to, we should part ways without letting it become a reason for bitterness between us. We shall always try to do our business ethically even if it means slowing things down,' Motu had said at the beginning of their partnership.

Pankaj had only smiled at Motu. He had said, 'My experience says that nothing is fair when it gets down to real business. We are still small and insulated. But to become the biggest software consulting company in the country we would need to do things very fast. In the process, we will have to step on toes, bruise egos, and kill competition. Don't expect it to be fair all along. Let's think of becoming ethical when we become big. For now, the challenge is how to become big.'

'For me, the biggest challenge today is to move out of this garage and find a decent place which we can call an office,' Motu did not completely agree but let it pass laughingly.

'We shall need more people to run this business. We should have someone to take care of the technical operations and someone to run the administration.'

They then decided to call Nitin, and Arjun who had only recently passed out of IIT.

'We shall do business in a way it has never been done before in India. Let's create a company where people would love to work and where every person has equal rights. We must do something that will change the direction in which our country moves in the future. Let the world look at us not as a country of black magic or snake charmers but as one of intellectuals who can compete with and beat them at their own game,' said a thoroughly enthused Motu to the new joinees.

Pankaj looked unimpressed because he had seen business being done up close, and he knew it was not all black and white;* Arjun was overawed by what Motu said, and Nitin was bemused as he didn't understand the depth of Motu's words. Motu himself looked determined to create the biggest, most powerful and ethical software company in the world.

'You still need to figure out how to get that leased line, which you have been struggling to get for the past two years and which is one of the first things you need to survive,' Pankaj said on his way out, smiling.

Nitin was very happy to have come out of hell and be back among friends. Pankaj had told the small group that he had caught the virus in Russia so that nobody felt cheated later. All of them accepted him without asking any questions.

Pankaj and Motu also decided the holding of each person in the company. As founders, Pankaj and Motu got the biggest share. Nitin was told that he was entitled to shares of the company too.

'How much is it worth?' Nitin had asked naively.

'Your shares amount to about one per cent of the total stock. We have given you these shares based on the importance of your contribution to the growth of the company in the future,' Motu had explained to Nitin.

'Oh!' Nitin was slightly disappointed with the small share.

'If we are able to grow our company to the size we envisage, this may run into crores of rupees,' Motu tried to explain the importance of what was being given to him.

Nitin was also given some papers to confirm his holding in the company. He trusted his friends with his life. Carefree as he was, he forgot both the conversation and the papers.

Strangely, Motu and Pankaj never discussed their holding. There was always a tacit understanding that whatever they achieved would be divided into two based on the firm belief that they would always work together happily.

⌇

Pankaj and Priya, both bruised in love, gradually came close to each other. Theirs was not love-at-first-sight as they had known each other for about twenty-five years. It grew slowly as both of them were not in a hurry. Their feelings for each other only simmered beneath the surface, never explicit.

Both of them knew that the bond they shared was deeper than just friendship. Pankaj, for whom it was the realisation of a childhood dream, savoured it like all childhood dreams. Scepticism, that the happy spell might be broken at any point in time was his constant companion.

In his college days, it had been the desire to conquer and add to the numbers which had been the controlling emotion in all his relationships, even with Sveta.* But this time it was different.

Both of them were happy in the stillness of their emotions, not wanting to fast-track anything. It was as if the idea of coition did not exist in their minds. The excitement they felt at the brush of their skin, the smell of their perfume, gave them a silent pleasure.

A few years passed that way and they had still not touched each other. 'It was about time we take this relationship to the threshold of expression,' Pankaj often thought. 'I would only do it once I become someone substantial.'

✍

One day Pankaj asked Motu to stay back after office to discuss the future direction of the company they lovingly called 'NumeroSoft'.

'Look, we are not going anywhere with this,' Pankaj almost shouted.

'Not getting where with what?' Motu tried to play it cool realising where the conversation was headed.

'We have spent enough time trying to get the show running. But where do we stand today? Nowhere. We are a bunch of zombies catering to the domestic *laalas*, who want to get the work done but do not intend to pay for it. This is not our dream! Do you think this is all you want to achieve?' Pankaj assaulted Motu with harsh words.

Pankaj dreamt big. He was not happy with the progress. A strength of ten people in two years and a turnover of fifty lakh rupees was no mean deal. But Pankaj was not satisfied. 'There is something we are not doing right,' Pankaj continued. 'We should move to the international market, target big projects overseas. If we keep on working here we shall die waiting for our next order.' It was difficult to stop Pankaj when he was in the mood to vent.

'You are right. I already have a few strands of grey in my head waiting for that fatso to release his order worth one-lakh-and-fifty-thousand rupees. I think he was counting till I visited his office fifty times to do that,' Motu chuckled.

'Fatso doesn't sound appropriate coming from you.' Pankaj laughed loudly at Motu's ever-expanding paunch.

It was a very pertinent cultural problem Indian business was facing during that time. Big people with even bigger egos wanted to show off their power. Acquiring new business meant the ability to nurse big egos in addition to the capability to do the job. Thus the opening up of Indian economy was a boon as it allowed young entrepreneurs with little investments and big dreams to try their luck in the international market.

'If we do not join the gold rush now we will be left with the wooden spoon. The more we delay things the more we are left behind in the race,' Pankaj was back to business, pointing to the newspaper article in front of them, which covered Infosys' growth into a hundred-million-dollar company.

'We have six months to try whatever comes to our mind. If we fail, we will have to give up everything and go to the Himalayas,' Motu had said.

They decided to overhaul their whole strategy. As part of their plan to get big, they sent out emails to all their friends who were working in the US and Europe.

'*Saala*, nobody replies when you need them the most,' Motu cried after a few days.

'I have a friend who works in a big pharma company as an IT consultant. Let me speak to him and see if he can find something for us,' Arjun chipped in. His friend turned out to be far more reliable than Motu's. He promised he would help as much as he could.

'He just happened to be in the right place at the right time,' Arjun said.

'This is the biggest opportunity of our lives. We cannot let it go at any cost,' everyone shouted in unison.

Such was the level of excitement that all of them could not sleep the whole night. They realised that it was their first chance of doing something meaningful with their lives. The details of the project arrived through email. It was a 2MB email which took almost an hour to download on the slow ISDN line.

'If we have to make it big, we need to get a better Internet connection. Nitin, can you get that leased line which has been pending for so long now? Can you make it happen in this lifetime?' Motu said in irritation.

'Bribe him if you need to. Nothing happens unless you are ready to grease any palms. Motu does not understand that ultimately, it is the end that matters. We will help so many people with a better life if we succeed,' Pankaj later explained to Nitin in Motu's absence.

'Motu will kill us if he comes to know we have circumvented the law.' They giggled like kids.

The pharma company sent a hundred-page document to them.

'Is this some kind of exam?' Arjun asked.

'They want to see if you actually studied at college,' Pankaj said jocularly. Motu and Pankaj divided the document into three parts just the way both of them along with Priya prepared for All India Quiz Competition* when they were kids. The technical part went to Arjun, the second on domain knowledge to Motu and the one on IT infrastructure to Pankaj.

It took them one week to send their final reply. It was all done over email, a far cry from the visit of NumeroSoft's only official LML to the *laala's* office and waiting for him to be free to discuss his own project (which he never had the time for).

'Let's wait for their feedback. If we get this, we'll need a pharma expert who understands the industry inside out. Replying to an RFI (Request for Information) document is one thing, but actually knowing pharma is a different ball game. Let's find someone quickly before they call our bluff and realise we don't know a thing about how a pharma company works,' Pankaj said.

As part of preparation for bigger things Pankaj authorised the first bribe from the company. Motu was flabbergasted to see the ever-elusive leased line installed in less than a week's time. Of course, he didn't know it had taken Pankaj and Nitin twenty thousand rupees to pull the last one kilometre of the Internet fibre to their garage.

❧

The project was under the direct supervision of Alex, one of the fastest rising and most powerful IT managers in the company, who, at the young age of twenty-six, had a budget of ten million dollars at his disposal. So high were the expectations from him that he was being groomed to become the CEO in ten to fifteen years' time. He worked at a breakneck speed and belonged to the school which believed there was no substitute for hard work. He abhorred people who used unethical ways to enhance their careers. He knew that his idealism could become a deterrent to his success, but for now his bosses were happy with him. He was sometimes surprised to see how his path got cleared exactly at the moment he thought he was running into someone who would stop his meteoric rise and smiled to himself on seeing how desperate they were to keep him there.

Pankaj knew (from Arjun's friend) that if he could convince Alex that 'NumeroSoft' was the right partner for him, they were set to go a long way. He had a hunch that this was their big chance, if only they played their cards right. It would turn into something monumental that would change so many lives. The only problem was to find the right pharma expert. With this pressing problem at the back of his mind, he went for his evening meeting with Priya.

Priya was not in a very good mood due to her professional problems. She was an idealist and her own boss. Of late, she had gotten into a tussle with the hospital management. She wanted a free hand in treating her patients but the big hospital chain which had taken over the management of their hospital, wanted to run it like a business. The doctors were continuously pestered for meeting targets, which once achieved were revised every quarter to a higher, more unachievable figure. The doctors were being forced (and lured with high rewards) to become money-making machines instead of the compassionate people they were taught to be. Due to the relentless pressure, even the most ardent of doctors were slowly converting into mercenaries.

'Our hospital was fine till this huge chain decided to take us over. The only thing they care for is money. It has become an unwritten rule that we are not expected to discharge a patient till we have extracted every single dime out of him.

'I can't tell you how much I hate this. Just a few days ago the size of my room got reduced by a few square feet. Every doctor's cabin is being squeezed to make space for more cabins. I don't like the place now,' Priya continued to vent her anger while Pankaj held her hand and listened quietly.

'Then why don't you leave the place?' Pankaj offered the easiest way out.

'I can still serve people if I am inside the system. But I am really tired of fighting. The way things are, I will have to move out of this place sooner than later.'

'What will you do after this?'

'Don't know yet. Will figure it out when the time comes,' Priya replied.

Pankaj began to smile which annoyed Priya, and she called him a maniac and a few other impolite things.

'You know, Pankaj, you are an unsympathetic bastard? What do you find so amusing about it?'

Pankaj did not give any reply. He had smiled because he knew, what Priya's next job would be if the plans at NumeroSoft materialised.

They waited for Alex's email every day, sometimes waking Arjun at midnight or early morning requesting him to check his email. After waiting for a few weeks in which all their hopes had dissipated, they finally received the much-awaited email from him informing them that they were amongst the few shortlisted companies. What followed in another email from Arjun's friend was, 'NumeroSoft is the smallest ever company to have been shortlisted for any project by us.' He had also added, 'Don't screw up this one. This will be your only chance to enter our list of preferred vendors and make it big. Our total IT budget for the next five years is one-billion dollars. If you can manage to take even a miniscule of this amount, you have made it.'

Arjun replied to his friend saying he had forgotten and forgiven the hundred rupees (along with the interest) that he owed Arjun since their days at IIT.

'Wow! You are so bighearted,' someone exclaimed while Arjun was typing the reply.

'We are not in a position to take the whole budget this time but we should become so strong that we don't leave anything for the rest of them after five years,' Pankaj said with a steely resolve in his eyes.

All the others were so afraid of the enormity of the challenge nobody said anything except Motu who too looked determined not to let the opportunity pass. Nitin wanted to party but was discouraged by the stern look in everyone else's eyes.

'It's too early to celebrate. We have only started,' Motu almost barked at him.

'We need the domain expert we were talking of earlier,' Arjun reminded all of them.

'I have a plan. Do you think Priya can fit the bill?' Pankaj asked. Most of them were surprised.

'Look, we are beggars. We have no reputation in the market, so we need to be realistic. At the moment, Priya looks to be our best bet. I haven't yet spoken to her about it. Can't say if she will like the idea. I wanted your consent before I spoke to her,' Pankaj said. As he explained them how Priya could be useful he saw an increasing number of receptive nods from the people present in the room.

'I am a doctor in case you have forgotten,' a baffled Priya told Pankaj when he offered her the job.

'Yes, and a very conscientious one. That is the reason it will be increasingly difficult for you to survive in a hospital. To be fair to your management, anyone who has put in money will want it to multiply. So whether you like it or not, for some people running a hospital will always be a business.'

Priya was listening to him intently.

'You are only twenty-eight. If you promise to give me the next fifteen years of your life, I mean professional life, I promise to give you your own hospital at a place of your choice, anywhere in the world.

Priya asked for a day to think. Pankaj knew that no amount of money could make her change her mind. That is why he decided to offer her something that touched her soul and then left the rest to her and god.

Priya took one whole week to decide. Everyone at NumeroSoft was nervous all this while, not sure whether Alex would wait so long for them. When she finally said yes, they were overjoyed. What added to the celebrations was the screen saver – 'Priya, will you marry me?' – which flashed on all the computers in the company, including Priya's. Priya was first surprised, then smiled coyly and went ahead and kissed Pankaj, not giving a damn about others' presence in the room. What nobody knew was that Pankaj had resolved not to ever propose to her if she refused to join NumeroSoft.

By the time Priya got down to work, only three days were left to the deadline. What followed was a phase of non-stop activity during which no one slept for two consecutive nights. The technologists spent their time refining the response to the detailed RFI over and over while others like Nitin kept awake to keep the momentum going through continuous supply of omelettes, bread pakoras, tea and coffee. Finally, one hour before the deadline, they were able to send their five-hundred page email to Alex. Priya's entry to the team had taken the quality of their response to a different level. All kept their fingers crossed, hopeful of clinching their first overseas order.

That is the good part about not knowing who your competitor is. It lets you grow in confidence, allows you to make an attempt at the impossible and dare the invisible enemy.

༅

Alex did not reply for a few days and everyone oscillated between extremes of hope and despair not knowing what awaited them.

Such is the human nature that till the time you find one way of doing things many promising possibilities exist, but once you traverse a certain path it seems to be the only course you have. This was also happening to the ten samurais of NumeroSoft They had started weaving their dream of going international around the success of the project they had not yet acquired. Finally, the succinct response from Alex arrived.

It simply read – 'Congrats! We have selected you as one of the three companies shortlisted for the final presentation. We expect you here next week on Friday.'

'Who will go?'

Motu decided that he alongwith Priya, Arjun and Pankaj would go for the final presentation.

'Let's get ready for travel!'

To their dismay, they realised that they had completely forgotten about passports and visas. With a little more than seven days to go only Arjun, who had been to the US for two-months while he was at IIT, and Priya had a passport. Pankaj's passport had expired. Arjun was spared from going to the embassy as he still had a valid US visa.

Another period of frenzied activity began. To get their passports ready, they relied on the network of Priya's father who knew a few powerful people, who further knew a few more powerful people, which set the machinery moving. Their passports got made in record time. By the time they had the passports in their hands it was Monday.

For their visas they requested invitations from Arjun's friend who continued to be evasive till Arjun got stern with him and told him that he could revoke the hundred-rupee loan he had cancelled.

With all the necessary documents ready they reached the US embassy in New Delhi at seven in the morning to meet the visa counsellor. She was not in a very good mood and was refusing visas to almost everyone.

'How does it feel?' Pankaj asked.

'Shitty! Waking up so early has spoiled my whole biological cycle. My bowels have revolted. Don't blame me if the counsellor smells something funny and refuses you visa today,' Motu blabbered, and the others looked at him with disgust.

'What will happen to us?' Priya whispered to Pankaj standing close to him.

'Just speak fluent English and remember all the facts. Don't worry. You can pull it off,' Pankaj advised her, while Motu eavesdropped on their conversation.

'It will not make you inferior if you join the conversation, Motu. And, Pankaj, do I need to remind you that I have been practising the language since the time I was born,' Priya scoffed.

'Why did you ask then?' Pankaj said and all of them broke into laughter.

'I am reminded of the day when we went to our school teacher asking her to allow us to participate in the quiz competition.* Pankaj, you were so nervous then, quite unlike what you are today – a confident young man,' Priya said fondly.

'What does a student from a Russian university have to do in the US?' asked the counsellor.

'I'm going there on a business trip. I believe all my papers are in order,' Pankaj tried to push his papers through the window.

'I will take what I want. And to me, your papers don't look in order. Why don't you try for your visa some other time?' She returned his papers to him

'Madam! If I don't get this visa I will miss the only chance I have to make something out of my life. I will rue this moment forever, analysing it and tearing it apart to see if at all I was at fault. The only conclusion I will come to, is that I was not at fault and still I suffered. America is the land where the biggest dreams have been realised and I know Americans support all big dreamers.

'I also know you wouldn't want me to blame you for all the missed opportunities of my life. I urge you to not let your conscience be bugged for something as small as a legitimate visa and instead become a part of my thanksgiving speech when my company becomes a billion-dollar enterprise,' Pankaj held her glance and challenged her authority, putting everything at risk.

The counsellor was a god-fearing, conscientious lady, in a foul mood only because of the fake cases she had had to handle before Pankaj. In those fleeting moments she remembered how much America had done for her by pulling her out of the ghettos and putting her in this seat. As Pankaj spoke, her own life flashed through her mind. The earnestness in his speech and her own sense of fairness did not allow her to reject his visa.

'You may collect your visa on Monday,' she simply said.

'Thank you, ma'am. But it would be of no help if I don't get it by the day after tomorrow as I am flying out on Friday morning. Can you please help with this as well?' Motu and Priya looked the other way, pretending they did not know Pankaj.

'Okay! Is that all, or you still need me to service some other request?' she said half-smiling .

'Yeah, just one more. Please do not reject the visas of these two people behind me. We are all flying together.

Motu and Priya were sure by then that she would reject Pankaj's visa too and bar them from entering the embassy for the rest of their lives.

But that did not happen. What happened instead and became a part of NumeroSoft folklore was that in those times when people did not get more than a six-month business visa, the three of them got ten-year multiple entry visas to the United States of America.

༄

The four of them flew to New York headquarters of the pharma company to meet Alex. They were confident that they could turn it around, partly because they had not seen the enemy. What they did not know was that among the shortlisted were two of the biggest software companies, one from the United States and the other from India. Strategically, it was a very big account for all of them though the amount of business from this project was small. Alex had decided against all the existing policies to outsource a software project for the very first time. This made the US company very apprehensive because it was on the verge of losing a multi-million dollar source of revenue. The other Indian software company knew that it was an entry for them into one of the most profitable pharma domains, and NumeroSoft clearly understood it was their most important chance to enter the big league. So, all three of them were ready to go to any extent to get a piece of what Alex had to offer.

'So you are the Indian company which will save Alex billions?' the representative of the US company said to the four of them.

'Yes.' Motu being the tallest (and broadest) of the four tried to measure up to the six-feet-four-inches tall American.

'I haven't heard of you before. How big are you?'

'We started only a few years ago. We grew very fast to twenty people in two years,' Arjun lied.

'What? Twenty? Who allowed you to participate in the bid?' The American had a hearty laugh thinking that his chances had suddenly improved from thirty-three to fifty per cent.

'Wipe that smile off your face because you are going to lose this account. And we may be a small firm today, but we would be a hundred-thousand people in the next ten years,' Pankaj said taking charge.

'And we are not twenty but ten people. Still we will snatch this account out of your fucking hands. Just wait and watch,' Motu added.

Priya chose to remain silent but stood in stolid support behind the three of them. Had Alex happened to walk past the waiting area he would have felt compelled to give them the project for their sheer determination. They were called in for the presentation. The other two companies were already done with.

'Another reason why we should grow big ASAP. We won't have to wait all that long to get in. I have a feeling we were called only to fill in the required numbers. It's already 5:00 p.m. and it's a Friday. We will have to see how long can we hold their attention,' Priya whispered to the three of them.

Alex was a tall, bespectacled, balding young man who exuded power even at his young age. All the people on the other side of the table were far older to him but awaited their turn to speak when Alex was around. He indeed was the decision-maker and the man-in-charge.

'You have one hour to present your case. Let me reiterate that you are the smallest company ever to have been shortlisted for a project by us. So, you must tell me what is it that you can do better than the other very reputed companies on the shortlist.'

Pankaj acted on his instincts. He knew that since Alex was young, he was impressionable. He guessed that Alex would be more willing to break away from the traditional pattern and listen to what they had to say once he was excited by their offer. He took a calculated risk by deviating from their very carefully prepared introductory script and said, 'Two of the people here belong to IIT. And getting into IIT is tougher than securing admission in the famous MIT or Stanford. The lady on my right side is a doctor from the top medical college in India where only a handful are selected out of the three-hundred-thousand who apply. I was almost a failure in college till I decided to get my act together and got a historic red degree from my university which no other foreigner had secured till then.

'We have a whole dossier of information to share with you. We want to suggest the most innovative way to run this project and if we only have an hour to present it, we might as well not do it.'

'Let's see what you have to offer. We shall decide if it is exciting enough to cancel our weekend party,' Alex replied.

They took turns to explain their parts of the presentation. Each of them spoke very well and came across as thought leaders on their topics. Alex seemed impressed with them. Pankaj stole a glance at his watch. It was already one-hour-and-forty-five minutes past the allowed time when Priya finished with her presentation.

'What are you guys going to do now that the tough part is over?' Alex asked.

'Well, we are free now. We only have to catch a plane in the morning,' Priya replied.

'Then let's go out and have dinner together. I will have to cancel my date with my girlfriend but I would love to spend time with like-minded people. And no visit to New York is complete without visiting Four Seasons in Manhattan,' Alex made an offer they could not refuse.

'Cut down on the wine and anything hard. Else we may go bankrupt before we even start making profits from this account,' Motu whispered to the rest of them on their way to Four Seasons. The four of them found Four Seasons a fantastic place to eat.

'Why do we have to pay?' Motu cribbed.

'Because he is a future client and we need to respect that,' Arjun said.

They ate and talked. Alex did not think twice before ordering a three-hundred-year-old wine bottle while each one of them squirmed in their seats. Pankaj suddenly remembered his date with Priya at the Nirula's when he had counted the money in his pocket every time Priya ordered something.* He thanked god that this time he did not have to worry about the return ticket.* The dinner went on for more than three hours during which they discussed the nuances of doing business in India and how offshoring would shape the face of the new economy.

'I had faced stiff internal resistance when I spoke of outsourcing our software projects to India. Two people left as they did not support the idea. By putting my foot down on this I am putting my career on line. If this experiment does not succeed, I am as good as dead. I shall be relegated to second string positions in second-rate organisations. This is the most important decision of my life,' Alex confided in them while calling for the bill.

They fought furiously over the thousand-dollar bill and the hundred-dollar tip. Alex won finally.

'If you do not let me pay this bill my career may be finished even before it has started,' Alex said, taking out his credit card.

The four of them looked confused. 'We are not allowed to accept gifts more than twenty dollars in value. And since we have not decided who are we going to give this project to, it is not ethical for me to let you pay for the dinner,' Alex summarised his dilemma. He told them they would have his decision in the next week.

'What are our chances of bagging this project?' Motu discussed on the flight back home.

'Very bright, I'd say,' Priya guessed.

'But he did not let us pay for the dinner as we were still not his chosen vendor.' Pankaj sounded doubtful. Arjun was also sceptical. Motu, tired and oblivious to what was being discussed, dozed off with his mouth wide open, for once not caring what the Americans thought of him.

Others, confusion written large on their faces, did not sleep as comfortably on the eighteen-hour long trans-Atlantic flight.

They did not have to wait long for Alex's decision. After spending the longest weekend ever, they received Alex's email on Monday evening as soon as New York opened for business.

'It looks that he is equally anxious to start this project with us,' Pankaj said while opening the email. He wanted to read it in front of all of them.

'Guys, I am extremely sorry but we will not be able to work with you on this project. I was really impressed with your capability to deliver but I could not get the buy-in from the rest of the team to outsource it to a small company as yours.' The mail was apologetic in tone.

Arjun got to know from his friend that Alex wanted to work with them but found himself on a weak footing to push two big decisions at the same time – one, outsourcing and the second, to give the project to a very small Indian company with less experience, which was a huge risk in the opinion of Alex's boss. So he had to relent on one point to score a victory on the other.

'He liked you immensely and fought really hard for you. He specifically asked me to tell you that he was really saddened by the way things finally ended,' he told Arjun on the call.

'What about the five-thousand dollars that we spent on this trip? Will they reimburse it?' Nitin asked.

Each one of them was in tears. It was the first time in the history of NumeroSoft that their office was closed at five in the evening.

❧

For the next couple of months they worked like a dispirited, headless organisation. It was as if NumeroSoft had reached the end of its journey. It also affected their domestic business, which when neglected, began to decay as well. All of them felt betrayed and no amount of counselling helped.

'I think we should close shop and go our own way,' said Motu while they were discussing the future of their company.

'Yes, it is a tough job running your own business. I feel we are not really cut out for this,' Pankaj added.

'We have a lesson to learn from this. We should never pin all our hopes on one dream,' Priya said.

'But isn't it premature to declare ourselves dead? We are still in our twenties and have a long way to go,' Motu interjected when the blabber refused to subside.

'Not together,' Pankaj said.

During the discussion they decided to give themselves one more month to see if they had the courage to keep on working with the *laalas* for the rest of their lives.

But no miracle happened in that one-month period. Meanwhile, they had let it be known to all the employees of NumeroSoft that they should start looking for new jobs.

They felt extremely disturbed because they knew that they would be able to run their own lives well, maybe not as successfully as their peers but still well enough for them to have a comfortable life. But the other employees would find it difficult to survive. What particularly moved them was the helplessness of the office boy who fed a large family of eight with his solitary income and Nitin, who thought they were his family.

'I'd rather die than go back to Kolhapur. Please don't shut this office. Winning is not always important. We are able to sleep in peace and have fun together in the evenings. So how does it matter even if we are not the best in the world,' he pleaded.

For the first time in their lives, Motu and Pankaj understood what it meant to live with the weight of other people's expectations.

The morning saw sad eyes everywhere in the office; some probably had shed tears already. Like all the others Motu had also come to say a final goodbye but on seeing the gloomy faces of everyone he felt compelled to change his mind.

'We can't close the office like this. We know that together we have the capability of changing the course of a thousand lives. Perseverance increases the probability of success immensely. All we need is a good break. Let's work hard. The right opportunity will definitely come,' Motu took centrestage.

Nobody was convinced; the pall of gloom was too thick to let them look beyond the present.

'Do you remember, Pankaj, I would have never cleared JEE if I had not believed in myself? Because I wanted to do it, it happened and you became my vehicle to IIT. You would never have been able to get the coveted red degree in your university if you had not believed you could do it. Then the dean became your vehicle. It's all in the mind. We shouldn't give up too soon,' Motu said, but his team still looked doubtful.

'Even if you believe it's ridiculous, for my sake, let's give ourselves one more year. I can't do it alone. If we aren't able to get our act together, we shall go our own way to do our own thing. But I need you all at the moment,' he begged.

That clinched it. They knew another year at NumeroSoft would not make a difference to their lives, but since Motu needed them there was no question of refusal. And Motu always knew that if they could stick together things would happen on their own. The first big storm at NumeroSoft had passed.

They again immersed themselves in working with the *laala*. They entered his office with the usual zeal, always walking out with a firm resolve to outgrow him as soon as they could.

It was the third month of the promised one-year extension when business was good but not roaring that it happened. Everyone was busy at work. Motu was taking stock of the number of releases for the day while Pankaj was trying to understand SEO to get them on the top of the listings on the search engine and improve their chances of getting new business. Arjun was working on a complex architecture for a project from a *laala* who wanted all the latest features in his product and that too at a meagre cost of one-lakh rupees. 'The same product would have sold for a hundred thousand dollars in the US, but the *laala* doesn't want to take his money out of his underwear,' Arjun had cried out loudly after coming out of his office.

Nitin was struggling with the hiring strategy to get the best guys from the market when suddenly they heard a strange groan which steadily rose into a high-pitched scream. It was Pankaj.

'Are you dying?' Priya almost dived for her long-forgotten, non-existent stethoscope.

'What is happening to you now? I always told you SEO was beyond you,' Motu yelled at Pankaj.

'Idiots, Alex has written to me. He wants me to call him right now.'

'What's the big deal in that?' Nitin asked.

'It is almost 4:00 a.m. in New York. This has to be something extremely important.'

Everyone gathered around Pankaj when he went to the conference room to call Alex. 'Hey, Alex! Shall I say good morning, or you haven't slept at all?' Pankaj said.

'It's been a long night, Pankaj. I am in the middle of the biggest mess of my life. The outsourcing experiment I tried with the other Indian company has failed completely. Now my ass is in the frying pan and if I don't do something quickly I am gone for good.'

'What happened?' Pankaj asked, suddenly on alert.

'Well, this big company did not have the resources to take care of a very complex project. They are capable of handling large projects but not complex ones, which need more expertise. They have messed up big time. I have fifteen days now to set this whole thing right and if I don't do that …' He did not complete the sentence.

'Can you guys come over and see if you can get this thing working?' Alex said finally.

'When do you want us to be there?' Pankaj asked.

'Can you come to my office tomorrow morning and start cleaning the shit?'

It was 6:00 p.m. in India already. In order to be in New York the next morning they had to leave immediately so that they could be at the airport in less than six hours.

'Yes, we shall be there.'

'And if you are really as tough as you had said, I think we shall be able to pull ourselves out of this,' Alex said.

'Ask him about the money,' Arjun gestured.

'At this time he needs friends and not businessmen. Let's help him now and business will follow,' Pankaj replied.

○

The moment remained etched in their minds as that was when their lives changed just as Motu had predicted. They began to enter the real world of corporate business moving away from the *laala*. The team of four – Motu, Pankaj, Arjun and Priya – packed their bags in a hurry and left for the airport.

'I think I have forgotten my underwear. You may have to loan me one,' Pankaj whispered to Motu when they were half way through to the airport.

'Mine may be too big for you. Instead of solving Alex's problem, you will keep fidgeting with your crotch in New York. May not be a very good idea while trying to win over a lost account.' Motu's eyes twinkled mischeivously.

'What should I do then?'

'You can try Priya's, she is just about your size. You are anyway going to share everything with her in life,' Motu said and burst out laughing.

'What are you guys talking about?' Priya wanted to join the discussion.

'Shall I tell her of your suggestion?' It was Pankaj's turn to get even. The horrified look in Motu's eyes made him laugh, leaving Priya and Arjun intrigued for the rest of the trip.

They reached Alex's office in the morning. What bothered them was the grateful look in his eyes and the weight of expectations it put on them. 'What is the problem?' Motu asked after the pleasantries were over.

'The first and the biggest problem is that no one understood what we wanted from the project. We want to make a unified web-based product which our more than a hundred-thousand employees spread across the world could use. But it is far from that. After a lot of tweaking, it began to behave like the original planned version but the code is so badly written that the pages take years to open. Even the links on the pages do not work. How big a screw-up is this?' Alex looked totally hapless.

'Prima facie I think they didn't understand the intended functionality of the software and the architecture for it was not developed accordingly. Somehow they rewrote some parts of the code just to get it up and running. It's like a house with no foundation. Umm ... forgive me for being blatant but this looks like the mother of all screw-ups,' Motu summarised it for Alex.

While they were discussing the various issues Arjun got busy looking at the various screens of the software.

'I don't think you have used the correct programming language for this. I would have used .Net for making this. It's new and very effective in solving business problems such as yours.'

'We have not flown here to discuss problems. Let's propose solutions instead,' Priya interjected.

They sat down to discuss the way ahead. The session continued deep into the night, the whole of the next day and further into the wee hours of the morning. Nobody gave a damn about the sleepless nights and the jet lag.

'It's like being back to college. As if we are appearing for the semester exams,' Motu said. After almost sixty hours of brainstorming, with intermittent power naps, they arrived at a broad consensus on how to go about saving Alex and his project.

'Firstly, we need to ensure that the code runs and does not crash. We know that their next internal release is almost six months away. As a long-term solution, Priya has to understand their business completely during this period. Meanwhile, I will make a plug-in so that everything works on .Net and rewrite the badly done parts of the code so that their product achieves a decent level of performance and then take it from there.'

'So let's get started with salvaging the product and Alex's reputation,' Arjun said. He and Motu were most enthusiastic about the first phase of the 'salvage operation' as it entailed playing with technology which excited them the most. For the next two weeks the rest of the world ceased to exist for them.

It generally took new vendors over two months to get registered and get a seat in the office. But it just took one day to get their passes made. That gave them the right to work in the office till as long as they wanted – a small reminder of how influential Alex was.

'We are part of the privileged class,' Priya commented to Pankaj while they were working in the office. Arjun and Motu were out on a small break.

'We may very soon not be, just like the other Indian company, unless we deliver on all the fronts,' Pankaj reminded her.

'Musk suits you better than any other fragrance,' Priya said when Pankaj moved close to her to show her something on her laptop. They had been given a cubicle of four where they had been sitting with their four kg laptops for twelve hours at a stretch.

They looked at each other longingly, their hearts suddenly beating faster in that precious stolen moment of love. Pankaj touched the back of her hand which was on the keyboard and pressed it softly. The effect was electric. They could have continued for eternity but the laptop screeched as the keys got pressed due to the pressure on Priya's hand.

Strange, how my touch on your hand reacts on the hair on your nape.'

'This is not fair. We should be out in the famous Central Park enjoying the beauty of New York instead of sitting here trying to solve someone else's problem,' Priya complained.

'Sometimes the uncertainties of the promise score over the joy of completion. Do you still want your hospital?' Pankaj reminded her of her biggest ambition in life.

'Left alone for a moment, the two of you forget everything about work,' Motu said, entering the cubicle with a cup of black coffee in his hand.

The two weeks they spent on the product worked wonders for it. The performance of the web pages improved considerably and the product was now in a decent shape. Alex, to their surprise, had given them complete freedom to find a solution, not interfering at all in their work.

'The *laala* would have stood on our heads, monitoring us with his CCTV-like eyes,' Arjun could not resist commenting on the way business was done in India.

It was time to invite Alex for a presentation. Pankaj did not think twice before dialling Alex's number at 10:00 p.m. as they had standing instructions from him to call him even in the middle of the night, if they thought they were ready.

Alex reached within one hour of receiving the call, very excited about the prospect of being back in control and at the helm of affairs.

Motu and Pankaj collectively presented their short as well as long-term plan to Alex. Then Arjun took over and explained him about the fixes they had made to the current version of the software to make it look decent.

'This will run and give you some breathing time. Meanwhile, we shall start a clean-up operation at the backend in the next six months. At the time of the next release you'll have one of the most robust software systems in the world that will support as many users as you want for the next ten years,' Pankaj said.

'Ten years is a very long time in the ever-changing software industry,' Motu reminded everyone of the significance of the ten-year guarantee.

Alex was speechless at the end of the presentation. For the first time in days his face turned the original crimson from the ashen look he had been sporting.

'Outsourcing does work,' Alex finally said and everyone burst out laughing more out of relief than anything else.

'Now do you think we are capable of doing business with you?' Motu could not resist asking.

'Of course! You guys are meant for bigger things. I will make sure you get as big a chunk of the IT pie from us as you can handle. From now onwards, your only worry should be scaling up to meet the challenges of growth.'

Then Alex did something he had never done in his life. He hugged his business associates, all four of them, as a sign of gratitude. It was an overwhelming moment for them. They had come to Alex only as a vendor. They departed as friends, a bond which grew stronger with every passing year.

∽

The flight back home was long but not boring. Priya and Pankaj wanted to have their seats together (and away from Motu and Arjun) without making it too obvious.

'Why don't you take an aisle seat in the next row? You will need more space. The one in our row is already taken up,' Pankaj suggested to Motu.

'I can request a swap if you want? We can sit together and analyse the meetings,' Motu replied, feigning innocence. Priya looked at Motu in mock anger and he got the message.

They sat together; their arms entwined, Priya's fingers caressing Pankaj's palm, her head resting on his shoulder and the brush of Pankaj's lips on Priya's cheeks. All this while, they tried to evade the naughty eyes of Motu and Arjun, which they thought were always preying on them. Their love for each other grew stronger by the time the flight to New Delhi landed.

Within fifteen days of returning home, Priya and Pankaj got married. There was no resistance from Pankaj's family with both his sisters and mother approving of the marriage wholeheartedly. Nobody cared that Priya was previously divorced, which endeared Pankaj's family more to both him and Priya.

'She is the best sister-in-law we could have found in the entire world,' commented Gudiya, his younger sister who had come with her Muslim husband. 'I proved you wrong. I am still very happily married,'* she told Pankaj when the two of them were alone.

'Don't embarrass me. I had realised a long time back that marrying within your religion does not necessarily guarantee happiness,' Pankaj told her suddenly remembering his association with Sveta.*

'Pankaj, you have chosen the best girl in the world. But you never let anyone know that you liked Priya. So the accident and not going into IIT were not the only reasons behind your depression.'* His mother poked him in the ribs.

'No, Mama,' he replied sheepishly and the look on his face told the whole story. Everyone, including Priya, had a hearty laugh at his expense.

'I never thought I could marry you and share the same bed with you for life. This is the culmination of a twenty-five-year-old dream,' Pankaj said hugging Priya tightly as if he would not ever let her go.

'That means you have loved me since you met me in class I, lover boy!' replied Priya cheekily, doing some back-of-the-hand calculations.

'No, maybe twenty years then,' Pankaj replied shyly.

'You mean class VI? That's still too early to think of love. Don't you think so?' Priya did not let him off the hook.

He could never tell her how much she had meant to him. They did not sleep at all during their first night together, as if catching up on all the lost time.

They could only take a short holiday to Goa where they stayed at the Taj. Priya was so impressed with their hospitality that she decided to stay at the Taj whenever she visited any Indian city.

'We should come back to Goa. It is such a lovely place, the people are so nice.'

The short duration of the trip irked them a bit, but both of them knew that NumeroSoft needed them because of the explosive growth ahead.

⌇

Motu, on the other hand, parried all questions on marriage. 'My work is my first love,' he would always say.

'I can never get the girl I am looking for. She should be very intelligent, grounded, as hard working as I am, and who does not want to get married just for the heck of it,' he confided to his very close circle of friends which included Priya, Pankaj, Nitin and Arjun.

'With your shape and size it is not going to be easy. Both you and your waist are in early forties. And the kind of attributes you are asking for may not be found here in India, perhaps not in the world. All such women are booked early,' Priya took a dig at him.

'If you have forgotten, I am in early thirties and my waist size is only thirty-eight,' Motu complained.

Let's wait for one more year and you will prove my prediction right.' Everyone joined Priya in the chorus of laughter.

However, Motu proved everyone wrong. In the next one year though he grew in age, he managed to reduce the size of his waist by two inches. But marriage kept on eluding him because of the high standards he had set for his girl.

~

Alex was right that their biggest challenge would be to maintain the high growth rate. An unprecedented number of new projects started coming in steadily from Alex's company. Delivering these projects successfully helped them build an impeccable reputation which further got them new referral customers. The first thing that they happily did was close down all of *laala*'s business. It gave them immense pleasure when they gave a firm kick in his butt by refusing to work with him anymore. The *laala* not knowing where to go with his business then offered them double the price for doing the same work.

'*Laalaji* will forever be the blood-thirsty vampire no matter what. So let's not get lured into working with him whatever the temptation,' Pankaj cautioned the rest to which everyone readily agreed.

As the company grew, Nitin worked very hard to find a new space, build it and move NumeroSoft's office there. The new office was ten times the size of their last office. They took a calculated risk by moving to a new office. Motu predicted that they would outgrow that space in a year's time which indeed came true. They had to find more space in a neighbouring building which was again five times the size of the office they presently occupied.

The next challenge they faced was the biggest one for any software company in India. It was the regular hiring of brilliant people. In a still-nascent industry where there was no pre-existing talent, skill development became the biggest barrier to growth. They realised much earlier than others that brilliant people could only be hired from colleges. This paid off beautifully as it was easiest to mould the youngsters into NumeroSoft's culture of hard work and heroic performance. Within no time they had grown from ten to one-thousand. With NumeroSoft growing at such a scorching pace they began planning for a size of ten-thousand people, which initially everyone would have laughed at sitting in second-hand chairs in that small office, but now that thought was not a distant reality anymore.

Arjun played a big role in stabilising the ever-increasing workforce and giving almost a hundred client releases per week. He sometimes rued the fact that he was getting away from his first love of coding. He had become more of a management person overseeing that everything worked to precision.

'Your passion will have to take a backseat if you want to run a business successfully. It is difficult for both to co-exist peacefully,' Pankaj had advised him.

While Motu and Pankaj planned and executed strategies to expand their business, Priya played a big role in expanding their pharma practice. Getting business from Alex's company meant that doors to the other cash-rich pharma companies opened easily for them. Over a period of three years, they managed to get entry into five such big accounts with an equal potential to grow. Alongside, their friendship with Alex grew as did Alex's position in his organisation. He had become the assistant vice- president with a shot at vice presidency next year, when the present vice-president was set to retire. Whenever he came to India he stayed either at Motu's or Pankaj's place and the same happened when they went to New York. The only thing not constant in their friendship was Alex's girlfriends who kept on changing every time they went over to NY.

'People in a hurry have a huge libido and need to give constant releases just like people managing software companies,' he had offered a simple explanation.

And so, NumeroSoft was on course to become the biggest software company in India. With everything going right for them, they had the gumption of thinking that someday they would be the biggest in the world. What they had not counted on was greed, hatred, jealousy, destiny and the role those 'seven hours' had to play in Pankaj's life.*

Life continued as usual but for certain developments which were about to change the course of their lives. With no one realising the process started with Pankaj's trip to Russia where meeting Kapil and Sveta changed him forever.

༄

The need to go to Moscow arose because NumeroSoft was short of ready cash which explosive growth demanded. All the money they made either remained with their customers because they paid late or went into building new offices. Pankaj had returned from Russia abruptly with the intention of going back once he had convinced his mother to accept Sveta.* As things turned out eventually, he never went back to settle his account with Kapil. At a rough estimate Kapil owed him a few million dollars, and that was enough to ease the liquidity pressure in NumeroSoft.

The flight to Moscow was uneventful more so because he wore a charcoal-coloured suit which gave him the demeanour of a businessman and got him some respect from the air-hostesses onboard. He smiled to himself remembering the past flights to Moscow as an awkward, underconfident, young man.*

Moscow had changed tremendously. There were new constructions, swanky office spaces, multiplicity of foreign cars and an ever-increasing number of foreign companies everywhere. The sense of pride which the Russians had lost in the second-half of the twentieth century had returned after Russia began to find its place in the new world order. With opportunities aplenty, people found meaningful ways of working.

It was summer time. There were many people on the roads showing skin. Pankaj enjoyed the show on his way to Domodedovo Airport for his flight to Volgograd.

As happens with all small cities, growth came to Volgograd as spilled-over remnants of what the greedy big cities spared. Except for that, it still looked the same sleepy town it had been so many years ago. The Padfaak still teemed with foreign students and the university was bustling with activity as usual. With the emotional moments of the past years in Volgograd playing in his mind, he entered Kapil's office ready to give him a happy surprise. The office building on Komsomolskaya Street, where he and Kapil had started with a humble two-room office, was now almost completely occupied by the company staff.

'He has been tremendously successful. He matured after all,' Pankaj thought with pride that came from being a part of building something up.

As soon as he entered the office Pankaj got the shock of his life. In one cabin in a big leather swivel chair sat Ajay* wearing an immaculate business suit. He looked his same mean self as during his days of supreme power. What was more shocking was that Kapil never told him about Ajay in his infrequent calls to him.

'Oh! So you managed to be a part of my company after all. Your audacity is amazing,' Pankaj said rudely. Ajay chose not to say anything but smiled smugly. No more words were exchanged between the two.

Kapil emerged from his cabin and hugged him. The embrace was not as tight as Pankaj had thought it would be. 'You never told me you are coming,' Kapil complained as they entered his cabin.

'I thought I'd give you a surprise, but instead got one myself. What is Ajay doing here?' Pankaj asked.

'I was all alone when you returned to India. I had nobody to help me run this business. When you decided not to return I was left with no choice but to pick him up as a partner,' Kapil explained.

'But of all the people ... why him?' Pankaj almost shouted. Everyone in the hall had stopped working. Sensing trouble, the burly Russian security officer sprung to attention. Ajay too came into Kapil's cabin fearing a scuffle between the two.

'You get out of this room. This is private and you are not invited,' Pankaj shouted at him. Kapil signalled him to leave.

'Pankaj, I didn't have anybody with the skills to run this expanding business except him. I can also shout at you and ask for an explanation as to why you did not return. But like a good friend, I did not complain and instead rebuilt this business, piece by piece. Ajay helped me in this. Now, I can proudly say that we are the biggest sellers of FMCG products in Volgograd and half of Russia,' Kapil explained the whole situation to Pankaj patiently.

Pankaj was quiet for a few moments. He could imagine Kapil's plight at being left in lurch and forgave him for involving Ajay in his business. He also realised that it was Kapil's business now and he had no right to question his decision.

'Yeah, you are right. After I left, it was no more my business. I understand. Please forgive my outburst,' he apologised.

'Don't worry about that. We are friends. But now tell me what brings you to Russia?'

Pankaj told him about NumeroSoft, how their business was expanding, how he, Priya, Motu, Arjun and Nitin were working very hard to make NumeroSoft the number one software company in India.

'Rapid growth needs cash. I thought I'd take the money I earned here and invest it into our software business. Many of our plans have gone into cold freeze due to the lack of ready cash,' Pankaj concluded.

The earlier uneasiness on Kapil's face was replaced by unhappiness. 'Pankaj, I don't think I owe you any money. You had left the business to die. Had Ajay and I not taken care of it, the lending sharks would have come to India chasing you for payment. You should thank me that I saved your life instead of shamelessly asking for money,' Kapil spun a completely different story.

'I trusted you, how can you …?' Pankaj could not finish the sentence.

'I trusted you too, Pankaj, and see what you did to me. You knew I did not know swimming, still you left me in the middle of the river and went away,' Kapil replied.

Kapil had indeed matured. Since nothing was on paper there was no point fighting with him. He had lost his conscience and the will to give Pankaj his due.

'A pig will always find filth and make it his home and if he doesn't find it he will create it around him. That's what you have done to Kapil,' Pankaj said to Ajay on his way out. Ajay gave a silent smile knowing that he need not react as he had already won.

Pankaj was shaken to the core. The only other thing on his agenda was meeting Sveta. He had long nurtured a subdued, passive desire to see her once again ever since he came back to India. He wanted to see with his own eyes if she was doing fine. Now that he was within a few kilometres of her there were doubts in his mind whether he really wanted to meet her. For the only reason of burying the ghosts, he decided to visit her.

He went to the university and found that he had missed her by a few minutes. With nothing much to do and a flight to catch only the next day, he went to her home, not knowing whether he was welcome there or not. But this time, he was intrepid as he did not have a hidden agenda unlike the last and only time he had visited her home.*

He rang the bell, shivering partly from the chill in the wind and partly from not knowing what awaited him. Sveta opened the door.

They kept on looking at each other for eternity. She still looked the same, except her hair was shorter and the creases on her face deeper. It took her a bit longer to recognise him. It was the kind of reaction you get when you see someone unexpectedly. Tears began to roll down his cheeks. To his dismay she didn't show any warmth.

'Why have you come here?'

'You had cut me off brutally. The scar never healed. Part of you always remained with me and I can't seem to escape it. I came here to liberate it, to cremate it so that it does not haunt me anymore,' Pankaj said.

'You are not welcome here any longer. I have buried your memories long back. I am in love with someone else now. You are a stranger to me. Please leave,' Sveta said.

There was neither softness nor familiarity in her voice.

He still gave his number to Sveta asking her to call him in case she ever needed him. She took it without actually wanting to. The brush of her skin did not evoke any warm feelings in him.

After travelling thousands of miles with the excitement of meeting two of the most loved people from his past, he had walked out of both places within a few minutes of walking in.

Pankaj realised he had made a mistake by trying to walk down the memory lane. He left Russia without a friend, with a raw wound torn open, never to be healed again. The flight to India was as sad as those in the past.

⁊

After returning to India something inside Pankaj snapped. He felt betrayed both by Kapil and Sveta. The tenderness he had always felt for his loved ones was gradually replaced by a feeling of bitterness. Not that he didn't realise this, but he did nothing to save himself from falling into that abyss of hatred and anguish. Slowly but surely, his priorities began to change with money and power displacing friendship and love. What could not be won with love was to be conquered with money and power.

'He has changed ever since he returned from Russia,' Priya told Motu one day. Pankaj's behaviour was troubling her for quite some time, and she felt a compelling urge to confide in someone.

'I can see that. He has become ruthless. Did you hear what he said when Nitin asked about Kapil? He said that Kapil is dead for him. Something must have transpired in Russia. But he isn't telling anyone what happened there. Let's hope it's just a passing phase.' As time proved, Motu could not have been more wrong.

One month had passed since Pankaj's return. He worked diligently and solved the monetary problem by convincing the bank that he was running a profitable business. That was when Pankaj and Motu first met Jaanvee, the fast rising banker.

'I am going to run the biggest software company in India. If you play your cards right you can earn your bank great profits and yourself a great reputation by banking with me,' Pankaj sold himself to her.

Earlier, his statements reflected sincerity and confidence. Of late, he reeked of arrogance and over-confidence. Slowly, the people who had stood by him began to drift away. Instead calculative, ruthless and shrewd businessmen, who only cared about money, became his close associates.

Within six months of his return from Russia Pankaj, for the first time in the history of NumeroSoft fired an employee for something very trivial. This led to the first big argument of their corporate life. Though nobody liked the fired employee, the manner in which he was chucked out was questioned and heatedly debated.

'Pankaj, this is not right. The guy has a family, that too a large one. We can't ask him to leave like this,' Motu said when he came to know of it.

'We cannot be socialistic when we are in business. I think you should also gear up to take such harsh decisions in the future,' Pankaj replied.

'It is not a question of being socialistic. Our decisions impact several lives, so we need to be careful. Remember, we had agreed we shall always take good care of our people and make them feel proud of the company,' Priya chipped in, baffled by Pankaj's impulsive decision.

'But he blundered big time. Can't you guys see that?'

'Mistakes do happen, but the guy is sincere in his work. We can try him in some other department. He will be useful to the company,' Priya replied, slowly getting on a stronger footing.

'Now what do you want to do? Override my decision, make me a fool in front of the whole organisation just for the sake of a useless employee?' Pankaj roared.

'He has responsibilities to shoulder. You can decide on this one, but I want you to know that none of us supports you,' said Priya pointing towards Motu, Arjun and Nitin.

The decision to remove the employee was not revoked, but he was given a healthy severance package. As time passed Pankaj's dictatorial attitude became more intolerable.

The circumstances surrounding the employee's removal strengthened Pankaj's belief that money and power would, from thereon, be his only constant companions. That night, for the first time since their marriage, Priya and Pankaj slept in separate rooms. Priya wanted to embrace him and discuss the turn of events at office, but Pankaj, who didn't like being questioned, deliberately kept away.

After three months, Pankaj called everyone for a meeting.

'We need to bring in a financial controller. I have observed that we are too soft with money. We need to hire someone who really understands its value. If we continue the way we are doing things right now, we shall never be able to make it big.'

'If making it big means sleeping in different rooms I'd rather not do it,' Priya thought.

'He is meandering. The way he is trying to shape the company is not how we had intended it to happen. Hope he does not mess up his life now just like I did in school,' Motu reminisced about his old days at school.*

Arjun and Nitin saw the friend they had loved so dearly and a businessman who had actually commanded their respect suddenly look like a stranger. But no one said anything as they had no ground to refute him.

Many people were interviewed for the post of financial controller. Some of them were really brilliant. The characteristics of the person were discussed in great detail and Priya thought if they made a caricature of the person based on the final description he would greatly resemble Ravana. They dithered over the final selection till Pankaj again dug his heels in and shortlisted three – two men and a female.

Out of the two males Pankaj rejected one because he was less experienced.

Of the remaining two, the male, Salem Mohammad, actually came very close to what Priya had imagined. He was huge, dark, in his early thirties with the beginnings of a paunch which showed promise of growing enormous with the passage of time. What actually differentiated him from others was his menacing grin. His teeth were very white, in stark contrast to the colour of his skin. His canines stood out prominently, as if they were ready to bite into the opponent and tear him to pieces. Nobody knew that apart from his other qualifications, his intimidating physique was one reason why Pankaj had liked him immensely.

'So what can you do that others can't do better?' Pankaj came straight to the point.

'In addition to everything else that is required of my profile, I can save you a lot of money,' he said with an impish smile. Pankaj liked that.

'When I work, I only see the numbers I am asked to achieve. Anything else, including people, becomes a part of the blurred background. I am a soldier who fires when the general orders and gets him victory at any cost.' Salem had realised what Pankaj wanted to hear.

When asked the same question the lady replied, 'I can help to make this company a great place to work in, where everything is done democratically and the welfare of employees is kept in mind. People will love working here.'

For Pankaj, 'democratically-run company' and 'employee welfare' did not matter anymore. He only wanted two things – money and profits. Salem was a frightful dog waiting to be unleashed and the lady, a financial whizkid. One was a doer, the other a thinker. Pankaj needed the doer more.

This was the second time she had met Pankaj, but it was the first time in her career that she had been rejected in an interview. Her name was Jaanvee.

∽

Things began to change after Salem joined NumeroSoft. The first strange thing to happen was that he got a cabin right next to Pankaj, replacing Arjun who had occupied it earlier. This raised a few eyebrows and a lot of concern. Pankaj justified it by saying that he would need Salem as he would be working very closely with him. But no one believed Pankaj. People in NumeroSoft began to feel threatened for the first time.

'If you love life you need to be a little evil. Good deeds will give you moksha. Evilness will make god give you a second chance at life,' became Salem's most famous words.

NumeroSoft, where everything used to be very transparent and open, became a secretive organisation which made people suddenly feel insecure. The sense of belongingness began to disappear. What also added to the mystery was that Pankaj did not clearly define Salem's role in the organisation. Over time, employees began to polarise between Pankaj and Salem on the one hand and Motu, Priya, Arjun and Nitin on the other.

Insecure people became sycophants and aligned themselves with Pankaj and the rest sided with Motu. This demarcation grew distinct with time. Without wishing to, people were caught in a divisive war which threatened the harmony of the workplace.

'We don't look like a software company anymore. This way we might become the biggest but never the greatest. This wasn't our vision when we started this company,' Motu said to Priya, Arjun and Nitin one day at lunch.

'There is so much politics in the company. People are confused and afraid now. These are ominous signs. If we don't do something about it, god knows what will happen,' Arjun agreed.

'Salem is not good for the company. He is too dangerous,' Nitin added.

At home, Pankaj had also distanced himself from Priya. Sleeping in different rooms had become a regular feature. It was as if Pankaj had turned impotent. She began to badly miss those small, stolen moments of intimacy in office and at home, those glances full of yearning for each other. She remembered his searching eyes that made her feel wanted, those tired moments when he gently flicked away a stubborn lock from her face to look into her deep black eyes and discover that they had a tinge of brown in them. She wanted to be loved by him but Pankaj seemed to have lost all interest in her. She did not discuss it with him hoping that things would return to normal soon.

At office, the time was ripe for something to happen; the only thing missing was a catalyst.

The first real thing that Salem did was prepare a blueprint for improving efficiency. It was nothing but a plan to get rid of less efficient people in the organisation so that NumeroSoft could reach a certain profit target. He called the exercise 'The Weeds'. Though it was meant to be a secret, it somehow got leaked which immediately sent panic waves throughout the company. People started calling Priya and Motu for details who had no inkling about what it meant.

'What the fuck is "The Weeds?" ' Priya and Motu stormed into Pankaj's office and demanded an answer.

Salem was by Pankaj's side. They were deep in discussion.

'Can we catch up after this meeting?' Pankaj asked curtly.

'We can't. The two of you are taking such big decisions without even bothering to consult us. Salem, could you leave us alone for a while? We need to speak with Pankaj,' Motu ordered Salem.

'He will stay here. He needs to know everything we intend to do.'

Priya and Motu were shocked. Motu did not respond for a few seconds even as Salem smiled smugly.

'I need to see that list,' Motu demanded.

'I can give you a copy tomorrow,' Salem said.

'You keep out of this. This is not your company. Pankaj, I need a copy right now,' Motu refused to budge.

'Don't get worked up over something so trivial. Salem is working really hard to get NumeroSoft in shape. Please show him some respect,' Pankaj said.

Priya and Motu left the room only after taking the list, completely dumbfounded by Pankaj's audacity. This was definitely not the Pankaj they had known and loved.

Motu showed the list to Arjun. Having interacted with almost all engineers on a regular basis he knew everyone in the company inside out. With his ears to the ground, he was the best person to know the calibre of NumeroSoft's employees.

'These are not inefficient people. All of them are hard working. Obviously, some will be more productive than others. But that doesn't mean those "others" are non-performers.

'You just can't remove them like that. Has Pankaj thought of hiring replacements? Why was I not consulted when this list was being prepared?' Arjun had many questions, answers to which eluded all of them.

'Let us fix a meeting with Pankaj. We should try to convince him as a friend. We need to find out what is going inside his head,' Motu suggested.

'Who will bell the cat?' Nitin asked.

'Priya, of course,' Arjun replied.

Priya could not disagree with the suggestion because she did not have the courage to tell them that they hardly spoke at home. She had no hope that Pankaj would listen to her.

_ᕔ_

'Pankaj, why don't we start sleeping in the same room?' Priya tried to massage Pankaj's head softly with her fingers; something which he always said relaxed him.

'I work late. You will get disturbed,' Pankaj replied curtly while still working on his laptop in the study.

Priya withdrew her fingers immediately. She did not want to degrade herself further by coaxing him to sleep with her. A lump was beginning to form in her throat and she feared it would choke her words.

'The guys want to have a meeting with you on "The Weeds" tomorrow,' Priya changed the topic.

'Sure. We need to get over it fast.'

'Without Salem,' Priya demanded, looking him straight in the eye.

'Okay,' Pankaj thought for a moment before replying.

The four of them met Pankaj the next morning.

'What's going on, Pankaj? Things aren't the same anymore. We used to have so much fun working together – planning things and executing them. Why have things changed so abruptly?' Motu said to Pankaj, the friend.

'Nothing has changed except that we have grown very fast. If we don't bring in some professionals now our dream will remain just that, a dream,' Pankaj replied calmly.

'But Salem is a beast. He is not the kind of professional we need. We are a company with a heart. Remember this is what we used to say,' Nitin urged Pankaj.

'Nitin, you are a kid. You don't know how businesses are run. If certain things are to be done, they have to be done. If in the process people are chucked out, so be it,' Pankaj argued.

'Have you carefully looked at this list? None of these people are really bad,' Arjun asked, pointing to the list which had names of more than five-hundred people Salem was planning to fire.

'I have seen the list,' Pankaj replied brusquely.

'Have you ever thought who will replace them?' Arjun prodded further.

'We are not replacing them. They'll just leave. We have so many people sitting on the bench, waiting for a project. They will take the load,' Pankaj replied.

'At this time we have no bench. And if we fire these people, the remaining employees will not be able to share the workload. You can't screw things up like this,' Arjun said.

'That's what you think. I don't need your opinion on this. People have to take more responsibilities. We can't afford to continue feeding useless people. Salem knows more about productivity than any one of you here. And look, Arjun, Gaurav and I made you into what you are today, so mind what you say. Don't tread on an elephant's foot. If it gets angry, you may get trampled underneath it,' Pankaj replied sharply.

Everyone was dumbfounded by the threat in Pankaj's voice. With nothing left to say they decided to leave.

'One last thing before you go, Salem is here to stay. No more questioning his authority and challenging his decisions,' Pankaj closed the discussion.

They were infuriated. Pankaj carried out one more of his dictatorial decisions, and they could do nothing about it. The abrupt firing of five-hundred people asserted Salem's increasing power in NumeroSoft. He carried out the operation without any retaliation from the ones who survived. In the absence of a strong leader, no employee questioned the manner of these removals. Everyone continued working as if nothing had happened, afraid of losing their own job. The protests were muted and were usually made on lunch tables. The earlier feeling of belongingness that bound the people of NumeroSoft together was gone forever. This did not worry Pankaj who had transformed completely into a hard-nosed, ruthless businessman who only cared about money. He ran the company like an empire where his verdict was final, never to be questioned.

'This is the last time I am keeping quiet. I will not take any more of Pankaj's autocratic decisions,' Motu told Priya after the incident.

'We had built everything up so painstakingly, not to see it disintegrate like this,' Priya too agreed.

While the current storm passed somehow, it left ominous signals that the next one would blow them apart. Nitin, always the non-violent and peace-loving person, prayed to god that nothing of the sort happened and sanity prevailed.

⌒

A few years back NumeroSoft had acquired a big customer, almost as big as Alex's company. Since it was an important account for the company, Arjun was directly in charge of the project. He did a great job by growing the account from an initial strength of five people to two-hundred-and-fifty people. The customer was very demanding and Arjun had handled him really well, ceding to most of his small requests and putting his foot down on the most important, undoable ones. The customer was happy with Arjun's contribution to the project. He had been able to show a fifty-million dollars' saving through the project in his organisation which earned him a double promotion.

Nursing this customer was a nerve-racking experience for Arjun which required skills and patience. The people working on his project were stressed out because the customer's demands were always wild and Arjun had to use all his persuasive power, and software acumen to keep him satisfied. The project made it extremely difficult for Arjun to concentrate on new accounts which needed greater attention through the initial transition periods to grow into steady accounts. He had spoken to the customer about reducing his time on the project, and he had not taken the news well. Instead, he had sounded upset and had given him a veiled threat that there were several other Indian software companies dying to take his account.

It went on like this till one day he asked for something impossible. In order to prove his worth to his company, the customer had promised to get new software delivered before the year-end. Since it was a high-visibility project, its success would increase his clout in his company tremendously. However, the biggest problem with this commitment was that he had not consulted Arjun at all before promising his CEO. The year-end was only six months away and according to Arjun's estimate, even twelve months weren't enough to complete work on the new software. It was a huge project and required detailed planning. When he had communicated this to the customer he got a very harsh email from him demanding to discuss the issue as early as possible.

It was Sunday night and Arjun was helping Diyaa with her first lessons in speaking. He hated receiving the call at that hour, but since it was important he patted Diyaa to sleep and got on a conference with him.

'What the hell is the matter, Arjun? You don't feel like working anymore?' the customer asked brusquely after the preliminaries were over.

'That's not the case. My biggest problem is that we still don't have the complete set of requirements. So I haven't been able to make a detailed execution plan,' Arjun tried to apprise him of his problems.

'If you want to do business, this is not important. The most important thing is getting business, everything else is secondary. The rest should automatically align itself around the end date,' the customer had said.

It had been a very disappointing day for Arjun. Diyaa had shown very slow progress. He had shouted both at the therapist and the trainer earlier in the day. He was now getting increasingly frustrated with the unyielding attitude of the customer and was ready to blow his top.

'But things don't work that way. I can't promise you good quality if I don't know what you want from me,' Arjun replied in irritation.

'Then double the shifts, double the people. Do whatever you can to salvage the situation. I am the customer. I give you the problem and you find ways to solve it. Don't come back to me with problems of your own,' the customer shouted.

'Doubling the shifts and people won't help too. If they work hours longer than what is humanly possible, it will adversely impact your code. Also, there are certain things which are not directly proportional to the amount of time spent. This is a recipe for disaster.' Arjun realised that he was getting into an argument but couldn't stop himself.

'Arjun, it is your job to find solutions to the problems I throw at you. That is what I pay you for,' the customer reiterated adamantly.

'That's fine. But my job also includes warning you of the consequences of your actions, and in my opinion they are not going to be pleasant at all,' Arjun shot back.

'You don't warn me. Just do what I tell you to do,' he shouted at the top of his voice.

'Let's get this straight. Single shifts or double shifts, this cannot be done in the time specified by you. If you want me to work on this, get the timelines extended,' Arjun did not budge.

'You lousy Indian, you don't know who you are talking to and what your refusal can do to your business. You will be out on the streets if I give this project to any other IT company.'

The condescending tone and the racist remark proved to be the tipping point. Arjun couldn't control himself further and said something he had never said to anybody in his life.

'You may not know but I was born on the streets and I am a son of the soil. It was my hard work and destiny that I reached where I am today. I am not afraid of going back to where I came from if that is what god intends for me.

'My destiny is not governed by threats from capitalistic bastards like you who don't give a damn about human lives and people's opinion. You can take your business anywhere you want or shove it up your ass. I don't care anymore.' Arjun slammed the phone down.

He felt relieved after the conversation, a feeling he had not experienced since he took charge of this account. The pent-up frustration when released gave him an exhilarating sense of freedom. He walked up to Diyaa's bed, kissed her and went off to sleep in peace.

Arjun's refusal to work with the powerful customer elicited different reactions from different people in the company. Motu, Priya and Nitin backed him completely, comprehending the real reason behind his firm stand. They too knew the customer was irrational, and he would have overstepped the boundary of 'Customer is King' for Arjun to have taken such a drastic step.

'Arjun, you don't have to worry even if we lose this account, we will gain many such businesses. What is more important is that we do business with like-minded people. Business, just like life, is all about being with the right people. Half your problems would disappear if you work with people who are on the same wavelength as yours,' Motu said encouragingly.

'He is right. Finding the right people is the biggest challenge we face in our lives,' Priya said, picturing Salem at the back of her mind.

'What will happen to people who are now on the bench, sitting idle because of Arjun's decision?' Nitin asked the question which was playing on everybody's mind.

'It doesn't matter. We shall keep all of them. It's not their fault that we lost this business. Our profits will certainly be affected, but we shall recoup the losses in the following years,' Motu replied, relieving the stress in the air.

'But what about Pankaj and Salem, how will they react to this?' Nitin asked again.

'Salem doesn't exist for me, but we do have to tell Pankaj. I think he will understand the circumstances and will respect Arjun's decision.'

They could not have been more wrong.

Pankaj was sitting alone, brooding over something when the four of them walked into his cabin. Of late, he usually worked alone or with Salem, rarely calling on any of them for advice; something he did very frequently in the formative years of the company.

'Pankaj, we have come to share a bad news with you,' Priya started the conversation. The hesitancy in her voice betrayed the uncertainty she felt about his response. In that situation nobody would have thought that they were husband and wife.

'What is it?'

Arjun then went on to tell him about the conversation with the customer, not missing anything.

Pankaj did not speak for long and sat poker-faced. He was trying to calculate the losses caused to NumeroSoft.

'This will set us back hugely,' Pankaj finally spoke, still not betraying any emotion. 'Who allowed you to take a decision on your own? I never gave you that authority,' Pankaj asked the question nobody expected him to.

'Authority comes with a sense of belongingness. I always thought this was my company too and gave it my very best. In this particular situation I didn't have the time to ask. It was like being cornered by a hooligan with a dagger in his hand. There was no time to seek help. I had to take a decision instantly,' Arjun tried to explain.

'I don't buy this. There are ways to stall someone. There was no need to decide without taking others in the loop. You must remember this is not your company. You are a worker and a minority shareholder here. Whether we have to continue doing business with a customer or not is a decision not for you to take. You are just supposed to do what you are told. And if you can't toe the line, find yourself another job,' Pankaj erupted violently, leaving everyone else stunned.

This was the first time that authority had been exercised so blatantly by anyone in NumeroSoft.

'In case it matters, let me tell you we fully support what he did,' Priya was the first one to speak.

'Maybe no one has told you but the customer was the most difficult and demanding we've ever had. His demands were irrational most of the times,' Motu told him.

'If you want to grow bigger you will have to get used to working with such people. Not everyone you work with will be an Alex,' Pankaj said.

'The important question is what should we do now?' Nitin pitched in.

'There is only one course of action. Arjun will have to apologise to the customer,' Pankaj said looking at everyone probingly.

'If everybody thinks my decision was wrong, I will do it,' Arjun relented, devastated.

'You don't have to apologise to anybody. Pankaj, I think you didn't hear what Motu and I had said earlier. We fully support Arjun's decision.' Priya stared hard at Pankaj this time.

'Then there is nothing left to decide. He should put in his papers and leave. One of us will talk to the customer and apologise to him,' Pankaj said standing up, indicating the meeting was over.

'That someone will not be one of us,' Motu replied pointing towards the three of them. Pankaj realised that the situation was not in his control anymore. He sank into his chair.

'Pankaj, you have been pushing your decisions down our throats for many months now. It can't continue like this anymore. We have to decide right now how we want to run the company,' Motu challenged him to a debate. 'How do you want to run the company?' Pankaj asked sarcastically.

'For starters, we need to throw Salem out. He doesn't fit into our culture,' Motu replied ignoring the sarcasm.

'That's what you think,' Pankaj said.

'That's what all of us think,' Priya said.

'Pankaj, please listen to us. This is our last chance to get things right. You don't realise but you have changed. All of us looked up to you for support because you always took wise decisions which benefitted everyone. Now you only think about money. For you, human beings are just employee codes. Can't you be the same Pankaj we loved and trusted so much?' Motu pleaded. He was in tears.

'So your love for me depends on my returning to my previous jovial self. Why can't love be unconditional?' Pankaj said suddenly remembering Sveta and Kapil.

'I still love you unconditionally,' Priya said hoping to break through the barriers Pankaj had created between them.

'In fact we all do,' Nitin added.

Certain moments come very rarely and fleetingly. If you catch onto them they have the power to change your destiny but if they pass, you rue them for all the great possibilities they held, yearning to have that moment back again for the rest of your lives. For a moment, everyone thought that Pankaj had mellowed; something which had not happened to him in months. In that short span of time everyone tried to appeal to his tender side. Suddenly, to everyone's horror, Salem entered the room.

'Pankaj, I needed your help on something,' he said. But when he saw the grim faces around, he asked if he could be of any help.

'You are not invited. Get out of here,' Motu shouted.

'He is as much a part of this company as I. He remains, here as well as in the company,' Pankaj asked Salem to stay. He had hardened back to his old self. Salem grinned and inched closer to Pankaj.

Nitin, undiplomatic as he was, could not resist saying, 'Don't think you are the only showman in town. You may take away all the applause today, but it could be someone else who does it the next time.'

Pankaj has had enough for the day. He said, 'Nitin, this is enough, no more histrionics. For everyone's information the company will continue to be run the same way. Nothing changes.'

'Then we will have to part ways.' Priya realised there was no way their relationship could survive now.

'That's your choice. I am not asking you to leave,' Pankaj replied coolly.

'But you have created conditions which are forcing us to leave,' Motu replied on his way out. That was the day when the four of them broke away from NumeroSoft.

For Priya it was a life-changing decision because she had to leave both her husband whom she loved madly and the company she cared for. What also devastated her was that Pankaj locked himself in his study, not even bothering to come out while she packed her bags or when she banged the door loudly indicating she was leaving. In fact, she went into the house again under the pretence of picking up her wallet. But Pankaj remained hidden in his study waiting for her to leave before he came out.

Nitin always rued the fact that he couldn't do enough to prevent the disintegration of the company. He thought it was his duty to keep Pankaj and Motu united. He vowed that if he ever got a chance he would do all it took to bring them together again. Arjun always blamed his outburst to be the primary reason for the separation. He felt extremely guilty sometimes even though everyone explained to him time and again that he was the catalyst and not the reason for the separation. Pankaj felt vindicated that his theory, that love was not permanent and people who loved each other one day may not want to see each other the next day, was not wrong. He also wanted to take revenge, a feeling he tried to suppress but which grew stronger with time. Pain and remorse were there, but as minority parts of the fluctuating emotions. Within a few days of the separation he got back to working harder, sans all the distractions, and more ruthlessly to achieve his ambition of creating the biggest software company in India.

It is said that there are only victims in a war. But in this war between friends, Salem was the undisputed gainer whose power in NumeroSoft multiplied manifold and he became more vicious. As Pankaj got busy in socialising, networking and trying to find ways to grow at a vociferous speed, he left the day-to-day running of the company entirely to Salem. While Pankaj grew NumeroSoft by buying out other companies, whether relenting or unwilling, Salem played the role of consolidating the merged companies into one single unit through ruthless execution. Those who dared to disagree with him were thrown out. Firing people became a way of life at NumeroSoft and fun at work a thing of past. Salem turned the company into an assembly line which churned out code and gave releases every day. NumeroSoft was merely reduced to a giant, aspiring to become an even bigger player, but without a soul.

∽

Motu, Arjun, Nitin and Priya then formed PureConsultants. Probably, thoughts about work ethics and fairness dominated their minds when they decided to name their new company. With enough meat on their resumes they could have found cushy jobs anywhere in the world. But all of them decided to make a second stab at greatness.

'We can't let our dream fizzle out so easily,' Priya reminded all of them.

'We just need to be careful about the kind of people we bring in,' Nitin added. 'We always were. But who would have thought that Pankaj ...' Motu did not complete the sentence.

Motu had always remembered Jaanvee since her interview at NumeroSoft and had made a note to himself that he would pick her up if and when he got an opportunity. The opportunity came by when he and Pankaj separated. Since Jaanvee was impressed with the work ethics of Motu and had heard the right kind of noise about him in the frequent corporate gossip sessions over network lunches, it didn't take her much thought to join PureConsultants when he made her an offer.

Time passed but Motu did not marry. 'Are you never going to marry? Vowed to celibacy, huh?' Priya asked him one day.

'Nothing like that. Once I did tell you about the kind of woman I am looking for. You don't find such women anymore,' Motu said.

'Oh!' Priya said.

'In fact, I had never meant to say this but since you are single now, do you think I am worthy of you?'

'First, mind your diet. One more bite of your extra-large Pizza and even Walmart will not be able to find a waist-size that fits you!' Priya said, buying time to think.

'I can reduce weight if that is an important criterion. I am a very determined person. You just have to say yes.'

'To be very honest, I don't know. I am very weak and confused at the moment.'

Priya was shocked. She had not expected to hear this from Motu, but the sincerity in his voice made her believe that his intentions were pure. But she still loved Pankaj and had no plan to remarry, continuing to believe somewhere deep inside that Pankaj would come back to her one day.

It was night and she had returned home. Sleep still eluded her. The more she thought about it, the more she realised that Motu's description of a perfect woman fitted her to a tee. She indeed had been the woman of his dreams. Now she could comprehend why he would always look sad whenever Pankaj and she turned romantic. She suddenly remembered that the smell of perfume on Motu was the same that she preferred on men. It couldn't have been by accident. She also remembered the forlorn look in his eyes when many years ago in school Bakshi sir had punished Pankaj for playing dumb charade and Priya had tried to protect him.*

'Oh, my God! He has loved me throughout,' she mumbled to herself at this sudden realisation. A burst of tenderness filled her. Her respect for Motu increased manifold because she knew that not having a temptation was simpler. Having it and still being able to resist it were signs of greatness.

'What can I do to make him happy?' she muttered to herself before she was embraced by sleep, taking her away from the painful decision for one more day.

The next day the two of them went to a quiet restaurant in the neighbourhood to discuss the impending thing on both their minds. 'So when did you fall in love with me?' Priya asked Motu tenderly, looking into his eyes.

'What? Is it important?

'Yes.'

'It was only after you and Pankaj decided …' Motu stammered, blushing at the same time.

'That was when you began to think about expressing it. I want to know when did you actually fall in love with me,' Priya asked again, smiling.

Motu's face turned deep red as if he had been caught stealing and had nowhere to hide. 'Maybe in school, maybe in college, I am not sure. It was so long ago,' he feigned forgetfulness.

'You depraved person! You used to ogle at underaged girls,' Priya said, laughing uncontrollably and inviting curious stares from the ones sitting nearby.

'Priya, don't embarrass me,' Motu complained, smiling sheepishly.

'Have you ever loved someone else?' Priya continued to embarrass him further.

'No. In fact, I never got the time. Maybe, I liked you too much to think of anyone else,' Motu spoke haltingly.

'Are you sure?' Priya was serious now. 'I still love Pankaj very much but I know it's important to move on. I don't want to disappoint you either. Since you are not married and have nothing to do except growing PureConsultants and loving me, I want to give you a reason to live.'

'So what have you decided?' Motu asked. His heart was hammering against his ribs.

'There is nothing to decide, Gaurav. You are one of the nicest and warmest persons I know. But it's neither my fault nor yours that I don't love you. Your chubby, smiling face and large frame make me feel safe and protected. It is an entirely different kind of feeling. It's similar to what I call the August feeling – the emotions you experience when you celebrate *rakhi*.' Priya was back to her teasing ways.

'On a serious note, characters are more permanent than isolated aberrations in behaviour. You will not change because of what you have said. In fact, I respect you all the more for the way you have conducted yourself throughout despite the perpetual conflict in your heart,' Priya said, more serious now.

'Then?'

'Let's do this. I know you will die if I say no to you and I want to give you enough reason to live. I will marry you when someone actually says that you know my job better than I do ...' Priya said.

'You mean I should know more about the pharma industry than you? That is impossible! You are the Maven, the expert,' Motu said exasperatedly.

'And that's not all. The second condition is that PureConsultants should reach the fifty-thousand people milestone before we tie the knot.'

'But that's again not possible in my lifetime. We only have five, six if we include the office help,' Motu complained.

'Okay! Twenty-five thousand. I am in the mood for charity today. But I can only go so far. That's all the concession I can give.' She smiled cheekily.

'Does it mean one or both the conditions need to be met before I can lay claim to your hand?' Motu asked.

'Both, sir. It's not going to be easy. If you are up to this challenge only then we have a deal. I am ready to sign on the dotted line if you agree,' Priya declared. She didn't refuse him directly but had put conditions impossible for him to meet.

'I am ready. If my love is true, god will help me achieve this miracle,' Motu accepted the challenge, knowing fully well the implications.

∽

Considering it an unethical practice, they did not solicit business from any of NumeroSoft's customers. A few did approach them but they refused and told them to continue doing business with NumeroSoft as it was an excellent company from a customer's perspective.

One customer who refused to be convinced by their rhetoric was Alex. He had come to know the whole story by first scratching the surface. After sensing that things were not as they were put forth by Salem and Pankaj, he called Motu directly for more details.

'That's how things unfurled,' Motu ran Alex through the whole story.

'This is sad. I was envious of the amazing relation you guys shared. I always wondered why I could not find selfless friends like you here in the US. I guess the warm curry you eat makes you guys much warmer and open to friendship. Do you think Pankaj is to blame for this?' Alex asked him.

'No, I think the circumstances are to be blamed. I still don't believe Pankaj could become so heartless,' Motu defended him.

'Let me tell you what I think of this though I have no right to comment. The direction in which NumeroSoft is headed is not the right one and the principles you broke away for, are absolutely correct. I will move all my business from NumeroSoft to PureConsultants whether they like it or not,' Alex said firmly. 'You guys are not the only emotional fools out here.

I'm anyway not going to work with NumeroSoft. Now you have to decide what you want,' Alex conveyed his decision.

'You leave me with no choice then. How will I ever repay this debt, Alex?' Motu had not told Alex how difficult it was for them to get new clients as people eyed them with suspicion. Salem too played a big role in it through all the negative campaigning he was doing against them.

'When we give something, there is always that desire to get something in return. Don't worry, I am not doing charity here. By the way, did I tell you that I am three steps away from becoming the CEO?' Alex informed Motu.

'Congrats! How many years before you get there?'

'Anywhere between five to fifteen years. Five, if I play my cards right and if the risk I am planning to take pays off.'

'What risks?'

'I need a product. It will save us a billion dollars at least. Will tell you when I have more details. Depends on when the USFDA comes out with the guidelines. I don't care if you sell it to other pharma companies, but it should work for me.'

That was when the Babe was discussed for the first time. And Alex's business once again removed all bottlenecks in getting new customers for PureConsultants, and they were on the fast track from then on.

Overtly, Pankaj took the news of Alex shifting his projects to PureConsultants graciously. Any suspicion that Motu had about rubbing Pankaj the wrong way died out over the next few years.

Phase III

Revenge is a dish best served cold. Hey avenger, don't forget god always sides with the innocent.

The Period – November 2008

With their life stories still not complete and in various stages of indecision and disarray, all the characters of the story moved towards the seven most important days of their lives – the days which would give each story an end and decide whether PureConsultants survived the brutal attack on its sovereignty or succumbed to the hostile takeover bid.

Prelude to Day 1 (covers the one-month period leading up to Day 1)

Jaanvee had so much going on in her mind. She assumed she would get a few grey strands in her head before her next birthday. In fact, she thought she saw two, hidden by a thick tuft, just above her forehead. Exactly a month ago Software Builder had made a public offer for the shares of PureConsultants at a price which was fifty per cent higher than the current trading price of the company. Its shareholding had shot up in PureConsultants from a mere half per cent at the time of making the offer to thirty-five per cent fifteen days before Day 1.

'This is a hostile takeover attempt. The shareholders will love it. We are under a very serious threat and may end up losing control,' Jaanvee cautioned the board at the time of the open offer for the shares.

'We have a tight management control. We should not be bothered with this piece of news,' one of the members tried to dismiss the danger.

'I did a scan of all the shares we hold together with our loyalists and I must say their offer is very, very attractive. With a high percentage of our shares in the open market it will be difficult for us to control the outcome,' Jaanvee said.

'If we look at it pragmatically, they need to buy fifty-one per cent whereas we only need to convince sixteen per cent of the shareholders to not sell,' Motu had said.

'Yes, but all the rumours floating in the market about the health of our company, the Babe being pruned, several key people leaving us, our share price falling by more than twenty per cent, makes their offer very lucrative. They can do serious damage. And who can rule out defections. Be prepared for a full-fledged war,' Jaanvee cautioned.

All of them agreed that defections could and would happen under extremely stressful and tempting conditions.

Software Builder too had guessed that the fight would be a bloody one. Fifteen days ago they had called for an extraordinary general meeting (EGM) inviting all shareholders of PureConsultants. It coincided with the closing of the public offer for the shares of PureConsultants. Since things were expected to go down the wire, Software Builder needed to get fifty-one per cent of the votes to take over the management control of PureConsultants. By then, it had thirty per cent of the shares in its pocket.

Jaanvee too had continued with her tireless campaign of convincing the bigger shareholders. The institutions, the banks and the promoters had promised not to switch sides, but she could not rest till the day of the EGM passed and they managed to retain majority stake. She was quietly confident that PureConsultants would sail through.

Two days before Day 1, Software Builder was sitting at forty per cent. There were five days of trading left. PureConsultants could still manage to win if only there were no defections and scandals.

Jaanvee had met BD and told him about her findings, her uneasiness after meeting San, without betraying any of her own conflicting emotions. It was plain, matter-of-fact reporting.

'This is sad. But we do not have enough evidence which points to anyone in particular. We need to wait and watch the situation more carefully. The only thing I am worried about is that we have a listing planned on the New York Stock Exchange sometime soon.

'All these happenings, these uncertainties may play havoc if something goes wrong at the last moment. We are going there for greater credibility, and if our listing gets postponed or bad news keeps pouring in we may never get a chance to go back to the NYSE,' Motu said to Jaanvee.

'What do we do with San? Why don't you try and speak to him and tell him about the reason behind your decision? I am sure he will understand,' Jaanvee requested Motu.

'This is not the right time. He is young and very ambitious. He will find his way and learn to live with the stress,' Motu replied.

'And who will show the Babe to Alex?' Jaanvee asked.

'Oh! I had forgotten that completely. This also solves your problem. Since San will be going with me to New York I can talk him out of his depression over the Babe.'

'BD, can you also check who could be behind this takeover bid?'

'Sure. Let me investigate.'

There was only one name that popped into Motu's head. At the same time, Motu found it extremely hard to believe that *he* could be the perpetrator. Over the years many things had changed. Once you change your circle of advisers, the way you think is influenced by the latest company you keep. Motu was extremely sceptical of his latest gang of advisers. That he would stoop so low was something Motu had never expected.

'Had you asked, I would have given the company to you anyway. But since you want to snatch it away from me, I will fight to the finish,' he murmured to himself, his resolve firmer.

Motu also thought of informing Priya, the chief marketing officer of PureConsultants, and the woman he loved about the whole episode, but decided to hold on till he was more certain of the facts.

He decided to do some research on the Internet. 'Search engines are like alcoholics,' thought Motu. If you put in the right amount of alcohol into them they would throw out all the information they had. And you could coax anything from a search engine if you knew what keywords to put in. He fed it with different name combinations, but to his disappointment it did not give any relevant results.

'Come on, baby, don't keep it to yourself,' he pleaded.

Then he typed another set of keywords. Voila! He saw twenty results, all of which led him into one direction. From the information he saw on the screen he began to see through the maze. But whatever he had gathered was still not conclusive.

'I think I have solved the puzzle. But let me do one more thing before I tell the world,' he exclaimed.

He then called one of his contacts who had worked with him earlier; something he hated to do but justified as necessary.

Moron was an old friend who had worked with both him and Pankaj. He was still working with Pankaj. He was a brilliant performer, knew his way with words and Salem and did not carry the baggage of a broken friendship which had affected the relation between Motu and Pankaj. He had the unique gift of easily maintaining friendship with everyone. Motu had nick-named him 'Moron' for his wild ideas and eccentric behaviour. Moron thrived on the attention it brought him. He and Motu shared a bond of trust and mutual respect. Motu decided to take this one favour from him.

'Hey, Moron! You still with Pankaj?' Motu asked after the pleasantries were over.

'Yeah, you know I don't have high moral standards like you,' Moron replied.

'Needed some inside dope from you,' Motu said haltingly.

'If it is not in conflict with my work ethics, I shall help,' Moron said and then both of them laughed.

Motu explained his problem and Moron promised to get back as soon as possible. 'Yes, that will be a huge favour, and the only one that I would ever ask of you. And it goes without saying that our conversation is classified,' Motu said in the end.

Motu knew he could rely on Moron. Though Moron had never expressed it openly, Motu suspected that if he was ever forced to choose between him and Pankaj he would pledge his allegiance to Motu.

Knowing he could do nothing else but wait, he began to plan for his trip to New York. He had two very important things to do in New York – the release of the Babe to Alex's company and the listing of PureConsultants on NYSE. Both were extremely important for the future of PureConsultants. The Babe was equally important for Alex. He was planning to spend over a million dollars on its launch and had invited leading people from the media and the industry.

'This is a show of strength, never before done in our company. If I get this one right, I am certain for the number two position with a clear shot at the CEO's in two years' time. God forbid, if the smallest of things go wrong, the position would be taken up by the CEO's favourite,' Alex had earlier explained to him the importance of the Babe's success.

'What is it about the Babe that will make this happen?' Motu had asked Alex.

'We are planning the biggest merger in the history of the pharma industry. This will create a two-hundred-billion-dollar behemoth. One of the most important things required for the two companies to merge seamlessly is the Babe. It will give the USFDA what it wants, keep it satisfied, and will take care of one of the most painful parts of the integration. You must keep this to yourself,' Alex had said.

'If I heard you right, you just now said that you have a shot at becoming the CEO of this company?' Motu had asked, exasperated.

'Yes, I do.'

'Don't worry, I will pull all stops to make sure nothing goes wrong with the Babe and the launch happens without any glitches,' Motu had placated Alex.

Thereon, the conversation had become more private. Motu told him about his love for Priya, and how she was becoming a distant dream with the passage of time. He told Alex about the two impossible conditions she had put.

'She wants to see the man in you and you cry like a child,' Alex had modulated his voice to imitate Marlon Brando from *The Godfather*.

Motu had prepared for months for the Babe's presentation to the world. After his conversation with Alex there was no doubt in his mind as to how much depended on her success. He was acutely aware of the grave consequences of her failure. He delved into her technical as well as functional aspects to understand her completely.

'Can't take any chances. What if one of you decides to take a day off?' he had joked with Priya and San when they pointed out his phenomenal interest in her.

✍

Day 1 (23 November 2008)

Jaanvee woke up after a fitful sleep. Throughout the night she tried to figure out what it was that San said on the evening he had broken down, which she could not place. She knew it was small, only slightly out of place but not right. It was like the perfect picture with a little speck here or a slightly overdrawn line there, which you register subconsciously, and which makes you remember the picture more for that little imperfection than for anything else.

She kept on rewinding the whole thing in her head repeatedly until her head started aching. Suddenly, it hit her. He had said something about BD which she found unusual when they discussed how to curtail the spending on the Babe.'

She recalled what he had said about Motu, '... the cold, calculative and heartless BD. They told me not to trust him in my darkest hour. The idiot that I was, I always did. Now I know how wrong I was.'

Motu had an impeccable reputation in the company. He was god for everyone in the office. He was respected for his hard work, ethics and honesty. San doubting Motu and his usage of 'they' in his outburst against him made Jaanvee suspect that someone was misleading him. She was sure it could not be anyone from within the company. It must be an outsider. She knew San was impressionable. He was the easiest target if someone wanted to break into the top echelon of PureConsultants. Every bit of the puzzle fell into place and she instantly realised the gravity of the situation.

She switched on her laptop with trepidation. Her knees shook and she prayed to god that she was proved wrong. She googled for San and began to analyse the results. She knew the Web would tell everything about a person if one knew what and where to search. She began to get information: some useful, other not so, some that she already knew and other that she did not. Whatever she found was normal; nothing extraordinary that could implicate San.

Then, with quivering hands, she typed in the words that she had been avoiding so far, not wanting to see the results. She googled 'San and Sukumar' and waited for what seemed like an eternity but were only a few seconds. She wondered how she had missed that information earlier.

She was aghast to see the search results. San and Sukumar were pals from school days. They had known each other for years. San had been so successful in hiding all this information from her that she began to think of herself as a complete idiot. She now knew who the manipulator was but she suspected there would be more players operating behind the scenes. To takeover a company like PureConsultants not only meticulous planning was required, which San was capable of, but also the resources and a very strong reason. Both San and Sukumar lacked them. By now she was sure that there was someone else who was calling the shots.

'There's a master who is controlling them. And this is no ordinary takeover. Ordinary takeovers are plain vanilla swaps with the purpose, intent and action clearly visible. This is a vendetta. I should speak to BD at once. He must have an answer to this,' thought Jaanvee.

She then called Motu who was almost done with his packing. It was a Sunday evening, and he was humming the Beatles' number *And I love her* with the picture of Priya etched in his mind.

'BD, I have something to tell you. Thought you should know.' Jaanvee then went on to explain her findings to Motu. 'I think San is being led by someone. He is being brainwashed into becoming a turncoat. I suspect he is one of them,' Jaanvee concluded.

It was 7:00 p.m., one hour before he and San were to leave for the airport. 'Thanks for the information, Jaanvee. It only complicates things further,' Motu said.

He then called Moron. 'I need more help from you. And I only have half an hour,' Motu was shouting over the phone.

'Even god would have failed to deliver at such short notice. But let me try.'

Moron returned the call exactly after twenty-nine minutes. 'I had to bribe someone for the first time in my life. It cost me a promotion but I got what you wanted,' Moron was whining.

'I can hear you crying later. Can you give me the details?' Motu cut him short.

'You were right all along.' Moron then told him the whole story. 'San is the mole,' he said, concluding with a sigh.

In his last call about a month ago, Motu had asked Moron to find out whether Pankaj was behind all his problems. 'There is a company called Software Builder. Do you know if NumeroSoft has any relation with it?'

Moron had replied in the negative. Motu realised then that he needed to be more direct with his question.

'Is Pankaj trying to buy my company?' he asked.

'If he is, I am sure this must be classified. If you want, I can try to dig deeper and find out what is going on,' Moron had said. He had replied in the affirmative to all his questions a few weeks ago. Shocked by the revelation, he had kept it to himself. Now when Moron had given him the rundown on San, everything had moved from the realms of uncertainty. Things were crystal clear in his head.

The next person he called was San.

'You need some rest. Get your ticket cancelled. You're not going to NYC. Just email the code to me and Priya,' he said simply before putting the phone down. He also made two other calls – one to Arjun and the other to Nitin, giving them a detailed account of what had happened. He decided to break the news to Priya in person when they met.

∽

San seethed with rage when Motu put the phone down on him. 'First you cut the Babe to half. Now when it's time to show it to the world, you want to take all the credit. I will make you look like a fool in front of the whole world. Get ready for the bumpy ride, BD,' San muttered to himself while furiously working on the code. When he finally sent the code to Motu, he had a smug smile on his face.

He then made a call he had been putting off for months. 'Salem, you always wanted total commitment from me. I couldn't promise you my loyalty earlier as I had a conscience, even if it worked part-time. I was loyal to PureConsultants because it has done so much for me.

'Count me in completely now. I will try with all my might to destroy PureConsultants. In fact, I have already started the process which will vastly impact its share price in the next few days. More people will throng to sell when they see the company in trouble.' He cut the phone off, leaving a much contended Salem on the other side.

'Need to finish a few more things before I go off to sleep.' San returned to work on his system.

Nitin was very confused about Tanya's proposal. There was no doubt in their minds that they loved each other deeply. What worried Nitin was whether he had the right to love given his medical condition. He wanted to go all the way if it was medically possible. He decided to visit his doctor for advice and called him to seek an appointment.

Just after his call, the doctor gave Nitin's secret backer a detailed report on his condition. 'He is coming along fine. He also seems to have fallen in love.'

'Wow, he deserves it. He is one of the finest human beings I know. It's sad that we are not together anymore,' Nitin's secret backer rued before putting the phone down.

The doctor never questioned the backer's motive or his relation with Nitin. He knew Nitin's backer was one of the most powerful people in the country and from his confident baritone, the doc felt he did not like being questioned. Over the years the secret backer had also funded treatment of the other patients whom the doctor had recommended. Together they were contemplating opening a separate fund dedicated to the treatment of HIV-infected people. The doctor's respect for the backer had grown with years and with the knowledge that he didn't seek any personal gains by helping people.

'You look great,' the doctor said as Nitin entered his cabin.

'I feel great too. Never felt better in my life.'

'You have recovered well and are maintaining a healthy and steady immune cell count. If you continue like this you have a long life ahead,' the doctor said.

'I have come to discuss a problem with you, Doctor.'

Nitin then explained his situation to him in detail, hesitant at first but opening up soon with the doctor's encouragement.

'This is the dilemma that doctors are facing these days. We are not taught this in medical college but apart from administering medicine we also need to counsel the patients on their sex lives.' The doctor had long become a guide, a friend to Nitin.

'With huge advances in medicine, HIV patients can expect to live a longer life. Once the fear of dying subsides, the potency returns, of course with the help of medicines. Then they have a strong urge to lead a regular sex life.'

'What do you suggest?' Nitin asked tentatively.

'Go and enjoy your day. But the idea of two condoms is not bad. It will keep her safe.'

'Thanks, Doc, you are always so helpful.'

'How's work? Has everyone accepted you at work?'

'They have accepted me. But the company is facing a big crisis.' Nitin told the doctor about the gruesome fight to take control of PureConsultants by NumeroSoft and how friends were pitched against each other in this battle for power. 'I never expected this from Pankaj. I can't believe he is doing all this to defeat his own friend. This is abominable.' Nitin was agitated, and his hatred for Pankaj showed clearly on his face.

The doctor remained dispassionate and didn't involve himself in the discussion. He continued playing with the pencil on his desk as if weighing the words that he would speak next.

'Nitin, there is something I have been meaning to tell you since long. But I would be breaching someone's trust if I make this revelation. But I think the time has come to share this information with you. You always thought I was treating you for free. I did not charge you my consultation fee and gave hugely expensive medicines to you on the pretext that they were free samples from big pharma companies.

'You readily accepted what I fed you, never questioned why I did it. If you thought I was doing it, you could not have been more mistaken. I am a good person, but not as good as you think. I am too self-centered to have thought of helping you to such an extent.'

'If it was not you then who …? You mean it was Pankaj all along,' Nitin asked disbelievingly as reality dawned on him. He ran out of the office on the busy street and began to cry. He was followed to his car by a very black, preying pair of eyes filled with loathe.

✍

Nitin called Tanya after the visit to the doctor. She was so excited that she did not give him the chance to speak.

'I have been out shopping. Bought myself the most aesthetically done lingerie available in the market.' She was transparent as ever.

'Aesthetic or provocative?' Nitin played along.

'You will see soon.'

'You didn't even wait for the doctor's verdict.'

'I was sure of my research. Anyway what did your favourite doctor say?'

'He said to exercise utmost care but we can go ahead, and it is …' The shrillness in her cry almost tore his eardrum.

'I had something else to tell you as well, Tanya ….' Nitin then told her about his friendship with Pankaj. He had never told it to her earlier because it pained him to talk about his broken friendship with Pankaj.

'On the one hand he fights with us and tries to finish us off in business, and on the other, he helps me live my life with dignity, bearing the expenses for my treatment without letting anyone know, ' Nitin cried.

'He loves you as a friend. … Isn't there a way you can bring everyone together again?' Tanya asked.

'You are right. I must do something to unite the two of them. That is what I always wanted. I'll invite both Motu and Pankaj on my birthday saying that we shall be celebrating it at my house. They will not be able to refuse. I will then try and convince Pankaj to drop this hostile takeover for old times' sake,' Nitin said.

'Do you think Pankaj will agree?'

'I don't know, but I don't have any other option. Let me give this a try. Until you knock, you won't know whether the door will open.' Not used to thinking, his brows furrowed at having to go through that complex exercise.

Motu reached NYC safely but he was nervous about how things will unfold. Priya was at the airport to receive him.

'How are you?' Priya asked softly.

'I always feel great when I see you. But the situation is so daunting that I am really scared,' Motu confided in her.

The two of them hugged each other. For a fleeting moment Priya felt Motu's warm breath on her nape.

Of late, Priya felt pangs of guilt when she thought of Motu – for not being able to reciprocate the love with which he always took care of her smallest needs. She sometimes cursed herself for imposing impossible conditions on Motu. She also cursed herself for her girlish pride, though she was well past that age, which prevented her from going up to him and simply telling him that she was at a stage where whether she loved him or not didn't really matter. What mattered was living together and sharing small moments of joy. She also cursed Motu for his gentlemanly behaviour and how he always expressed his emotions with restraint.

They were always tentative when they talked about anything except work or weather. Today it was going to be all work, and so they greeted each other with a confident smile.

Both of them knew the importance of the next two days in New York. First, the Babe had to perform and live up to Alex's expectations and second, PureConsultants was going to be the bell-ringer on the NYSE. Both events were big enough to give goosebumps to the biggest tycoons.

'We have so much work to do,' Motu said when they sat in Priya's car.

'It's unusually cold for this time of the year,' Priya said while swirling the car in the direction of her home.

'Your hunch was right. There indeed was a mole in our organisation. San betrayed us,' Motu told the complete story to Priya diluting the part about Pankaj.

She was so shocked that she couldn't react. 'It was Pankaj after all,' she said after five minutes.

'It must be Salem who is pushing this. Let's not blame Pankaj,' Motu tried to placate Priya, but failed to convince her.

'He can use his own brains. He is not a child who can be led by anyone,' Priya shouted hysterically.

'Will you be able to drive?' Motu suddenly found himself teary-eyed, remembering all those wonderful moments the three of them had shared.

'I am fine,' Priya replied, controlling herself.

The rest of the thirty-minute journey was filled with silence.

⟡

Motu was putting up at Priya's home. A hotel was never an option; since they were on very good terms Priya had asked Motu to stay at her house while in New York. As soon as they reached home, Priya went to her bedroom and began to sob.

'Are you okay, Priya?' Motu knew she still loved Pankaj. This would shake her to the core.

'I'll be fine. Just give me a couple of hours.'

In the meantime, Motu connected his laptop to check San's email and give last-minute touches to his presentation. After he was done he shut the laptop down. Priya was still dazed by Motu's revelation.

Motu made some soup and invited Priya to eat. 'This is called hospitality. The woman of the house sleeps while a jet-lagged guest cooks for the two. It is the darkest era in the history of mankind.' Motu tried to cheer Priya up, but she only managed to give a faint smile in response. After the dinner, Priya went back to her state of stupor while Motu decided to sleep to adjust to the difference in time zones.

He woke up with a start thinking it was morning already. The time was 2:00 a.m. He was restless but was not sure why. 'Maybe because of the difficult day ahead,' he thought. Uncannily, he realised that he was not tense because of all the impending things but because of something in San's email which was out of place. Then he recalled that it was related to the time of the email. He opened his laptop and looked at San's email again.

It had arrived at 3:00 a.m. IST, whereas he could have sent that code immediately after their phone call.

'Oh, my God! He must have played with the code. Damn, how could I miss it,' he cursed himself.

He immediately sat down and began to install the code emailed by San on his laptop. The application opened up nicely. He began to start testing it with a prayer on his lips. The user interface was just like he had last seen it. Everything looked perfect. 'Time for some extensive testing,' he thought. He opened the menu and clicked the option which would start the first part of the planned demo. The screen displayed the expected data. Motu clicked the next button to go further. The next screen opened, and everything looked good there as well. He walked through all the basic screens but did not find anything unusual.

He turned the laptop off and went back to bed to try and catch on lost sleep. But he was still not satisfied. Sometimes, not finding a problem where you are dead sure one exists does that to you.

'I can't be worried about this so much. I am too old a hand to be having pangs. Then what is it that is bothering me?' Motu was perplexed. Then suddenly it hit him. The information on the screens he checked looked very familiar, as if he had seen the data before. But the version of the application he had was supposed to pull fresh data from the Internet in real time.

Motu went back to his laptop and looked at the data again. He realised that the reason it looked familiar was because it was the same dummy data that he had seen at the first demo of the application many months ago. With an impending sense of doom, he quickly changed values and pressed the save button. Then he reloaded the screen to check whether the changes he had made were saved. As he had expected, the data could not be saved and the same dummy data smiled back at him as if mocking him for wanting something else.

'Damn, Damn, Damn! The application that I am going to demo for the most strategic deal in the history of PureConsultants is a dummy application!'

Motu cautioned himself not to panic. It was still possible that San had installed the very initial version of the application instead of the latest one by mistake. 'Since I had asked him to copy the code as well, I think I should try compiling the code to create a new version of the application, and use that for the demo instead.'

In his early days Motu himself had been a great programmer. He located the code, issued the compile command and waited for the application to compile so that he could install it. What he saw next made him rub his eyes in disbelief. The screen had thrown up error after error – a total of five-hundred-and-seventy-three in all.

'San would have taken the latest code from the repository and put it on my laptop. Could it be that one of the developers on the team had by mistake made changes to the code and not tested it? No, this is not possible. The development had stopped almost a week ago. Only testing had to be carried out,' thought Motu, his mind analysing the problems from all angles. He had to find the exact reason for these errors.

After rejecting all possible theories, he concluded that it was a deliberate act of sabotage and San was the real culprit.

'There is no way I can fix fifty errors in one night, leave aside five-hundred-and-seventy-three. My only hope is to get help from India. One of the possibilities is that Arjun transfers the code to me from India,' Motu thought. It was still not going to be easy.

'If luck is on my side, I might get a few hours to compile it before the presentation,' Motu encouraged himself.

'Priya, you can mourn later. I need your help urgently. It's a two-hundred-billion-dollar emergency,' Motu shouted and immediately regretted the slip of tongue. He remembered Alex telling him that the information was highly confidential.

Thankfully, in her stupor, Priya did not take notice. 'What happened?' she asked.

'The code is not working. It may be impossible to figure out where the problem lies,' Motu said.

'How much time do we have?' asked Priya.

Mercifully, the presentation was scheduled in the second half of the day. They still had twelve hours to fix the problem.

'Can we do it?' Priya asked Motu.

'I am out of touch with the code. It is a Sunday in India. We will need time to gather all our people there and get them to one place first,' Motu explained.

'Just cut the crap and tell me if you can make this thing work?'

'I don't know. I can try but the time is too less,' Motu said. 'I am calling Arjun now. It is almost evening in India. Let me catch him before he goes out to the mall with his daughter.'

'Arjun, this is an emergency. Cancel everything you are doing and get back to your laptop. Get your best guys inside the office and wait for my next call. How soon can you get everyone in one room?' Motu asked him in an urgent voice.

'Give me an hour. I will try to organise everything.'

'We have a free hour. I will try to troubleshoot in the meantime,' Motu said.

Motu began to do some extensive search on the Internet. At the same time, he tried to recall whatever he had learnt on the subject.

Arjun was actually planning to take Diyaa to the mall for another accidental meeting with Muskaan. For this emergency, he had to cancel his plans abruptly.

'Diyaa, let me drop you at dadu's house where you can play till I get back. I have some emergency at work,' Arjun told an overexcited Diyaa, who correlated the visit to the mall to a surprise meeting with her mother.

'No, Papa, I want to be with you. We don't have any time together on the weekdays, and you have never shown me your office. Also, now we are not meeting mama. You owe me this one,' Diyaa said, concealing her disappointment.

'Okay, let's go.'

'Papa, shall I take my water bottle, chocolates and chips?' Diyaa asked.

'No need, it shouldn't take much time,' Arjun replied.

In hindsight, Arjun's guess turned out to be the most incompetent guess he had ever made. They were not able to return home either in the next twenty-four or forty-eight hours.

The drive to PureConsultants' office on Sunday was a far cry from the madness of the weekdays. The roads were empty, and the light chill of November evening almost gave Arjun a false sense of well-being.

'Not the time to go in a comfort zone,' he thought.

He realised he must have the most competent people in his team if he wanted to solve the puzzle made by the sharpest brain in the trade.

By the time he reached office he had made ten calls and managed to convince five of his best men to reach office, the other five were away on errands which made their return impossible in a short span of time.

Motu called Arjun as soon as he and his team reached the office. 'What is the first thing we should be doing now?' he sought Arjun's advice.

'Let's fetch the latest code from the repository for you,' Arjun said. Motu hung up, knowing it would at least be a few hours before the code upload to his laptop would be complete. Sleep was out of question.

In about fifteen minutes Arjun rang back. He sounded scared, in stark contrast to his reassuring last call.

'I cannot upload the code. The team says the code was put under a password, and each person had his own password to access it. Everyone has used his password, but a 'permission denied' error pops up each time. I think the passwords have been changed. The only person who could have done this is San.

'Is there a way we can reach the code?' Motu's patience was wearing thin. 'No, there is no way the code can be uploaded. We are back to square one,' Arjun admitted defeat.

'So are we declaring the Babe dead?'

'Right now we are stuck with a code which, in its present form, doesn't work. We don't have access to the repository. Given the time constraint, I fear we have reached a dead end,' Arjun said, tired.

'I can't accept this. I have a demo in less than five hours, and we cannot concede defeat like this. Let's start using our brains. Look carefully at the code again,' Motu egged Arjun and his team on. He started reading the list of errors. As he went through the list, he began to notice a pattern.

'I think most of the errors are coming because there are certain missing modules which the code cannot find. Can you and Priya recall how the application is structured?'

'It is made of several interdependent modules. Each module is dependent on some other modules, which in turn are further dependent on more modules, thus forming an interconnected web,' Priya explained.

'That means the code is compiled module by module. When all the modules are compiled, the application is ready to be installed,' Motu elaborated on the theory.

'While one module is being compiled, it will look for the availability of the modules it depends upon (which should already have been compiled), and when it doesn't find them, it throws an error,' Arjun added.

'Since you are sitting on the final code, BD, you should start tracing which modules are missing. Each error should lead you to the missing modules. By following this trail you can reach the perpetrator of all the problems,' Arjun said.

Motu then began to sift through all the errors. It was a very difficult task to try and find the common link between a few hundred of them, made more difficult by the constant ticking of the clock at the back of his head. It was four hours before they were to leave for the presentation.

Arjun waited anxiously for the results. He could not leave office as BD might need his help anytime. As it was getting late, he sent Diyaa to a sleeping room with an enthusiastic and cooperative office help. A very reluctant Diyaa left with tears in her eyes. Even at such a small age, she wanted to be a part of all the action and excitement. Since he had nothing else to do he began to think of Muskaan and the crossroads at which their relationship stood.

Motu worked on the problem painstakingly. As suggested by Arjun, he successfully traced the missing module which was causing all the errors. He looked at his watch. Only two hours were left for the demo. His heartbeat and the creases on Priya's forehead were increasing with every passing minute.

But by no means was the job over. What he had been able to do till now was to localise the problem. He now knew where exactly the problem was. The errors in this core module were causing problems in code compilation, leading to errors in all the other modules. Motu had to find the missing code for Module Z (as he called it) in order to fix the error.

'I have found the problematic module. Do you think you can find the code?' Motu asked Arjun on the conference call.

As Motu had anticipated, they couldn't find the code. All the files for the module were predictably missing, thanks to San. In the little time he had before he sent the email to Motu, he had used his hands-on knowledge of the application to delete the code for Module Z.

✎

With only one-hour-and-forty-five minutes to go, Motu was on the brink of giving up.

'What are our chances now?' Priya asked.

'Alex will never become the CEO. I might as well leave for India. The Babe is dead,' Motu replied hopelessly as he walked over to the mini-bar, pulled out a couple of beers and sank into the chair.

Just then Jaanvee called him. 'I heard what has happened. Could I help in any way?' she asked Motu.

'I don't know,' Motu replied but still quickly ran her through the relevant parts of his struggle over the last hours.

'I have come to know him very well over the last few months. He must have left us a teaser somewhere. He wants to defeat us in combat, not when tied down. He would try to outsmart us instead of not giving us a chance at all. Look for clues in any of the conversations you had with him or anything that you know in common. It has to be something only the two of you know as he blames you for the problems with the Babe. You just need to recollect your thoughts.' Jaanvee was emphatic.

'If I am getting it right, you and San had an argument over a particular module. You wanted to use an open source component which was free, but San wanted to write his own,' Priya recalled a stand-off between the two which had almost turned ugly. Motu had finally relented but he wasn't very happy about it.

'Yeah, I remember it now. I just couldn't believe why he suggested that, since the open source module apart from being free on the Internet, was a standard well-tested component which could not fail. But since he was leading the Babe, I didn't want to overrule him.

'San insisted on writing the code himself; he took over a month to do that, and strangely, had never let anyone review it. I also remember hearing some complaints from his team members regarding that. I found it strange at that time because that was a standard rule which he had himself suggested a few years ago. And it was Module Z,' Motu recalled everything clearly now.

'So the question is, why didn't San let anyone look at the code? Why was he hiding it? He had coded a module in a record one-month's time which had all the features of the world class open-source module, and it performed equally well. What he had written was every developer's delight and instead of showing his proud possession to the world he hid it. Why?' Priya kept on asking all the questions in the right order to lead them to the elusive answer. It was forty-five minutes before they were to leave.

Motu kept toying with the question, but couldn't make sense of it. Then a thought struck him like lightning – San wasn't hiding anything. In fact, he was hiding the lack of anything being there.

Motu bolted out of his bed and turned on his laptop again. He had a very strong hunch that San never coded Module Z. Instead, he had gone ahead with Motu's original suggestion and had used the open-source module. At the same time, he proclaimed to the world that he had coded it himself.

'If my hunch is right, then I just need to go to the website of that open-source module, download the code, merge it with my code and compile the entire code again. This must work. It is a long shot, but now I think this is exactly what the bastard must have done. Motu quickly copied the files after downloading them from the Internet. Motu had also got Arjun on the call in case he needed any help. All of them were holding onto their breath as Motu gave the 'compile' command, which a few hours ago had given 573 errors. When the process finished, the screen flashed the words 'compilation complete, 0 errors'. Without missing a beat, Motu immediately installed the newly compiled application and gave it a test run – the three palpitating hearts suggesting as if they had run a marathon. All the screens worked as expected. The data too saved properly. Voila! They heaved a sigh of relief.

'If you promise not to tell anyone, I'll skip the shower,' an excited Motu said to Priya as they hugged each other.

'Of course, but only if you promise to maintain a distance of at least five metres from me for the rest of the day.'

They had a hearty laugh and hurried to get ready. They knew the importance of time as they were already running behind the schedule.

Muskaan looked forward to the surprise visits of her ex-husband and daughter. Inspite of herself, she had begun to like these intrusions in her private moments at the mall. Not finding them, she cut short her visit and went back home, thinking about all the good times she had shared with Arjun and Diyaa before the sudden discovery of Diyaa's problems.

And so ended Day 1 and Day 2 began, both intertwined as people worked across different time zones on an unusually nervous Sunday. Motu, Priya, Arjun and a host of others were kept awake by the most critical demonstration in PureConsultants' history which was scheduled for the next day. Jaanvee went to sleep, realising that San would defect and take his two per cent shareholding in PureConsultants to Pankaj. She was somehow also depressed because BD had called San a 'bastard'. She made a mental note to call him again the next day and beg for the first time in her life to not sell his stake to Pankaj. His two per cent would take the shareholding of Software Builder to forty-nine per cent and the balance two per cent, she imagined, would not be difficult to manage with Salem having satanic powers to play murkier as the game progressed.

℘

Day 2 (24 November 2008)

The day was to begin with a small speech from the CEO. Alex was seated next to him, signifying how close he was to addressing such meetings in the future. Alex was agitated because Priya and Motu had reached just five minutes before the scheduled time giving him some extremely nervous moments.

'Is everything okay?' he asked them.

'Apart from not catching a wink in the last sixty hours everything else is fine,' Motu smiled, promising him a juicy story as an excuse if he forgave the two of them this one time.

'I hope you don't sleep through the presentation,' Alex said stiffly.

'Why did he grimace when he met us?' Motu asked Priya when Alex moved away.

'It was more you than us. I think he came too close to you for comfort and realised you hadn't bathed,' Priya commented. Both of them suppressed a giggle to avoid drawing attention.

'This product is very important to us strategically. It will lead to a substantial amount of saving on the current expenditure of the company,' the CEO said, which made Motu and Priya a little anxious. They were far from their usual confident selves.

'When he addresses the next public meeting, he will quote revenue figures of two-hundred billion dollars,' Motu blurted out with a twinkle in his eyes, realising he could no longer hide anything from the woman he loved.

'How do you know? Are they buying someone out?'

'Wait and watch,' Motu did not spill all the beans.

'This is my account, my domain and I have been handling this for so many years now. I am surprised you know something that I don't,' Priya whispered to him.

Motu winked at her and told her to be quiet, warning her that they may be thrown out even before they had a chance to demo the Babe.

All of them were relieved as the presentation reached the end, and the software did not act up even once. Alex too had sensed the nervousness in Motu and Priya. That, in turn, had made him very anxious, making the two-hour period of the presentation one of the most nerve-wracking experiences of his life. For a moment he was forced to think that it would have been good if they were strictly business partners and not friends.

As the presentation progressed, doubts began to disappear. Everyone was elated by the end with Motu, Priya and Alex more relieved than happy.

'I have another news for you. Now that there are no reservations that this product will be a success, I want you to make a unified system which can be reached through a single page across our more than three-thousand offices worldwide. Roll this out at all these locations, provide training to our people, and maintain our software for the next ten years,' Alex announced to them in private, brimming with happiness.

Motu reached out for his glass of water as his throat had suddenly turned dry. He instinctively knew that when translated into numbers, this would mean hundreds of millions of dollars worth of revenue for PureConsultants. Simply put, it was something PureConsultants had never done before and would catapult them to the big league.

A single tear of joy escaped his eyes. Alex extended his arms to hug the two of them. No words of gratitude were required. The three of them enjoyed their well-deserved moment of victory, not caring about anyone else in the hall.

'I want you to not disclose this information for the next two weeks. Hope you understand,' Alex requested Motu, who shook his head in acquiescence.

'By the way I am in Mumbai on the twenty-sixth. Can one of you fly down and present this product to the India Pharma Conclave being held in the Taj? Basically, I want to show this product to other companies, besides other things. This may help your cause when you actually begin to sell it in the open market.'

'I will come. He has too much on his plate in the later part of the week,' Priya said, knowing Motu needed to be in the office and see PureConsultants through the battle of control.

'That should be ideal as you are the one who knows the Babe inside out,' Alex warmed up to the idea.

On the way back, Priya could still not resist asking Motu, 'How much is this worth?'

'I don't know, but if we are talking about a ten-year deal, this must be worth five-hundred-million dollars at least, maybe a billion dollars.'

'That is huge. How many people do we need for this?'

'Anywhere around ten-thousand people. More importantly, this will also help us win many more of such multimillion dollar deals. We shall have a twofold increase every few years going forward.'

A loud wheezing sound escaped from Priya's lips. 'I told you to be careful with the information you give me when I am driving. You could have killed both of us with your indiscretion,' she said, and they burst out laughing.

By the end of the day, both Motu and Priya were exhausted. They had to wake up early the next day for what had been till a few hours ago the biggest moment of their lives – now dwarfed by Alex's announcement.

Motu was going to ring the opening bell to mark the completion of the listing process of PureConsultants on NYSE. It was a historical day for him as well as for Priya, Arjun, Nitin and Jaanvee. They would all have been here in NYC had it not been for the dire circumstances the company was faced with. Listing on NYSE would give PureConsultants greater credibility in the international market and also the banks and financial institutions.

'Arjun, can you be in the office till the opening ceremony is over? I have a feeling it's not over yet.'

'Okay. My gut is churning too. If another scandal breaks out, this very important day of our lives will be ruined.'

With that call the day ended for Motu and Priya. They only had a couple of hours left before they woke up for another very hectic day. Motu went to sleep, his mind readying for the big fight the next day. On the other hand, Priya was completely relaxed, as if she had achieved salvation. She had realised something which she decided to share with Motu at the end of the week after the EGM when both of them would meet again in India in peace.

Jaanvee had closely monitored the stock position throughout the day. There were no untowardly movements, the market sentiment stayed neutral, not swaying either way. She was satisfied till 3:00 p.m. when she suddenly got the news that three per cent of the shares had changed hands. She dug deeper and realised that Sid's bank had sold off all its holding to Software Builder. Software Builder's holding in PureConsultants now stood at fifty per cent.

'The bastard finally switched sides. It explains his reluctance to help me when I needed finance the most.'

With four days of trading to go, Jaanvee realised the chances of winning were bleak. She threw her hands in the air in despair. She knew they were lucky that the launch of the Babe didn't experience any hitches. They may not be as lucky the next time. At this stage, she would not put her money on PureConsultants foiling the takeover bid.

Oscillating between hatred and love for San, she decided to postpone her call to him for one more day.

⌒

Day 3 (25 November 2008)

Motu woke up with a start. It took him two whole minutes to figure out where he was. He reached out for his watch and saw the time. It was 4:30 a.m. He had only slept for three hours. The excitement and nervousness which had kept the adrenaline high had not let him sleep early. Priya and he had talked late into the night and had gone to sleep reluctantly only because they had a very hectic and important day ahead. He had made himself an unusually large drink to help him unwind and go to sleep.

He tried to figure out the reason that had woken him. He realised it was a bad dream. He tried to recall the dream. He vaguely remembered that it was related to PureConsultants getting listed on the NYSE. When he thought further, he recalled that someone announced the postponement of the listing of its stock which had startled him out of his sleep. Motu had a premonition that things wouldn't go fine on the second day.

'I won't be able to sleep anymore,' Motu thought. He decided to wait for half an hour before waking Priya up. He saw her cuddled probably because of the slight chill in the room. He looked at her lovingly and covered her with the blanket.

'It seems I will have to spend my whole life like this, sleeping with you in the same room but not on the same bed,' Motu thought and smiled to himself, his face betraying an expression of pain. 'Let me take a cold shower. Else I will not be able to think straight.'

After a rejuvenating bath he switched on his laptop. He tried to open PureConsultants' website to see if all the information was in place. To his utter shock, the website did not open.

The website would be the most visible and easily accessible source for anyone, including potential investors and the media, who wanted information on PureConsultants. It was extremely critical that it properly received visitors at least on the day of the listing.

His PR team had created a lot of hype about the company and had planned to reveal some very exciting news through the site, such as the successful launch of the Babe, to coincide with the listing on NYSE. He remembered one of the PR executives had seen some errors on the website a few days ago and had said that some of the news websites she was working with found that the site was not accessible. But he was too preoccupied at the time and could not look at the problem properly. He referred it to his website team and forgot all about it. He also remembered receiving an email from the website team saying that all the pages were working fine and dismissed the reports as temporary Internet problems. With so many things on his mind, anything that was not escalated to him as a problem again, he presumed that it had been taken care of.

When he thought about it again, Motu remembered someone from the office complaining about some improper PJs on one of the pages of the website a few days ago. The website team had checked again and dismissed the report saying that the complainant's computer must have had a virus in it.

Still, Motu had requested Arjun to create a team to monitor the site closely and visit all the pages continuously to ensure that everything worked fine till the listing on the NYSE. That was the end of the problem. He did not hear any more on the issue after that.

Motu called Arjun again to apprise him of the current problem. 'Arjun, I cannot open the website. Can you see what the reason is?' There was fear in his voice.

'Let me check,' Arjun replied while quickly looking at the monitoring services he had made to check the website. All the logs showed normal operation.

'Everything looks normal. You are just anxious because of the listing today,' Arjun tried to soothe Motu's frayed nerves.

'I am scared. Can you try and look at the website without using the office network? Try using your iPhone,' Motu asked Arjun looking at the table clock again. Of late, time seemed to slip by very fast. He and Priya had to leave home two hours before the NYSE opened to be able to reach there on time.

It was time to wake Priya up. 'Get up, Priya! We are again going to have a very happening day.'

'What time is it?' Priya stretched her body lazily.

'5:00 a.m. We need to leave in exactly an hour.'

'And what is so happening about today? Hope all is well. We have had enough bad news yesterday.' Priya was still sleepy.

'There are two pieces of news. One is good and the other, bad. The good news is that I have taken a shower and am fresh like jasmine, and the bad news is that we have a website which doesn't work and we still don't know why.' Motu shook Priya out of her slumber.

⸎

Arjun typed the website address on his iPhone and was greeted with a 'Page Not Found' error. 'Strange,' he thought and tried again. The next time he was able to open the site, but instead of PureConsultants' home page, an advertisement appeared showing some pornographic stuff, a one-month free trial subscription and up to a thousand free screensavers.

Arjun called the website team and asked them to check it. Surprisingly, he was met with some very confused comments on the phone.

'But the website is working perfectly fine. In fact, all of us are on the home page.'

For some strange reason, the site was accessible from the office. Arjun told everyone to call home or their friends and ask them to visit it. In a few minutes, it was clear that someone had hacked the site, and it was done very smartly. When the website was accessed from the office, it worked fine as if the hacker was trying to keep them from knowing that the site had been hacked till as long as possible.

This was bad news because of the timing of the attack. Arjun logged onto the server and scanned the server logs, looked at all the active processes, and also examined the website code to see what caused this aberration. He drew a blank. Arjun and his team concluded that the website should be working fine as they could not detect any problem. Nevertheless, he decided to restore the website code from the backup, in case there was something he had missed earlier.

After an hour, the website was restored with the older code. The result was the same. When he accessed the website from the office network it worked fine, but when it was accessed from outside it showed everything except what it was supposed to show.

He realised that his initial guess about the website being hacked was wrong. He tried to recall the computer lessons learnt in school. Every human readable address for a website (such as *www.pureconsultants.com*) is mapped to a numerical address on the Internet (such as 192.168.1.11). Actually the numerical address (also called IP address) is understood by the computers, and used by them to communicate with each other. So when someone types in the web address of the website, his computer tries to find the numerical address corresponding to it. There are special servers called DNS servers where mapping between the human readable address and the IP address is maintained. When a computer needs to find the IP address of a given human readable address, it asks a DNS server for the relevant information.

Arjun knew the numerical address for the website. He opened his laptop and issued a command to get the IP address of PureConsultants' website by typing in the human readable address. The website returned the correct address. Then he configured his laptop to use the Internet connection from his iPhone. He issued the same command again, and it came back with a different numerical address. That's where the problem was. He put that numerical address in his browser after getting connected to the office network, and was immediately shown the hacked version of PureConsultants' website. Someone had created a copy of the website, and had somehow managed to change the DNS server settings. As a result, when the website was accessed from outside the office, the wrong IP address was given by the DNS server.

Normally, DNS servers are controlled by third parties, but in PureConsultants' case Arjun had hosted the server in his office and controlled the DNS for the website. This meant that someone had hacked the DNS server. Arjun immediately logged onto the Linux computer which hosted PureConsultants' DNS server and started looking at the processes. After a few minutes of digging, it was clear that there was a rogue program which was intercepting all the DNS queries. If the queries came from outside the office network, the rogue program gave the IP address of the fake site.

It was less than an hour before NYSE opened.

'BD, this was a DoS attack,' Arjun explained to Motu as soon as he was able to do a complete diagnostic of the problem.

Motu and Priya were ten minutes away from the NYSE when Arjun called. Priya was at the wheel. She had already warned Motu to give her any shocking information gently lest she banged into a car coming from the opposite side.

'What is that?' Priya tried to remember, having read it somewhere a few months back.

'DoS is "Denial-of-Service". It happens when someone takes control of your website and makes it unavailable to its users. I think the purpose was to make a huge dent in our reputation just before our high profile listing on the NYSE,' Arjun explained.

'It is not only about listing. It would have affected our share price too. It is meant to make us the laughing stock in front of the whole world.

'And how difficult is the solution?'

'This is easy to fix. We'll have to configure a new DNS server, and restore the website database from the safe copy of the backup, and finally replace the compromised server,' Arjun explained the whole process to Motu.

'How long before you can fix it?'

'One to two hours.'

'Two hours is a lot of time these days. Try your best and keep me updated.' It was five minutes before NYSE opened for the day.

'How could someone manage to break into the network?' Priya asked Motu.

'Three important things were needed to pull this off – access to our website code because the rogue website was similar to our own, and to our DNS server as it would be impossible to put the rogue program on it without the highly secure password to access it.

'Access to the website code was available to the entire website team, but very few people in the company had access to the DNS server. But it was the third thing that differentiates the perpetrator from the rest of them.

'What is that?'

'The skills to create a rogue program similar to the one running on the DNS server. For that you need a very skilled person,' Motu explained the whole scenario to Priya.

'Then only two people in the company could have done this. One of them is Arjun. He is obviously not the one behind it, and the other is San. He is amongst the smartest people in the world; he led the website team for a while and also had access to the highly secure password. He had created backdoor access into our systems and exploited them to create this hack,' Motu was getting extremely agitated.

'Can't we get him arrested?'

'I think he has covered his trail well. It'll be difficult for us to pin him down. If we want to catch him for good, we need to wait for him to make a mistake,' Motu replied.

'It might be too late when he makes that incriminating mistake. The bastard might destroy us completely by then,' Priya rued.

'We should inform Jaanvee. This will greatly impact our share price both in India as well as on the NYSE,' Priya advised Motu.

'Round II definitely goes to San,' Motu said as they entered the NYSE. They eagerly awaited Arjun's call.

What happened after that was something no one at PureConsultants wished to remember. Motu did ring the opening bell at NYSE, not with pride but with trepidation. After that he answered questions from a hostile media which bombarded him with accusations. He was asked that if the CEO of a technology company could not manage his website, how would he safely deliver other people's software. He had no answer to the questions. He felt like a scantily-clad female unwillingly thrown out on the street and ogled at by thousands of passersby. It was Priya who did not lose control and came up with some kind of cover-up.

'The reason our website is down is because of the unprecedented number of people who suddenly decided to visit the website. In hindsight, I agree we did not anticipate the traffic. But I have just received an SMS telling me that the website is up, and the problem has been solved.

'I have also been told that we can handle five times the current number of visitors now,' Priya ended with a reassuring smile, taking strength from the message she had received a minute back from Arjun.

The media-men broke into a smile too. The damage control exercise was successful. They had to wait and see how the incident got reported in the press.

'Are the spoils even?' Motu asked as they drove to the airport to take their flight back home.

They had chartered a plane to India. It was a nonstop flight which would take a little under fourteen hours to reach India. It was very expensive but with so much happening around them every passing minute, they did not want to miss any action and had decided to take a chartered flight.

'I don't know but we tried our best. Was I right in not giving out the correct information to the media?' Priya asked a question of her own.

'Of course. It is not a fair world. The bastards who are out to get us are not fair either. We know in our hearts that we shall protect people's faith in us till the very last moment of our lives. It doesn't matter if you lied, because telling the truth would have been disastrous. It would have resulted in panic selling on the bourses, resulting in people losing money for no real reason. As long as we are there to handle the crisis in the company, don't worry your conscience too much about it,' Motu sermonised. 'By the way you were incredible today,' he added in the end.

'I have always been incredible. Don't know what took you so long to realise it,' Priya responded in a lighter vein.

'I know it for the last twenty-five years. It's only you who don't see the signs,' Motu tried to speak but his cellphone rang. It was Nitin.

'Can you come down to my house as soon as you reach India? I have something very important to discuss with you. It is also my birthday and I would love to celebrate it with you in the evening. And, no excuses please. I shall not take more than half an hour,' Nitin pleaded with Motu.

'Is it urgent?' asked Motu. Though he didn't want to spend any time outside the office at this crucial juncture, he couldn't refuse Nitin because he had always felt guilty about not being able to do enough for him.

'I'll try to finish it in half an hour,' Nitin, in his excited state, did not mind the rebuke at all.

Then he called the next person on the list. Calling him was much more difficult than calling Motu, but he had to do it nevertheless. 'Hello, Pankaj! This is Nitin,' he tried to control the quiver in his voice.

They won praise from some sections of the press which bought Priya's line on PureConsultants' military-like response in solving the problem. About half the news disseminated was negative. Since it was already past 4:00 p.m. in India when the DoS attack was reported, the Indian stock markets were not affected by the bad news. It was possible for Jaanvee to know the complete effect of the attack only after they opened the next day. Earlier in the day, she had expected the cheers to sway the investors back to their camp, but things would be entirely different on Day 4 now.

She was thinking of her next line of defence when her cellphone rang. 'Why are you fighting so hard when you already know you have lost?' It was Salem.

'We will see. You are not dead till you actually stop breathing. You still have a long way to go, Salem,' Jaanvee retorted. 'And by the way, what is the purpose of your call?' she asked coldly, not feeling as confident as she sounded.

'I wanted you to speak to someone. Someone who will break that last line of your defence,' Salem said, laughing.

There was silence on the phone for a few seconds. Then San came on the line. 'San, don't do it. If you defect then they will hold fifty-one per cent of our shareholding. We'll be finished,' Jaanvee pleaded.

'I have been forced to do it. I have been betrayed and BD needs to pay,' San replied curtly.

'Hasn't he paid enough already?'

That was the end of the conversation between two people who had loved each other till a few days ago.

'You son-of-a-bitch, you had no right to destroy my world. Sure it wasn't ideal, but atleast there was no pain,' Jaanvee shouted after disconnecting the call. It was going to be a long lonely night for her. It was also the last day of her one-month old Blackberry phone, which was not made to handle the impact of hitting the wall with full force and fury.

Nitin could not sleep too. He was very excited about the next day, and the immense possibilities it presented. He knew that he could change history if Pankaj and Motu reconciled their differences. He kept awake till four in the morning and had barely slept when he was woken up by a sudden, unnatural sound.

At the end of Day 3, Software Builder was holding forty-five per cent of PureConsultants' shares. Some hectic lobbying by Jaanvee forced a few investors to align with PureConsultants. The sad thing was that the impact of the DoS attack was to be felt the next day after the markets in India opened.

✍

Day 4 (26 November 2008)

5:00 a.m.

Arjun woke up with the premonition that there would be another serious attempt to disrupt business at PureConsultants, and that this time it was going to be closer home where hundreds of software releases went out to the customers every day.

'I need to be wary. This is my turf and I have to ensure that nothing goes wrong,' he said to himself.

Motu and Priya decided to catch some sleep till their flight landed at the Delhi Airport. Motu loved to sleep and was yearning for this break. He was jetlagged from his trip to New York, and had hardly slept in the last seventy-two hours.

Jaanvee went to sleep at 5:00 a.m. and did not wake up early. She could afford rising late as for her the action would start when the stock markets opened at 10:00 a.m. All night, she had monitored the news in the US press. When the NYSE closed PureConsultants' stock had taken a beating and closed at twenty-five per cent below the day's opening. The result of the US bourses had given her the shivers. She knew it would be a very volatile day for trading in India. She prayed that when the shares changed hands, they didn't land up with Software Builder.

7:00 a.m.

Arjun arrived at work early as he wanted to be closer to the battleground. A few employees had already reached office who worked for customers in Australia. Everything looked normal with people giving him warm goodmorning smiles which he replied to with a curt nod. The one thing that was out of turn was the frequent complaints by employees about the slow speed of their computers, and that it was taking them unusually long to finish their work.

Arjun was tired of the early-morning complaints and the impatience of his colleagues.

'Sometimes they say the computers are slow and the Internet is not fast, at other times the access to servers on the network is slow.' Without realising, Arjun went into a complaining mode himself. He did not encounter any of the problems that others were facing. Thus he dismissed the complaints as routine discontent and went back to work.

10:00 a.m.

Starting early, Arjun finished a substantial amount of work by 10:00 a.m. Then he decided to meet the five-hundred freshers from different colleges in India and demonstrate a key project to them as part of their orientation. He requested the code to be installed on one of the auditorium machines. Arjun always looked forward to such interactions as it gave him a chance to meet brilliant and fresh minds who were unaffected by convention yet. This sometimes gave him many ingenious ideas. It also made him feel younger and full of energy.

Arjun started the program after the lights dimmed and the projector turned on. He knew that since it was a beta release, it would take a few minutes before it loaded. Beta release follows the alpha release. It is given to a select set of voluntary users before the fully tested version is delivered to the client. It sets the expectations of the target users that the software would have a few problems. Strangely, it took much longer than usual.

'Damn! Someone must have fiddled with the code and made it slow.' He began to discuss other things with the group to distract them from the delay. It took the program five minutes to be loaded. Arjun went through the demo, which didn't go very well since the application continued to run slow. Arjun thanked his stars that he was giving the demo to internal employees and not to a client.

After the demo ended, an infuriated Arjun summoned the team working on the project and asked them if they had made any changes to the program without authorisation.

'We have not made any changes, sir. The program is as fit as ever. The problem must lie somewhere else,' the project manager replied.

'It cannot be the computer. It worked fine on my laptop last week. Looks like it is not a usual problem. Let me try and get to the bottom of this,' Arjun signalled that the meeting was over.

Arjun fired the monitoring command to see the programs which were running on demo machine. He did not find anything out of turn. The usual windows services were running in the background. Then he looked at the processing power and memory the programs were consuming. Still everything looked normal. He started the demo application hoping it would run properly, but again experienced the same glitches. He typed the monitoring command again and saw an entirely different picture. Suddenly the computer started behaving as if under an attack – its processing power consumption and memory utilisation rose tremendously. Just starting the demo application could not have had that effect. Something inexplicable was eating into the computer resources, making the application run slower.

He typed another command and noticed that one of the processes, which looked like a windows service, was suddenly using more memory than before. Apart from that, he found that the rogue process was also sending out a large quantity of data over the Internet, thus slowing it down. He used the search engine to see what the process did, but to his utter surprise, found no documentation. It was strange that the Internet did not have any information on it. He tried to search more, but gave up in frustration because even the Internet was running slow. It became clear to Arjun that it was a virus. His gut churned because he feared PureConsultants had not seen the likes of this virus before.

The thought that he could not find anything on the virus still nagged him. He called up his Special Threat Assessment and Rescue Team (START) to run a scan on the computer to detect and kill the rogue virus. After a few hours, what they reported was depressing. None of the anti-virus programs they used could detect the virus, leave alone eliminate it.

'This is something new and very intelligent, sir. We need an expert's help to tide over this one,' the START head announced. It was difficult to digest that the team comprising his best men, who loved creating and destroying viruses, was actually admitting defeat.

'Assess the extent of damage. Go look at the other machines. And switch off the demo machine. We need to do all we can to prevent this virus from spreading,' Arjun told START. He had realised the seriousness of the problem at hand. He knew that START was right. This was something he could not handle on his own. He decided to call the best in the game.

ᔐ

11:00 a.m.

The flight back home was very relaxing after a few crazy days. On board, Motu and Priya talked about the old times, reminisced their childhood – the quiz competition and the days leading up to it; their separation after the introduction of French language in school and the joyous reunion; their going separate ways to pursue education and then reuniting to start NumeroSoft.*

'Life gives you joy through simple things. But somehow we always end up making things complex. Or maybe the joy stops when you become big in your life,' Priya asked Motu, her eyes brimming with tears.

'Yes, small is simple and simple is beautiful. Simple things are easy to understand and enjoy,' Motu agreed with her.

The moment remained etched in their minds for as long as they lived, made priceless by the fact that it was one of the last few they shared.

They parted after landing at the Delhi Airport. 'Papa is not keeping well these days. I will visit him for a couple of hours before I take the evening flight to Mumbai,' Priya said.

As soon as Priya left, Motu called Arjun.

'We are under a severe virus attack. The whole network is down, and we have still not been able to locate the source,' Arjun explained the situation to Motu.

'How bad is it?'

'The worst. It is so bad that I would have to call Musky to attend to it. We cannot handle it ourselves.'

'Do you need me? It will be some time before I reach office,' Motu asked.

'I think if Musky can't handle it, nobody in the world can,' Arjun replied.

Motu couldn't agree more with Arjun. Muskaan indeed was the best in business. Next, he called Jaanvee. She did not reply which was very surprising for Motu, but before his brain went wild thinking of all the possible reasons she called back.

'My phone has a new ringtone. Did not realise for a few seconds that it was ringing,' Jaanvee apologised.

'What happened to your Blackberry?'

'I lost it.' Motu failed to sense the turmoil behind what Jaanvee said.

'Anyway, how's the stock market doing?'

'Not a good day at all. Had there been a circuit breaker for individual shares, we would have hit it at the start of trading,' Jaanvee replied.

'That was expected. The only interesting thing now is to see who is buying.' Motu kept the phone down sadly.

12:30 p.m.

Motu straight away drove to Nitin's home from the airport. He was not in the mood to be away from office and all the action and was very agitated with the timing of Nitin's meeting. There were two lifts in operation. When he pressed the call button, he saw one returning from the tenth floor where Nitin lived. As he began to press the bell to Nitin's apartment he saw the door ajar and went inside. What he saw gave him a series of shock – Nitin was sprawled on the floor of the bedroom, smattered with blood and Pankaj was kneeling by his side, trying to revive him.

'He has been shot,' said Pankaj as he spotted Motu.

'Is he dead?'

'Not yet. We need to call the ambulance. Let's hope that the bullet hasn't pierced his heart,' Pankaj replied.

Motu called the ambulance immediately and then made the next call to the police. The police arrived first. 'Both of you will have to come with me to the police station. I need to take your statements,' the police officer said.

'He is not dead yet. First get him to a hospital, and then you can take us anywhere. But make sure he keeps alive,' Pankaj shouted at him.

'Don't teach me the law. I know what to do,' the police officer said brusquely.

'If anything happens to him, I will make sure you never get to attend office again, even if I have to speak to the commissioner of police. And I mean it.' Pankaj was red with rage.

'Inspector, you can take us wherever you want. But first let's get this guy to the hospital and into safe hands. Then we shall do whatever you say.' Motu did not let the stress show and his calm voice somehow restored order.

The police inspector too for the first time noticed that the two gentlemen in front of him were wearing hugely expensive suits and did not look like killers. One was carrying luggage too. From the tag on his luggage, it seemed he had come straight from the airport. He understood that manhandling them could put him in trouble. Realising that it may be too late by the time the ambulance arrived, they took him to the hospital in the police jeep, with Motu holding his head and Pankaj his dangling legs on their laps.

'So how are you doing?' Motu broke the long and awkward silence between him and Pankaj.

'Not bad. And you?' Pankaj replied.

'Not bad either.'

They did not speak to each other after that. Both of them prayed for Nitin's recovery on their way to the hospital.

They called a lot of people which made things move really fast and Nitin reached the ICU still alive. After making sure that the best doctors were attending to him, they went to the police station with the inspector. The inspector knew the two of them were very powerful and influential people, but he had to follow the procedures.

'Sir, I will need to keep the two of you in the police station for some time.' The inspector sounded apologetic.

'Sure, do your job.'

2:00 p.m.

'Good afternoon. Can we speak for a few minutes?' Arjun's voice was controlled.

'Yes, we definitely can.' She was polite. Her voice still sounded melodious to him. It was strange he had to call her under such stressful circumstances.

'Musky, we are under a virus attack and my team says it is one of the worst we have seen. I need your help. I assume you have not rusted over the years and are still the best,' Arjun could not resist taking a dig at her though he knew the truth from the corridor radio.

'If it is work, you know I will help. About me being the best, only time will tell.'

'How soon can you come here?'

'Give me two hours. I have a couple of important things to finish,' she replied.

'Okay, come as soon as possible.' Arjun did not like the fact that she had something more important to deal with at the moment. What he never came to know was that she had to fly off to Italy the same night, and she needed some time to inform the client that she would not be coming and a junior would replace her instead. The client, incidentally, was one of the largest banks in Italy and her biggest customer.

∽

Going to the police station was not the best experience for Motu and Pankaj. But they had seen so much in life that it did not seem disastrous. For Motu, it was his first brush with the law, and he badly wanted to be with Nitin instead. For Pankaj, the police station brought back memories of the Volgograd prison,* where Nitin, Kapil and he had spent a whole night. But that incident was different. They had picked up a fight with Khalid and Hassan for stealing their food at Padfaak. However, in this case there was a possibility that he could become the prime suspect for the attempted murder of Nitin. But strangely, Pankaj was not anxious for himself. He was only worried about Nitin.

Motu too was thinking about the same thing. His mind raced to find answers to two questions that were haunting him.

Who could have shot Nitin and why? With life coming to a standstill and nothing else to do in a 6x4 cell, Pankaj and Motu began a conversation.

'How's life been all these years?' Motu tried to break the ice. Though they had spoken sporadically on the way to the hospital, the conversation had centred on the incident and Nitin's safety.

'Fine,' came the monosyllabic reply.

'It's been years since we sat like this and talked.'

'We have never sat down like this and talked in a police station. Maybe you did this with someone else.' It took Motu a while to understand the joke. Both of them then laughed uncontrollably. It was the carefree laughter of yesteryears – uninhibited and unrestrained.

'Nitin had called me for an important meeting. How come you are here?' Motu asked Pankaj.

'The same. Maybe he wanted the two of us to meet,' he replied.

'Will it take Nitin's death to unite us?' Motu sighed. There was no anger in his voice, only regret for all the wasted years.

'We have gone too far ahead on our separate paths to be able to simply walk up to each other and shake hands. Even if I want to revive the old days, it cannot happen all of a sudden. Other people's lives are intertwined with ours and my decisions will impact all those allied with me,' Pankaj replied, slightly pained.

'Then let's not hurt each other at least,' Motu almost begged.

'I still love you, Priya and Nitin. What I am trying to do to your company is strictly business. Please don't take that personally,' Pankaj's voice was very soft, the likes of which Motu had not heard in years.

'Then why do it unethically? There are better ways of doing it.'

'I had left the modalities to Salem, and I think he is an ethical man, though slightly hard and impatient.'

Motu then narrated all the events leading up to the last few days where the attack on PureConsultants was blatant and completely unethical with the means defying the end.

Pankaj sat through the story impassively. He said finally, 'I think Salem went overboard. But excesses do happen at times. We all know the world is not a fair place to live in. I guess it's too late to stop the juggernaut now.' His looked helpless. Motu forgot all about his own suffering and felt like giving Pankaj his unconditional support.

Pankaj then switched the topic. 'I just remembered I am hungry. Care for some food?' he asked. Motu looked at his watch and realised that he too had not eaten in the last twelve hours.

'Do you still love aloo parathas? Maa makes them as delicious as ever, and I can ask Priya to bring them over,' Motu said excitedly.

'Inspector, how much time before our lawyer comes?' Motu asked the police officer.

'It may be a couple of hours. He said he is caught in a jam caused by a political rally,' he replied.

'Then please give my cellphone. I need to put something in there,' Motu said, pointing to his large belly. He then dialled Priya's number. 'Priya, when is your flight taking off?

'Still a few hours. Why?'

Motu quickly told her the whole story.

'Who could have shot him?' Priya was shocked.

'We are speculating too. For now, the relief is that the bullet missed his heart.'

'Priya, will you have time to pick aloo parathas from maa's place and come over before you go to the airport?'

'Do you think you are doing the right thing?' Priya asked apprehensively.

'I don't know. My heart tells me to do this but my mind tells me to be cautious. For this one time, I have decided to listen to my heart.'

'Okay, then let's follow the stupid heart and ignore the wise mind.'

Priya reached the police station within an hour.

The three of them met again, this time under completely different circumstances, making them so preoccupied with the things at hand that they had little time to delve into the past except for the brief interlude that opened the floodgates of memories.

In a brief span of time they remembered everything from their childhood to their present situation; ruing over lost chances and smiling over all the beautiful moments life had gifted them.

Then Priya decided to break the silence. 'What a waste! Life was full of so many possibilities till we decided to ruin it. We could have done so much together. Things could have been so different, so beautiful.' She raised both her hands in sheer exasperation, tears streaming down her cheeks. The long-lost friends understood each other's pain and anguish.

'The parathas are as delicious as ever. Kudos to your mom!' Pankaj remarked.

'Everything is still the same, Pankaj, nothing has changed,' Motu said.

'I have to leave. I have a flight to catch,' Priya said with a quiver in her voice.

'Where are you going?' Pankaj asked.

'Mumbai. I've a meeting to attend. Will be back tomorrow.'

'Still staying at the Taj?' Pankaj asked, smiling.

'Yes, as usual. I still love all the things I loved ten years ago.' Nobody missed what Priya meant.

'Before you leave, I want to say that all of us should continue with our karma and do it honestly. If, in the process, it hurts someone we should acknowledge it was strictly business. You guys are still dearest to me.' Pankaj said. He extended his arms and the three of them hugged each other before parting.

The inspector took their official statements as soon as the lawyer arrived. 'Since he has been shot from the front, Nitin must have seen the attacker. You guys can understand that you are also under suspicion. We'll nab the culprit very soon. In the meantime, you two shouldn't leave the city without informing the police.'

⌘

5:00 p.m.

The initial few moments of the meeting were awkward till Arjun and Musky decided to get busy with work.

'How far has the virus spread?' Muskaan asked.

'It is present on every machine.'

'How many machines do you have?'

'At least ten thousand. And the number of complaints is increasing every minute.'

'My machine does not have the virus because I do not connect to the office network very often. Otherwise, I would have figured out this problem a lot earlier,' Arjun summarised.

Muskaan looked at one of the infected machines and spoke to some of her friends in the antivirus industry. Soon it became clear to her that none had seen this virus before, and it would take them a while before they could do anything about it.

'Let's try to turn off the process ourselves,' Muskaan asked START without hoping for a victory. The virus was indeed deadly, and the moment they killed one process, it popped up again under a different name.

After a few hours of troubleshooting Muskaan declared her findings, 'This virus has been living inside these computers for quite some time now, lying dormant, waiting for its chance to strike on this day. Also, each virus was programmed differently. So all of them were not triggered at the same time. It spread slowly. That's the reason nobody realised that there was an attack. It is a time bomb set to explode today on all PureConsultants' machines.'

In a few hours work came to a standstill. 'You will not be able to send out any releases today. All the computers have gone on strike,' Muskaan declared to the small team in the room.

'How soon can we solve this?' Arjun asked her.

'I noticed that the virus is sending out data to the Internet. I am setting up tools to monitor traffic on your office network,' Muskaan started reading messages that went to the Internet from PureConsultants' office.

'This is going to be a long night and we still don't have any kind of control over the virus. I think we need to spend a lot of time tomorrow before we are finally able to pin this down.'

6:00 p.m.

After Priya left the police station Motu and Pankaj called the hospital. Nitin had gone into a coma and had not gained consciousness even once since he was admitted. When they reached the hospital, they also got to know from the investigating officer that a certain suspicious character had been seen following Nitin till the entrance of his apartment block a number of times in the last few weeks. One of the security officers at the gate remembered him enquiring about Nitin's apartment number. More investigations revealed that he had successfully bribed the ubiquitous press-wallah when his initial attempts at getting free information failed. The security officer gave them a detailed description of the stalker. Suddenly, it struck Motu that Ramlal could be behind the attack on Nitin. Earlier, when the information of Nitin's ailment spread in the office, Motu had investigated as to who was behind it. He was informed that it was Ramlal who told his sympathisers in office about Nitin's condition. He must have followed Nitin when the latter visited his doctor. Motu told the investigating officer about the tiff between Ramlal and Nitin. 'You can get his photograph from PureConsultants' database and check if it matches with the description of the stalker.'

Later, it turned out that it indeed was Ramlal who had shot Nitin to take his revenge. His hatred for Nitin had grown over the months because of his inability to find work and consequently being ridiculed by family and friends. He went out of control over a two-day alcoholic binge where he got to hear some really nasty comments from the fellow drinkers. In his moment of anger, he borrowed a pistol from someone and went to Nitin's house. The original plan was to wait outside and shoot him whenever he came out. However, since Nitin had called Motu and Pankaj to his house he did not venture out at all. So, a half-drunk Ramlal forced his way into Nitin's house and shot him around noon.

Motu and Pankaj were later absolved of any guilt when Ramlal admitted his crime in the police station after much grilling. He was subsequently charged with an attempt to murder.

Motu had called Jaanvee from the hospital to know of the day's progress.

'I am afraid the news is not good. Something or the other is not letting the share price recover, which makes Software Builder's offer increasingly attractive for people. We lost another three per cent to them today. They now hold forty-eight per cent of our company.'

'What if we make a counter offer at a higher price to buy back the shares?'

'I think they will increase the price too. Moreover, we don't have the hard cash required to pull it off. We will go bankrupt,' Jaanvee replied.

'Now that things are set to go down to the wire, scan the list of shareholders and see if there is anyone who can still be stopped from selling. Get back to me as soon as you can,' Motu told Jaanvee.

⟡

8:00 p.m.

Tanya had been outside the ICU ever since she got the information about the gun shot. She looked dishevelled. She prayed to god to give Nitin the strength to come out of the coma. Whenever she went to see him the only words she whispered into his ears were, 'There is a lot that you still need to do for spreading the hope that you have raised in the lives of millions who are suffering. All of us need you. Don't make me flush these unused condoms down the toilet. I will never forgive you for this.'

Everyone, including the media, was amazed by her belief that Nitin would pull through. The ICU was always brimming with hundreds of people who wished for his recovery.

'How can you die when so many people are praying for you? You will have to come back, and I know you will,' Tanya said, more to console herself. She had not cried even once since she had heard the bad news.

8:45 p.m.

The day was not over for Motu yet. Though he had gone home early trying to take it easy after a very unusual day, he was not able to retire to bed. He was sequentially going over all the happenings of the day. He fondly remembered the olden days and all the ill feelings that he harboured for Pankaj vanished. As usual he kept the television on, but the voice was muted. He did not want to miss any important news.

Lost as he was, he saw the breaking news in the third flash. It read 'Mumbai Under Terror Attack'. He switched channels to look for details but all the channels were giving inconsistent reports on the attack. He never believed terrorism to be a viable means of protest. Within ten minutes he saw news flashes which said that the attacks were carried out at multiple places. His heart skipped a beat when he heard that the Taj Mahal Palace was one of them. Immediately the phone rang too. It was Priya.

'We have been attacked. I can hear gunshots all around.'

'Where are you now?' Motu asked her.

'In my room. I am not going out till things are under control.'

It turned out to be her biggest mistake. They talked for some time and exchanged every bit of information they had.

'Pankaj had called. He is also worried. He offered to fly down but I refused.' In the first hour nobody realised the magnitude of the attack. By the time they did, the control had slipped into the hands of the terrorists.

'I can't call you anymore. The lights are off and my cell is going on a blink. I forgot to bring the charger in all the rush. Will keep smsing you.'

Motu was scared for Priya. She seemed calm. There was so much that they wanted to say to each other but ...

10:00 p.m.

It was close to 10:00 p.m. when Arjun saw Muskaan fidgeting in her seat. He knew the reason. It was time for Sorry's daily chat with Superhero007.

'You need something?' he asked her, smiling within.

'No, I just had a routine thing to take care of. But I guess it can wait till tomorrow,' Muskaan replied.

'So this is how you make your money?' Arjun decided to switch the topic.

'Basically yes, we make money by first giving large companies a big scare by showing them how easy it is to hack their networks, and then we take a lot of money to secure their networks,' Muskaan smiled as she replied. She had recovered from the anxiety of a few minutes ago. The conversation got disrupted when Arjun's cellphone rang.

12:00 a.m.

Motu was constantly sending Priya updates on the attack. With no details on the movement of the terrorists, it was impossible to get away. It was easier to try an escape in the initial confusion but now it would be suicidal to attempt one. Motu was devastated because he knew Priya was in danger and he could do nothing to help her. He squirmed in his bed and cried out aloud.

The last message he sent her before he involuntarily dozed off to sleep was – 'Things look under control. Reinforcement has also come in. You will be out of there in no time.' It was just the opposite of what he actually felt.

⁓

Day 5 (27 November 2008)

2:30 a.m.

Motu woke up with a start. He looked at his cellphone to see if there was any message from Priya. He was disappointed to find none. It had been like that for quite some time now. He did not even know if her cellphone was working or whether she was alive. He could not call her for the fear that it might give her away. Suddenly he remembered that he had a batchmate from IIT who had become an IPS officer and was posted with Mumbai police as a DCP. Calling someone on the ground whom he had known for so long made better sense than looking for an indirect contact at a higher level. He skimmed through the mails on his laptop and found the number in a few minutes. Motu was confident that he would help. In college, he was fondly called Kaddu. Motu had played the role of intermediary when Kaddu did not have the courage to propose to a girl in college. So Motu went up to the girl and had proposed to her on his friend's behalf. Because of his reputation in college he was not rebuked, but the girl had turned down his friend's proposal. The DCP picked the phone immediately on the first ring. 'Kaddu, how are you?' Motu asked.

'Who is this?' the DCP did not recognise him at first, his voice stressed. He did not put the phone down either as he realised the guy on the other side knew his college nickname and must be a friend.

'This is Motu.'

'I am no more a Kaddu. Serving the nation has made me lean and mean. What makes you call me so early in the morning? Is it an invite for dinner on the weekend?'

Motu told him the whole story and finished with, 'I love her more than anything else in my life. I am torn between my love for her and my duty towards the company. I just don't know what to do. Will it help in any way if I fly to Mumbai?'

'I will try to give you as much information on her as I can. There's no point in coming over as you will not be allowed anywhere near the place. Just be on standby in case she needs you when she is out,' the DCP said what Motu wanted to hear. He wanted Motu to relax and feel that things were under control. Motu couldn't have been of much help anyway.

5:30 a.m.

It seemed as though all the people directly or indirectly associated with PureConsultants were caught in a wrong planetary position.

Tanya had not closed her eyes even for a second ever since she had heard the news of Nitin being shot. She met the doctors every few minutes. Thankfully, they were extremely patient with her.

'Has there been an improvement in his condition?'

'Not much,' the junior doctor had replied half an hour ago. This was the fifth time he had given the same answer to the same question.

'What are his chances, Doctor? Be honest with me.'

'We should put him under observation for two to three days. If things don't improve the chances to resuscitate him will reduce drastically.'

'What do you do if Nitin doesn't respond?'

'We advice the patient's relatives to stop all life support systems as there is little hope of recovery,' the doctor avoided any direct reference to Nitin.

'That means you advice them to kill him.'

The flustered junior doctor didn't know what to say. He dismissed Tanya as another one of those unreasonable relatives and went back to work, vowing to avoid her at any cost during his future shifts.

10:00 a.m.

Priya was inundated with calls and messages, hundreds of them from family, friends and well-wishers, especially from papa, mama, Motu and Pankaj. She initially tried to return the calls but soon realised that her cellphone battery would discharge. Also, the noise she would make in the extremely silent hotel posed a huge risk to her own life. In order to save the battery, she switched off her phone, putting it on at regular intervals and communicating through smses. As the battery went low, she couldn't respond to their messages. They were all extremely worried. She had insisted that no one should try to come to Mumbai. 'It'll make me doubly scared. The fact that my people are waiting for me outside would make me do something rash,' she told everyone. The message that she sent to all who had called her was – 'I am fine. Will keep you updated.'

After the initial shock and fear, she was suddenly calm. 'It is life which is painful, death relieves the pain.' She comforted herself with the help of those profound words.

11:00 a.m.

Motu and Pankaj were both torn apart. They couldn't concentrate on work. First, the most loyal and faithful friend and then the woman both of them had admired the most were struggling for their lives and they found themselves incapable of helping either of them. They had received Priya's sms but they knew the situation was tense. Pankaj, as if waiting for something extraordinary to shake his insides, felt his love for Priya as intense as ever.

'Do you have any more news after she had sent the last sms?' Pankaj called Motu.

'I spoke to Kaddu, a college friend.' Motu gave Pankaj the rundown on his conversation with the DCP.

'I now realise how sometimes you can be so powerless,' Pankaj said.

'Yes, some problems and their resolutions are beyond us. We should just bide time and pray for nothing to go wrong instead of trying to play god,' Motu said philosophically.

'Yes, you cannot play god in your life forever,' Pankaj replied after a thoughtful pause.

'She has always been so special to us right from our school days*.'

'She'll come out of this alright. I know she will. She has to ...' said Pankaj in a choked voice.

Both of them did not talk at all about the impending hostile takeover of PureConsultants before putting the phone down.

'I never stopped loving you, Priya. It just got buried under the weight of a stupid ambition and betrayal by the people I loved,' and 'I know I will always be a friend to you but to me you will remain the most lovable person I have ever known,' the two of them said to their pensive reflections in the mirror after putting the phone down.

2:00 p.m.

Muskaan was deeply engrossed with the monitoring tool she had set up.

'See this. All machines were busy reading data from various servers. These servers host all your company's important data – code of all projects, employee records, customer records, finance, almost everything. In short, the virus has attacked the lifeline of your company. Residing inside your servers, it is sending data to all the computers on the office network, thus slowing them down.'

'Anything else that you have noticed?'

'Yes. All these computers are sending messages on the Internet to the same IP address. We have to find out who the owner of this computer is. I'm sure he is the one who has put the virus in all your machines.

'Do you know someone at the Internet Service Provider?'

'I do know somebody but I can't say for sure whether he will help. I have taken a few services from him earlier, but he is a very unpredictable guy.

Muskaan called the number but it went unanswered. 'We will have to wait till he returns my call.'

'Why don't we call the police?'

'Believe me, it will be a lot faster if we go through my contact. Let's wait for him to return my call. He's not the most reliable guy, but he never fails to return my call.'

Realising that the exercise to control the virus attack may well continue into the night, Arjun had called Diyaa to the office. She had not met him in the last few days and was getting restless. He had made arrangements for her to sleep in the retiring room made especially for people held up late in office. This way the mother and daughter would get to meet after a long time.

'Hello, Mama, how are you?' Diyaa asked as soon as she saw Muskaan.

'Good. How about you?'

'I am doing good too, Mama.'

Both of them talked excitedly for some time till Arjun sent her away with a junior technologist who loved children and had taken the responsibility of putting Diyaa to her afternoon sleep.

5:00 p.m.

It had been a whirlwind day for Jaanvee. She had made more than hundred calls to people who mattered, trying to convince them not to sell their shares as PureConsultants was still on a solid footing.

'We are on the top of the whole thing. It's only a matter of days before things return to normalcy. It's because of rumours and speculations that our share price is going down,' she said to one of the influential investors.

'But I may lose all my money if I don't act on those rumours. The buzz in the market is not in your favour. You are backing a loser, Jaanvee. You should also cash out and leave,' he replied.

'I would have had it only been about money. But this is about what I believe in, and I still believe PureConsultants is not a loser,' Jaanvee replied as she ended the call.

'Isn't there anything we can do to avoid this mayhem?' Jaanvee later called Motu and asked for help.

Motu was tempted to tell Jaanvee about the multimillion-dollar deal that would be announced by Alex next week but he had promised Alex he would refrain from revealing anything till a formal announcement was made. An upright man, he decided not to endanger Alex by leaking this information at an inopportune moment.

'Nothing at the moment. You'll have to keep on trying to convince people.'

'Then get ready for a losing speech. I don't think we can pull this through. '

♫

8:30 p.m.,

Muskaan's contact at the ISP returned her call.

'You seem to be on a vacation. What took you so long to reply?' Muskaan asked him sarcastically.

'Come straight to the point. What do you want from me?'

Muskaan told him the whole story and requested for the IP address of the computer where all the PureConsultants' data was being sent. 'Give me an hour,' he replied and hung up.

'Who could have done this and why?' Muskaan asked Arjun.

'Somebody who must have both the brains and the motivation to do it,' Arjun told the whole story to her. 'Can we do something better than waiting for your contact's call?'

'Well, finding an antivirus to patch this will take some time. So the best thing to do is find the IP address, confiscate the machine to which your data is going and stop the data flow. That should get things back on track for now,' she replied.

Arjun noticed that Muskaan was getting jittery again as the clock struck ten at night. They were both seated at his desk when she suddenly excused herself.

'Can I take a break for five minutes? I need to do something on my machine,' Muskaan said.

'Sure. I hope you don't want me to move away,' Arjun asked, trying not to smile. She was still seated at Arjun's desk; the two of them facing each other. One could not see what the other was doing on the machine.

Knowing why Muskaan wanted to be alone on her machine Arjun too logged onto his instant messenger.

'The day is extremely hectic and I can't chat for long,' Sorry told Supper.

'What happened?' Supper asked.

She informed him that she was with her husband and daughter, and that it was getting extremely difficult for her to concentrate on her work sitting so close to him.

'What is taking you so long, Musky? We have work to do,' Arjun said in a complaining voice, enjoying his moment to the hilt.

'Give me a minute. I need to finish this report,' a flustered Muskaan replied.

'I still find him irresistible. He makes me feel like a woman. You know I feel dishonest sitting in front of him and chatting with you,' Muskaan said as she stole a glance at Arjun who seemed engrossed in something very serious on his machine.

'Hmm ...' Supper replied, curtailing his answers to monosyllables as if he were hurt. His heart began to thump out of excitement, and he wondered if the noise would give him away. He looked at her fleetingly and found she was completely busy chatting Supper up.

'I think I should tell him I still love him,' Sorry said.

'Hmm ...' Supper was still not very forthcoming.

'Also I hope you'll forgive me for what I am going to say now. This will be the last time I am chatting with you,' Sorry wrote furiously into the messenger window.

'Are you done, Musky? Your one minute got over a long time back,' Arjun asked again. 'What are you working on? Is it so important that you can't delay it?' he continued with his teasing ways.

'I can't. Now can you stop disturbing me?' Musky was irritated as Supper had not replied till now.

'Hello!' she sent out a funny audible to cheer him up. To her surprise, she heard the audible back and the sound came from Arjun's machine. Not sure that she had heard it correctly, she sent the audible again in her chat window. This time, unmistakably, she recognised the sound coming from Arjun's machine. She looked at a flustered Arjun who was trying to control the damage by muting his laptop's speakers.

Not knowing what to do, Muskaan hid her face in her palms and began to sob. Arjun put his arms around her and let her cry.

'So this was the report you were working on,' he said, finally giving up all pretence.

'How did you come to know?' she asked.

'The Italian name was a giveaway,' he replied.

Then they noticed some commotion from the far end of the hall where Diyaa was talking animatedly to the junior technologist and coming towards them. Sensing that this was a special moment for the three of them Diyaa cried 'Mama' and tried to run towards them, tearing her hand away from the junior technologist.

She fell down after taking just one step forward. Only then did everyone notice that she had taken off her braces.

'You don't ever need to take them off for my sake. I love you even with them.' Muskaan was crying guiltily. She then kissed both Diyaa and Arjun, an unabashed display of pent-up love.

'I know you will quickly find a solution to the attack now that your 10 o'clock distraction is over.' Arjun grinned at her. Muskaan beat him on the chest sportingly. They reluctantly got down to work after some time. They had a hard time trying to persuade Diyaa, who was not ready to leave her mother, to go to sleep.

'Papa, she called me her baby, and that too twice,' she whispered into Arjun's ear on her way to the sleeping room.

10:30 p.m.

PureConsultants' shares took a beating on the stock for the fourth consecutive day. The news that they were reeling under a severe virus attack, and that work had come to a halt also got leaked to the press. Shareholders, acutely aware that something was not right within PureConsultants, sold their shares to Software Builder. Jaanvee was desperate to know when the virus attack would finally be tamed.

'Arjun, how soon can we expect to get out of this mess?' she hollered over the phone. It was clear that she was over the edge.

'I have some good news. Everything should be back to normal by tomorrow.'

'Tomorrow has twenty-four hours. Tell me the exact time?'

'Before the stock exchange opens,' Arjun replied cheerfully.

'Some good news in a long time!' Jaanvee shrieked with joy.

'How are we placed on the stock market?' Arjun asked, fearing the worst.

'We lost again today. I fear that we may lose control of the company tomorrow. But there is one more day of trading left. A lot can happen in one day, more so if people get to know we are back on our feet firmly,' Jaanvee replied cheerfully. 'Were you able to find out who did this?'

'Yes. I will have a confirmation very soon. He had covered his trail well the previous two times, but this time I have concrete information to nail him.'

'Who is it? Is it ...'

'Yes, I believe this too is the mastermind of San.'

Jaanvee put the phone down. She knew it was going to be another long and lonely night for her.

11:00 p.m.

Muskaan's contact did call as he had promised and gave them the IP address. It was registered in San's name. With solid information in hand they called the police and registered a complaint. A warrant was immediately issued and San's computer and ten hard drives were confiscated. The police told Arjun later that San hardly put up any resistance and gave himself up easily as though he was expecting the arrest.

11:30 p.m.

Jaanvee was shattered to know about San's arrest but she had to concentrate on the task given by BD. She searched through the shareholders' list to see if she could find anyone who could tilt the balance either way.

'We cannot afford any more surprises,' Jaanvee thought to herself. She almost knew all the names by heart. She scanned through the list once again when she saw one name which struck her as odd – a certain Mrs S Sharma. She looked for the address. The address mentioned was of Hoshiarpur. What alarmed her was that someone from a small town like Hoshiarpur was holding three per cent shares of a software company.

'BD, is Priya alright?' Jaanvee called him.

'I received the last message a long time back. I don't know what has happened to her. I want to be there but ...' Motu was trying to control his breaking voice. 'Anyway, I heard that San has been arrested. Will you be able to take this blow, Jaanvee?'

'How did you know?' Jaanvee asked in a weak voice.

'Your eyes gave you away. I have known it for months.'

'Let's pray for each other then. Tough time for both of us.' Jaanvee laughed dryly. 'I called you for something else. Do you know Mrs S Sharma from Hoshiarpur?'

'What about her?'

'I found this very regular name in the list of our shareholders. She holds three per cent of our company.'

Motu deliberated for a second and blurted, 'Of course, I know her! I have known her for more than thirty years. She is Pankaj's mother. Pankaj must have given her these shares.'

'Do you think you can convince her to sell her shares to us?'

'I am not sure but I must try.'

'That means you are going to Hoshiarpur tomorrow.'

'Why do I need to go?'

'You must meet her in person to convince her. There is no way I see it happening over the phone.' With their hearts heavy with pain, they went about doing their job, knowing that they could not let the people who had trusted them all along down. After trying Priya's number one last time and finding it switched off, Motu went to sleep with the phone lying under his pillow waiting for her response.

∽

Day 6 (28 November 2008)

4:00 a.m.

Motu woke up early to get ready for the trip to Hoshiarpur.

Arjun had no intention of waking early and kept on sleeping with both Diyaa and Musky snuggled up to him. All of them could afford to sleep a little more as the biggest problem they now had to deal with was the logistics of moving Musky back to their house.

Tanya had not slept for almost forty-eight hours now. She wanted to be the first one to hear either the good or the bad news about Nitin.

5:00 a.m.

Motu decided to drive to Hoshiarpur, as this would give him the chance to unwind and he still could be back well in time for the next day's EGM. He had always been fond of long drives, though of late he had not got the chance to go out on one. He loved driving on NH1 because it had a huge variety of North Indian dhabas.

1:00 p.m.

He reached Hoshiarpur after almost eight hours on the road. After the journey he realised that his body was not all that young anymore, and he was feeling tired. He knocked at Pankaj's mother's door with little trepidation. In the few seconds that she took to open the door he recalled every bit of what he knew about her.

Motu remembered Pankaj's mother as a very simple and homely lady. One thing he distinctly remembered about her was her obsession with honesty and morality, and she had always taught Pankaj to never sacrifice his morals. She was often quoted by Pankaj in his many conversations about his family. The thought gave him the added courage he so desperately needed to go to Hoshiarpur and seek her help.

'Who is it?' Pankaj's mother squinted to focus on Motu's face.

'I am Gaurav ... actually Motu, Pankaj's childhood friend,' he said.

Her face slowly broke into a smile. She looked older than her seventy years. Maybe living alone had added to her years.

'What brings you here, beta?' Her house was a simple but neatly done two-room cottage – a stark contrast to Pankaj's sprawling and luxurious house.

Motu told her the whole story. He reserved his comments about Pankaj, not giving an opinion on either his behaviour or his changed personality.

'It is difficult for me to understand what you are saying. I do remember him giving me some papers saying that whenever I needed money I could sell them. But I don't have much use for it ... I don't understand money.

'One thing that I know about money is that too much of it sours relationships. It seems this is what has happened with the two of you. Otherwise you would have asked for these papers from him and not me. Am I right?'

She was far more intelligent than Motu had thought. 'Yes, we very rarely speak these days. But I still respect him.'

'Tell me one thing, and I will give these papers to you. Do you think you are right and Pankaj is wrong?'

'Yes, I sincerely do. Otherwise, I would not have gathered the courage to come to you,' Motu said after a long silence.

'Then take these papers. How much are they worth?'

'A few hundred crores, at least. I just need them for tomorrow. I will return them later.'

'Doesn't matter when you return them. Ordinary people do not need money to find peace. Now that you are here, have dinner with me before you leave. Apart from my daughters rarely anybody visits me these days,' she smiled.

Motu was short of time but agreed to dine with her.

They talked about many things over a simple dinner of dal, vegetables, and roti. But to Motu, it was one of the best meals he ever had. It was already 8:00 p.m. when he got up to leave.

'Time for me to go.' He impulsively touched her feet, something which he had not done when he met her a few hours ago.

'Pankaj was right. He told me when he gave me the papers that they were worthless at the time he had bought them, but in a few years they will be worth a lot of money. It looks that he was right, beta.'

10:00 p.m.

Inspite of the sadness surrounding him he felt happy after meeting a pure soul like Pankaj's mother. He was overwhelmed by a deep sense of gratitude towards her. He also remembered that Pankaj had bought five per cent shares of PureConsultants. His mother had three per cent. So he had kept that two per cent for himself.

In the free time that he had in between, he had called Jaanvee and Tanya and sent an sms to Priya. He had encountered bad news on all the three fronts.

'We lost two per cent again today. If we subtract this two per cent that we lost to NumeroSoft and add the three that you got back, NumeroSoft and its loyalists still hold fifty-one per cent. They seem to have won.'

Priya had not replied to any of his smses leaving him extremely worried.

'They will tell me tomorrow what they intend to do with Nitin. The doctor also said that with each passing day his chances of pulling back are decreasing. These doctors are such fools!' Tanya said, her voice still brimming with hope.

With a cocktail of different emotions in his heart he began his drive back to Delhi contemplating what fate really had in store for him.

⟋

Day 7 (29 November 2008)

4:00 a.m.

Motu looked at his watch impatiently for the umpteenth time. He had hardly moved a mile in the last two hours. He had failed to factor in the time for traffic jams for the return journey. This jam had caught him unawares at 2:00 a.m. From what he understood, a truck and a bus had collided head-on. Both overturned, leaving at least ten people dead. The ensuing confusion led to a massive traffic jam which clogged the road for kilometres. There was no chance that anything would move before daybreak. By then it might be too late for Motu. He still needed four hours to reach Gurgaon, in time for the 9:00 a.m. EGM. With no other alternative left he called his DCP friend.

'You have specialised in calling people in the night. Do you derive some sadistic pleasure out of it?' the DCP said in a sleepy voice.

'Knowing the kind of person you are, I was sure you will not be asleep. Do you have any information on Priya, Kaddu?'

'The operation is being taken out of our hands and handed over to the special force. That's all I know for now.'

Motu thanked him and put the phone down.

6:30 a.m.

The traffic had still not moved. Motu needed a miracle to reach Gurgaon now. His mind was working at a breakneck speed but failed to find a solution. Then, out of helplessness, he looked at the heavens for help.

'Why did I not think of it earlier?' Motu rummaged through the visiting cards in his purse, praying that he had not misplaced the one he was looking for.

'Pawan, do you still run that inefficient helicopter service of yours?' he called up another one of his old friends, who picked the phone after ten rings.

'Yes, I do and I can bet that it is more efficiently run than your software company,' he said in his guttural voice. Both of them laughed aloud, just like two old friends do when they touch base after a long time.

'I will believe it if you provide me a helicopter immediately.'

'Generally, I take bookings in advance, at least not so early on a sleepy Saturday morning. Where are you right now?'

'Ambala. And I need to be in my office by 9:00 a.m.'

'A close call but let me try.'

7:50 a.m.

He heard the helicopter hovering in the sky over his head. He knew it was meant for him. He went to the nearby dhaba and began talking to the owner.

'How long have you been running this dhaba?'

'This was opened by my grandfather forty years ago. My father ran it for thirty years. I have been the in-charge for the last ten years. What can I do to help you, sirji?'

'Take these keys. Park this car in a safe place. I will send someone to pick it up soon,' Motu flung the keys of his black Mercedes at the dhaba owner in a hurry, who gawked at him for a long time.

'And how are you going, sirji?'

'In that helicopter.'

8:55 a.m.

Jaanvee had tried to call him several times in the last one hour but had found Motu's cellphone out of range. The EGM was going to be an open affair, and the seats in the auditorium were available only on first-come-first-serve basis. Pankaj and Salem had already arrived dressed in dark business suits. But there was no sign of Motu still.

Suddenly, she heard the distinct humming of the helicopter's propeller which intensified with every passing second. She went out to see the cause of the commotion. The helicopter was coming closer. Then she understood it was going to land inside the premises of PureConsultants. Everything came to a standstill waiting for the helicopter to land.

'Thank you, Officer. It was indeed the most comfortable flight of my life. I hope you did not have any trouble arranging things so fast.'

'To be honest, sir, I do not have permission to land inside the building. I am sure I may have some trouble with the authorities, but I will manage. After all, you are one of the best things to have happened to the Indian business. It was indeed an honour to be with you, sir,' the ex-wing commander of IAF said with a salute.

The meeting started exactly at 9:00 a.m. Both sides presented their documents. The verification of facts by the committee went on for almost two hours after which it was established beyond doubt that NumeroSoft, which was the owner of Software Builder, had indeed got control of fifty-one per cent of PureConsultants' shares. With this the reins of the company were transferred to NumeroSoft. Salem had a smug smile on his face but Pankaj looked troubled when he heard that his mother had pledged her shares to PureConsultants.

After the necessary verification was over, Pankaj was called upon the stage to address the company as its new chairman. He suddenly remembered the trauma of school days when he was pitched against Motu as the head boy and had won.* Fate had put him in the same situation again after so many years. The only difference was that this time it was of his own making.

'I would have been immensely pleased with this outcome a week ago. But in the last three days many things have changed. I have come to realise that I have lost all my friends. All the people who were dear to me have gone away for one reason or the other.' The crowd gasped at the completely unexpected opening line from Pankaj.

'My wife who had loved me so much is in trouble; my friend who was more faithful to me than anybody could ever be to anyone, is battling for his life, fighting a bullet injury. And the friend whose company I have acquired today still has love and respect for me after all that I have done to him.

'Even from a business perspective, it does not seem right to take over a company which is being run well and has a great future ahead on its own. I believe this takeover will only slow things down. So I, in my individual capacity, pledge my two per cent direct holding in PureConsultants to Gaurav and hand over the control of the company to him.'

Everyone was in a state of shock. Nobody had expected such a turnaround. Pankaj walked to Motu and hugged him tightly. They could not control their tears even though they were on a public platform.

'Pankaj, you are the only person capable of pulling it off twice. You had relinquished the post of head boy in school so many years ago and now you have done it again.* When will you give me a chance to repay you?'

Suddenly, Motu's cellphone vibrated in his pocket. It was Kaddu.

'The operation got over a couple of hours ago. Priya was found inside her room. Her eyes were closed and she looked in peace when we found her.'

Priya was dead. I also found an unsent message in her cellphone. It read – 'Though you haven't realised, both my conditions for marrying you have been fulfilled. You know more about happenings inside the pharma industry, (citing the news that Alex had shared with Motu which Priya did not know about) and even if it may technically take us a few more years PureConsultants will have twenty-five-thousand people very soon. So I accept your proposal and will marry you if I come out of this alive.'

The cellphone slipped out of Motu's hands.

'What happened?' Pankaj asked, fearing the worst.

'Priya is no more.' Motu managed to say before breaking down. Pankaj sank to the ground. People came running towards him.

'I also have another announcement to make and this one is for you, Priya. Gaurav and I will build a huge hospital in your name. I promise it will be the best hospital in the whole world,' Pankaj said before he sank to the ground again.

Both of them then excused themselves and went out of the auditorium to have their private moment of grief.

✌

The Day After (30 November 2008)

It had been a long night for both Motu and Pankaj. They had gone to Mumbai to get Priya's body, and by the time they reached Delhi it was past midnight. Kaddu was right. Priya indeed found peace in death. She looked serene with her eyes closed. If it were not for the bullet wounds, anyone could have mistaken her stillness for sleep.

They brought the body to her parents' place. Both Pankaj and Motu evaded the eyes of her parents throughout the time they were there. During their short stay not many words were exchanged. All eyes were brimming with tears but were trying to act brave.

'We will come in the morning, Uncle.' Motu hugged Priya's father. Pankaj had retreated into a shell. He was not speaking to anyone.

'Priya loved both of you very much. She spoke all the time about the strange relationship she had with you two. It had almost got confusing for her by the end. The last thing she said before she left was: "Papa, are there different shades to love? If Pankaj's love made me feel beautiful, Motu's makes me feel secure," ' Priya's father said.

Nothing more was said after that other than a promise to meet in the morning.

'I will come to pick you up,' Motu said when he dropped Pankaj outside his home.

Motu found it strange when Pankaj did not take his call. So he decided to go directly to his house to pick him up.

'Is Pankaj awake?' he asked the butler. Pankaj had long graduated to a level in society where he did not need the traditional Ramu kaka but a smart butler to manage his home.

'No, sir. The light in his room was switched on till late in the night. He must have been busy with something. So I decided not to wake him up.'

Motu entered the room and began to speak, 'Pankaj, will you get up now please? I know you don't like me. But you don't have a choice as I am never going to go out of your life. So get up,' Motu said, trying to cheer him up a little.

He knew that the fact of a few days ago was not true anymore. They were friends again. He had vowed to himself that this time it would be for good.

After calling him a few times, Motu reached out to shake him out of sleep. When his fingers brushed Pankaj's skin, a chill went down Motu's spine. Pankaj was cold and still. Motu noticed an empty bottle of sleeping pills along with a half-empty bottle of Scotch lying on the side table. He had tried to commit suicide. Motu immediately checked his pulse. It was very feeble, but he was still alive. He rushed him to the hospital – one of his many visits there in the last few days – and took him straight to the ICU.

❦

'He would have certainly died if you had arrived a little later,' the doctor said after the resuscitation procedure was over.

Motu heaved a sigh of relief and walked out of the ICU with drooping spirits. He wanted to feel happy that Pankaj had survived. But when he remembered that Nitin was in the same hospital fighting for his life and Priya was waiting for him to be present by her side when her last rites were performed, he was again filled with grief.

Epilogue

Pankaj did survive the suicide attempt. What his muscle and money could not do, Pankaj's and Motu's reunion did for them. Now NumeroPureConsultants is among the ten largest IT companies in the world. The company's vision statement says that they want to be the biggest in the next five years. They have established a big hospital in Priya's memory which only treats the poor.

Salem, who inspired awe in people because of his meteoric rise and the mystery surrounding it, was thrown out of NumeroSoft. He is now shunned by everyone and only discussed as a failure in gossip sessions in corporate parties.

Musky moved back to the house which had never closed its doors on her. Diyaa, buoyed by the return of her mother was an altogether different girl, finally discarding her braces forever. Arjun prayed that the joy surrounding him be permanent.

Jaanvee was still the dream woman of every intelligent man. She vowed never to be foxed by the wily ways of evil men again. She decided that her nirvana would only be through work and went back to working harder than ever. San was the sole reminder of her closest and most tragic brush with love.

San was forgiven by Motu because he knew that San was impressionable but not a criminal. San himself could not take the ignominy and the loss of respect and love. He has turned into an alcoholic, waiting for his liver to burst.

On the good side, Priya appeared in the dreams of Motu and Pankaj to tell them why she had to die the way she did.

'Both of you loved me, and I loved you too. It would have been impossible for me to choose one. So the only choice god had was to take me to him. Motu, I too have learnt the art of loving from a distance. And I can see everywhere from up here. I am especially keeping a watchful eye on your bedrooms. So, you better behave,' she said and disappeared laughingly.

That was the day Pankaj realised that Motu had loved Priya for so many years and had suffered in silence. He reminded himself again not to ever let Motu go away. Pankaj, who never believed in miracles, finally began to believe in them. After Priya's appearance in his dreams, his cellphone rang. 'Pankaj, forgive me for all the bad things I did to you. I am suffering now for them. Please forgive me.' The voice on the phone was hysterical.

'What happened? What is the matter?'

'I am dying. Ira too has left me. Please help me. I don't want to die. I love you, Pankaj, and I want to see you.' Sveta was delirious.

Before you crucify me, let me also tell you about Nitin and Tanya. The doctors had given up on Nitin and wanted to withdraw the life support systems, but Tanya did not believe that he could die. She brought him home. She converted Nitin's room into a hospital ward. Along with oxygen she gave him a daily dose of soul-stirring music through her iPod. She often took her dress off and snuggled up to him for hours with his head resting on her bosom, and gave him a piece of her mind.

'Either you wake up fast or I will keep nagging you like this for the rest of my life,' she threatened him daily.

A few days ago, deciding enough was enough, Nitin stirred out of coma saying, 'Seems like I have listened to this song at least a thousand times. It took him a whole of five minutes to notice the tears in Tanya's eyes and his own condition.

'Was it your breast that was touching my face when I woke up?' Nitin said in a weak voice.

'I knew this was the only way to get you out of a coma,' Tanya replied, crying.

'Did you marry?' Nitin asked hesitantly, fear clearly showing in his eyes.

'I knew you were not going anywhere. So I decided to wait.'

'How long have you been waiting?'

'Eight-hundred days.'

And so ends the story – happy for some and sad for others. But that's how life is, isn't it?